Eden Prairie, MN

Once Upon a Name: Tales of the Strange & Unusual

Lynn Rush, Alice Ivinya, Marie Reed, Jo Holloway, Alex Stubblefield, Sarina Langer Bekah Berge, Lyndsey Hall, D.M. Taylor, MS Weaver, R.S. Williams, Dani Hoots, Bethany Hoeflich, C.C. Sullivan, Susan Stradiotto, N.D.T. Casale, Sky Sommers, Arielle Willow, Ashley Steffenson, Elena Shelest

ISBN: 978-1-949357-34-9

Published by:
Bronzewood Books
14920 Ironwood Ct.
Eden Prairie, MN 55346

In honor of Elena Shelest, one of our own authors originally from Ukraine, and dedicated to victims of war and poverty who need hope and fairy tales in their lives now more than ever in these strange times

ABOUT OUR CHARITY

When the authors of this anthology gathered to write these strange and unusual tales, they wanted to give back in the way of literacy. Since the anthology work began in the middle of 2021, it has become the team's mantra to support literacy globally.

Book Aid International stood out as a leader with their belief that books have the power to change lives. The organization's mission is to give people around the world who lack access to books the opportunity to read for pleasure, study, and lifelong learning.

Book Aid International supports young readers and education. They provide books when conflict strikes, and provide books dedicated to creating better health by providing books to worldwide healthcare workers.

Books change lives, and this organization is there to ensure that happens. Every £2.00 allows them to provide another book.

To learn more about the organization or make your own donation, visit bookaid.org.

CONTENTS

LYNN RUSH

SOULLESS

A BLADE PIERCED MY SIDE AS I STOOD IN LINE TO GET THE MOVIE TICKETS. A fiery blaze chewed at my flesh like tiny fire ants, and I immediately knew it was a Tainted blade.

"Don't cause a scene," a familiar voice said from beside me.

No.

It couldn't be.

Could it?

I looked to the side and met my best friend's ice-blue eyes, and my cold, evil heart cracked. Okay, I didn't *literally* have a cold, evil heart, but most thought creatures like me did, so I just went with it.

"Rowena?" My voice trembled, but I tried to hide it by clearing my throat.

Her arctic glare could shatter an iceberg.

The tip of her dagger edged deeper into my flesh. If I stayed still much longer, we were going to have a serious problem keeping things quiet, because the poisonous blade affected my ability to keep my otherworldly side hidden.

The two guys in front of me stepped forward, closer to the ticket booths, but Rowena nudged me out of the line.

It was tough to sneak up on me, considering I'd been on the run from her kind for centuries, but she'd done it brilliantly. If Rowena was a Hunter, that meant her parents were too. That was how it normally worked.

How had I missed that? Sure. Hunters were normal humans, just humans privy to the supernatural world. It wasn't like they gave off an essence or anything, identifying them as Hunters. But still.

"Hey Rowena!" Tyler, a junior from our school's volleyball team, waved in our direction.

The traitorous Rowena Rowenfeld slapped on a wide, very fake, grin and said, "We'll be right back. Grab me some popcorn, will ya?"

"You're a Hunter?" I couldn't believe it. Rowena? How was this possible?

"You're not the only one with a secret."

How could I have been so careless?

When I came to this podunk town to hide, I vowed to keep to

myself. It was safer. Both for me and those around me. But I had gotten so bored I registered for high school just to do something.

Mostly I stayed away from my classmates, but Rowena was having none of that. She'd befriended me my first week there, and we'd been inseparable since.

Our friendship hadn't felt like a lie. But was it?

If she knew what I was, why would she have toyed with me all these months, becoming my friend? Why not just kill me straight out?

"And they say *I'm* soulless," I said, grimacing under the pain gnawing through my muscles.

"Your kind are. Monsters preying on the souls of the innocent."

None too gently, she shoved me toward the alley between the theatre and the coffee shop. What was she going to do, off me right here? While the latest Vin Diesel movie was playing on the other side of this wall? I could hear the thumping bass through the brick.

Hunters thought me soulless.

Evil.

A monster.

Yeah, well, I may be all of those, but I was also part human.

And I deserved to live.

The darkness of the long alley swallowed us up, and I allowed my true self out. A wave of electricity bit at my skin as I surrendered to my Wraith. Rowena was sneaky and fake, but she wasn't too bright, because in the shadows was where my kind thrived.

The void of darkness faded away as my eyesight adjusted, and I roared. With a quick jab to her side, I spun away. I found my footing, then kicked her lethal weapon to the ground.

Rowena jumped, planting her foot on the brick wall beside her and then kicked out, her size six sneaker connecting with my jaw.

A crack vibrated through my cheek and a sting burned my flesh.

Another Tainted blade? And at the tip of her boot?

Really?

I righted myself and faced off with my former friend as I ordered my wounds to heal. The poison slowed my healing, but luckily the cuts hadn't been deep.

Dang it. I liked Rowena. We'd had slumber parties and talked about the boys we'd wanted to date.

She so deserved an Oscar for her BFF performance.

She held up another weapon, a smaller knife, but the sulfuric tang of Tainted metal laced the air. It took a lot to kill me, but she was in possession of the very weapon that could. Three of them, actually.

All she had to do was pierce my heart with it.

"Some friend *you* turned out to be," I said, hoping to stall her so my wounds could keep healing. "Back away now, Rowena. I don't want to kill you."

"I'm ready to meet my Maker." She stood tall, challenging me. "My soul isn't damned to eternal fire."

"I wouldn't be so sure of that, *Hunter*. Your kind is just as evil. Blindly following your Council's orders without knowing the full story."

"You're Catlin Browneye, Wraith of the Northern Storms. That's all I need to know."

Dang! Rowena actually knew the full name I'd inherited from my mother when she'd died. But I doubted she knew the full truth about my kind. We weren't all evil killers like the stories portrayed.

"It's closed-mindedness like yours that make the human race destined for destruction." I sucked in a gulp of air, the oxygen infusing my muscles with a cool wave of energy.

Strength and confidence billowed from Rowena as she aimed her Wraith Killer at me. The legendary Tainted steel forged from the Hunters' cursed fires.

The very weapons that'd nearly made my kind extinct. And I knew because I was the last one.

The.

Last.

One.

A thread of energy connected us all. But the once vibrant thread was cold. Silent. No more hugs from Mom ever again. No fellow Wraiths to hunt with, to talk with, to . . . *anything.* I was constantly on the run, watching my back. Fighting for my life.

And alone. *Always* alone.

"I'm not what you think," I said, hoping to cut through the lies she'd been told. I really didn't want to kill her. "I may be Catlin Browneye, Wraith of the Northern Storms, but only my mother was a Wraith."

Rowena's bottom jaw dropped.

I held up my free hand and conjured a ball of electricity. "My mother influenced the weather. Technically, *she* was Wraith of the Northern Storms. At least before your kind crucified her."

Tears stung as images of Mom's bloody body flashed through my mind. Her lifeless eyes fixed on nothingness just before turning to ash.

Rowena relaxed her attack position, still not saying a word.

"My father was human."

"Impossible." She pointed her dagger again, assuming the attack position, but there wasn't much sincerity behind her eyes anymore.

Maybe our friendship wasn't a lie after all.

Could I get through to her?

"Weren't you at all surprised I could so easily be in the light at school? I mean, come on, you're a smart girl. You know Wraiths thrive in the dark because they have a hard time holding their human masks. How can you *not* see I'm different?"

"Spells," she said. "You used magic to hide your essence."

"Is that what you were told?"

She nodded, hesitation and doubt emanating from her.

"And you so blindly accepted it, despite knowing me like you did." I shook my head, offering up a laugh. "You don't know crap about my kind."

I had a lot of power, but I only had enough to keep the *physical* appearance of my Wraith nature under wraps, not my true essence. As a Hunter, she should have detected me the moment I stepped on campus.

In the next breath, Rowena's dagger cut through the air like a bullet. I dove into a summersault, then leaped into the air. Using my powers, I clung to the brick wall, several feet above her.

Her eyes widened.

"Didn't know I could do that, did you?" I teased.

She glanced up and down the alley, then back to me. "How?"

"Like I said. I'm not what you think." I jumped down, keeping a few feet between us. "And I'm also the last of the Wraiths."

"No you're not. There's a coven up in—"

"Destroyed by Hunters. Last month." Tears stung at the corners of my eyes. "I felt every death."

"Felt?"

Each stab. Each slice. But the worst part was feeling their last heartbeats.

I felt like I was going to die.

"Wraiths are connected. We feel each other, no matter the distance." I coughed through the tears clogging my throat. "I was out of school for a week after it happened I was so wrecked."

"Flu," she whispered.

That was the lie I'd told to excuse my absence. Each day, after school, she had brought me chicken noodle soup and watched movies with me.

"Did you really . . . feel their deaths?" She stood straight, no longer in attack mode, it appeared, but I didn't let my defenses down.

"It's like a thread, connecting us all. In death it turns arctic cold, then vanishes."

"There were ten up there."

"I know." Phantom pains ripped through my chest so violently, I gasped.

She shook her head. "I didn't . . . this is just . . ."

"What you were brainwashed to do."

"When they told me you were a Wraith I . . . didn't want to believe it." She sighed.

"Because we're friends. *Best* friends, Rowena. So you know I'm not evil like they've been telling you. Some of us are, sure. The ones truly succumbed to the Wraith's darkness. But not everyone. Especially not me, a half-breed."

She shifted her weight from foot to foot, nervously.

"How long have you known?" I asked.

"Father told me today."

"So you came up *here*?" I raised my arms. "To kill me at the movies? Without even talking to me about it?"

"I was shocked. So shocked. And scared for my friends." Her voice cracked.

"You thought I'd hurt them? But—"

"I studied the Wraith of the Northern Storms, Caitlin! Her darkness is legendary. Using her ability to influence weather and use lightning to cause death and destruction so she could feed on souls."

"Not true. She only stole the souls of evildoers. Killers. Rapists."

Rowena slouched. She must have had her doubts already to believe me so quickly.

"Did you know she used her abilities to influence the weather enough to bring rain to drought-stricken areas when she could?" I stepped closer. "Help snuff out raging fires threatening to destroy towns?"

The acrid tang of sorrow and regret blasted from Rowena so forcefully it made me stumble.

"That's not what you've read or been told about us, is it?"

She slowly shook her head. "You're all female. Evil. Stealing souls. Killing."

"Well, there's that," I joked.

"Have you . . . done that?"

"I've killed. Yes. Defending myself. And the only souls I steal are from evil people. I get revenge for those they've hurt or killed."

"But you need the souls to live."

I nodded. "I *only* take the souls of people who deserve it."

Suddenly a wave of lava-hot heat exploded deep in my chest.

Fire.

Pain.

My knees met the asphalt with a crack, and I fell forward. Palming the ground with one hand, I clutched my weapon in the other. Rowena was showing signs of accepting my claims, but I needed to stay alert in case she tried to attack me again.

My heart hammered deep in my chest, pulverizing my ribs.

Flashes of a guy—dark spiked hair, turf-green eyes, and a scar along the side of his face—ignited in my mind. A sizzling hot thread cinched my heart.

Searing it.

Marking it.

Wait. A thread?

"Catlin?" Rowena squatted beside me and rested her hand on my shoulder.

I got no sense of ill will on her part, and her amber eyes seemed clearer, more focused somehow. But still, I had to be cautious. "Stay back."

"I won't hurt you."

"You say that now, but once your programming kicks in again . . ."

She pulled out the tiny blade protruding from the tip of her shoe and tossed it down the alley. "What's happening with you?"

There was my friend.

I still stayed alert, though, as I mentally flipped through the images I'd seen in my mind's eye again.

The cinch around my heart tightened.

"I'm not alone after all," I said, winded.

"Sorry?"

I pushed up to my haunches. "A Wraith was just created."

"But how? I thought—"

"Wraiths are only offspring of Wraiths?"

"Almost like humans, but the creature is pregnant for only three months."

"That's true."

"Then how . . ."

"The first of our kind, millennia ago, was a human. Transformed."

"Human? No. The devil breathed it into life."

I laughed through the stinging, burning pain in my chest. She really was brainwashed. "Wrong."

"But then that means . . ." Her eyes widened. "It's happening like that again? How—"

"Just wait." I put my hand up, shushing her, as I stood. "It gets better."

"I'm not sure that's possible."

"Oh trust me. It *really* gets better." I grinned, my chest warming at the thought of not being alone anymore. "It's a *guy*."

"Wait, what?" She froze.

"The first male Wraith in history."

"I can't believe it. How? Where?"

"Right here in podunk." I shook my head and glanced up and down the alley. I'd come here to *hide*, the last Wraith in existence. But Fate must have had ulterior motives.

"Here? But . . . you . . . how?"

"Okay. I can see words are not your friend right now." I hardened my features and took a step toward her. "I need to know if you're with me, Rowena."

Her jaw twitched, and she threw a glance over her shoulder. Confusion radiated from her. I was asking her to defy her nature. What she was trained to do. What her family expected of her.

"It's okay." My heart sagged. "I'll get him on my own."

"I won't say anything. I swear."

Just when I'd found a best friend, and one who might be open to my misunderstood kind, I had to leave her.

"How will you explain not killing me?"

"I'll tell them I did." She winked and pulled out another knife from behind her.

"Do you have them strapped all over your body or something?"

"Pretty much." She nodded. "Do you trust me?"

"Not so much. But what'd you have in mind?"

"You heal fast, right?" She held up the blade. "Just a little slice."

"But we turn to ash when we're killed."

"I'll just burn something to get some. But I need some of your blood on my blade."

"You already jabbed me a couple times. Use that."

"Barely. Come on. I want to make sure I've got enough. This needs to look legit."

"Fine. Do it." I held out my arm. "Hurry. This guy has got to be freaking out. And I need to get to him before your *daddy dearest* finds him."

One slice and dice later, I booked it to the end of the alley. I was both excited and sad. Excited to no longer be the only Wraith in existence. But sad to leave Rowena. Sure, she had just tried to kill me. But I saw conflict within her. She might be able to accept my kind.

Maybe someday I could find her again.

One push from my super-charged legs and I cleared the back wall. Darkness shrouded me, and once I confirmed it was clear, I drew in a deep breath to get centered. *Where are you?*

A spark of energy flickered on my left. Just a flash of a muted blue color, but I knew it to be the direction I needed to go. Hustling onto the next block, the pull had me hanging a sharp turn.

"Aww!" a guy bellowed.

The sound came from the park on my left. It was dark, technically closed, but no one in town ever followed that rule. I bolted across the street and rammed into a wall of heat, anger, and electricity. It stole my breath.

"Hello?"

"Stay back," the guy said. His voice was deep but tight, laced with agony.

"I can help."

A tall guy, the one I'd had flashes of, stepped out of the shadows of the kiddy slide. Electricity hovered over his palms, his green eyes flashed, and wisps of darkness shrouded him like a black fog.

"You can't help this." He held up his hands.

Surrendering to my Wraith, I conjured two energy balls above my open palms. "I kinda think I can."

He drew in a quick breath, then flinched. "It's hot. My chest. It's a—"

"Thread. We're connected." I eased closer, letting my electricity fade. "You're like me."

He fell to his knees.

"I thought I was all alone." Tears stung my eyes. "So very alone."

"What's happening?" His gaze fixed on mine and something in my chest clicked.

His scar, tattered jeans and tough exterior told me life hadn't been super comfortable for him. It was more like a feeling, a sense.

"I'm so hungry." He clutched his stomach.

I nodded. "You need a soul."

"What? I . . . no. What?"

"It's okay. I can show you." I glanced around. "But we're not safe here."

His eyes flashed with a burst of energy, and a ripple of fear sliced the air surrounding him.

"Come on." I reached for his hand. "I can help you. Protect you."

He regarded my outstretched hand, but he didn't move.

"I won't betray you. You can sense that, can't you?"

He nodded, then slowly took my hand.

"You're not alone." I helped him up. "You never will be again."

LYNN RUSH

New York Times & *USA Today* Bestselling Author, Lynn Rush, is a full-time writer, wife, and trail runner living in the Sonoran Desert, despite her fear of rattlesnakes. Known as #TheRunningWriter, Lynn can't resist posting epic sunrise pictures while running in the desert with her trail sisters, even if she has to occasionally hop a scorpion. When she's not running or writing, she's watching movies that fuel her everlasting love of superheroes, vampires, and all things *Supernatural*. The books she reads usually carry the same theme, but this former college athlete loves reading sweet sports romances as well. She's madly in love with her Ironman husband of 20+ years who is the inspiration for what true love is. You can find her on social media as @LynnRushWrites

ALICE IVINYA

GODDESS OF SMOKE AND STEEL

Lea Lectricheart, Goddess of Destruction, Bloodlust, and Nightmares, sat on the crumbling wall and purred. Her tail flicked against the rumble, and dust and smoke coated her black fur with the delicious smell of annihilation. She hadn't been this happy in a long time.

She stretched out and yawned, her front claws raking the stone, then jumped to a higher vantage point. The old library was the tallest building left standing. If two remaining walls and a few blackened roof beams qualified. It was cracked open like an egg, its shell jagged and fractured, revealing its precious contents to the sky. Rows and rows of priceless knowledge collapsed into glorious, smoking ruin.

Lea smiled and licked one paw, reveling in the taste of the particles of burnt parchment that had gathered on her fur.

The rest of the city sprawled behind her. The houses were mostly wood and thatch, perfect kindling, and here and there she even saw a few embers still glowing, though the army had left two days ago. The great castle of gray stone was now empty and blood-drenched, the dead bodies long cleared for burial by survivors. Survivors who had been too haunted to remain here for long after the grim deed.

The invaders hadn't left the temples standing either. All the carefully carved and decorated stone structures weren't so pretty anymore. Each was dedicated to a god or goddess that had let the city fall. Useless. Now they were ruins that spoke only of *her*.

She was the one who vanquished all. She knocked a brick off the wall with a swipe, letting it fall far, far below and smash into pieces. Another purr shuddered through her body.

She closed her eyes, rotating her ears to enjoy the silence of a dead city. She half wished the invaders were still here to entertain her with the symphony of ringing steel, the whoosh of all-devouring fire, war cries, and screams. She loved to touch their hearts, igniting their rage and bloodlust, causing the descent of the Battlefog, which made men and women forget who they are and become monsters.

But she would settle for the quiet of a job well done.

"Hello? Is anyone there?" The hoarse voice startled her, though she did her best to hide it.

Lea twitched her tail in annoyance. How *dare* anyone disturb her peace. Her basking in victory. Her . . .

"I heard something. Please, if you're there help me! Please!" The voice was muffled.

Lea's amber eyes sought the origin of the annoyance. Behind the wall was the remains of a third or fourth floor, most of the floorboards sloping sharply down to a sudden drop to the collapsed bookcases below. In the corner was an area that was still level, and a mound of dusty curtains of ruined velvet and shelves rested against the remains of the exterior wall.

The cat sighed and hoped whatever had made the noise would soon suffocate or starve or whatever else forgotten survivors did.

A thud reverberated along the floorboards as something under the mound of debris hit the floor. Hopefully, it would hit hard enough to cause the whole floor to collapse. Then she could go back to basking in the dust-fogged sunlight.

"Hello? Please! I'm trapped. Please help me!"

A desperate pounding erupted through the floor causing her teeth to jar. She unfurled and stretched, flicking her tail in the air viciously enough to show how displeased she was with the interruption. Her paws hit the floorboards without a sound, and she wove around blackened books and broken furniture to the mound of material and shelves.

"You shouldn't be alive," she stated, though even a simple human should have realized that.

The pounding stopped. The male voice that seeped through the curtains was giddy with relief. "Hello! You have no idea how grateful I am to hear your voice. I've been trapped for days. I'm not sure how many; there was lots of smoke, and I think I passed out. Please, help me."

Lea sat in front of the pile and started to groom herself. Her tail still flicking with a mind of its own ruined her appearance of calm. "Are you almost dead yet? Or do you require assistance? This floor won't take much to fall."

There was an uneasy pause, then rasping; desperate laughter tickled her ears, making them twitch. "Very funny. I know you're not a Svorik invader. Your accent is wrong. Let me out. Anything of mine of value, you can have. I've been to court a few times. I could introduce you to the court bard who knows everyone. He has the king's ear. I—"

"Dead." Lea shrugged her slender shoulders and yawned. "The bard, the king, the court . . . dead."

The disembodied voice took a while to process this. "So who is in charge?"

She grinned to herself, letting the points of her canines scrape her bottom lip. "I am."

Much to her annoyance, another wheezing laugh made the curtains shake. "Very funny, now you really must help me. I've not eaten or drunk for days, and I think my leg might be broken."

Lea eyed the dusty wall and the blackened city and thought about leaving the human to his fate, but the sun was red with dust, swelling as it approached the horizon. It would be a shame to waste such a view. It was one of the most beautiful sunsets she had seen in thousands of years. This was the best vantage point in the city, and now, even the rivers reflected the red sunlight, filling them with fiery blood.

She glanced at the mound of debris. If she freed him, he could see how hopeless resistance was. He could watch the sunset as his will to live faded. The perfect accompaniment. Then she would leave him stuck up here and continue on her way.

She crouched and changed her form to the one she preferred when meeting humans. Red silk cascaded to the floor, slit to her thigh. Gold cinched her waist and shone on torcs around her neck and arms, bringing out the richness of her dark skin. Her braided hair was twisted around a crown of two gold serpents, their horned heads rising to hiss at each other across her temple.

Her human form never failed to impress and terrify. The problem was the object she wished to terrify was buried under an awful lot of debris. She sighed. Normally humans were more than capable of doing the dirty work for her. With a little bit of encouragement anyway. But right now, they were all dead or useless.

She closed her eyes and lifted her arms, feeling for the life trapped beneath the rubble. His pulse was weak, his heartbeat fast, one leg trapped underneath a locked chest full of books, his kneecap and tibia smashed. No, he would not be long for this world.

She mentally grabbed a purchase across his body and made him vanish and reappear before her. Her fingers tingled from lack of practice. She couldn't remember if she had ever rescued anyone before. Oh yes, there had been that bloodthirsty pirate who she had needed to lead the raid. But a bystander? No, this was a first. But she wasn't rescuing him, not really.

A lanky boy of about twenty lay before her, gasping and bewildered. He was covered in dust and soot, so it was hard to tell the color of his hair or clothes. He wore a pair of dirty round spectacles. As he stared up at the Goddess of Destruction, he took them off, wiped them on his clothes, then returned them to his nose even more dirty than before.

"Gods above," he breathed.

Lea swished her skirts for dramatic effect and loomed over him, ready to taste his fear. "I am—"

"You're Lea Lectricheart, Goddess of the Battlefog."

Lea snapped her mouth shut, annoyed at the interruption of her grand introduction. Maybe it would be best if she just threw him off the roof after all and enjoyed the sunset alone.

She glared in warning. "I—"

"I am so excited to meet you," the boy said with far too much enthusiasm. "Honored. Truly honored." He pushed his glasses back up his nose and attempted to stand before remembering his leg was broken. He collapsed back down, hissing in pain.

Well, that wasn't the reaction she had been expecting. She normally received begging or terror or dark requests. Maybe he was delirious from dehydration and pain.

The boy realized she was staring at him and lurched. "I am so sorry; I forgot my manners. I am Leif, a scholar and librarian." He gestured over the smoking ruins as if the library was still standing.

Lea wasn't sure how to respond to such unnecessary knowledge and turned back to the glorious view as the sun gorged itself while it lowered, becoming fatter and redder.

There was a scuffle behind her as the boy attempted to do something. She didn't turn, but let her form return to that of a cat. It suited her mood.

"You *are* Lea Lectricheart!"

She tensed, her tail swishing, and planned where over the city to drop him.

"I've been studying you for five years. Every book you're mentioned in, I've read. They said you were unknowable, the hidden goddess, but there are records of you in many books if you know where to look. And can speak enough languages."

This surprised Lea. There were no official temples dedicated to her anywhere in the world. Nobody had altars in their houses to the Goddess of Destruction or wore symbols of her around their necks. But she had always told herself it didn't matter because most worshiped her in the most integral depths of their hearts.

Besides, why would she need a tiny temple of stone, when a whole city could become an altar of worship to her?

She narrowed her eyes over her shoulder at where he had begun dragging himself over the floor. "You've . . . studied me? Why?"

"When I was twelve, I was allowed to choose my topic of specialization. I chose you. You are far more interesting and influential than the other gods and goddesses. I've even written a book about you. It's"—he turned to point into the main room of the smoking library and then his arm sagged—"Oh yes, doesn't matter."

A warm glow ignited in Lea's chest. "You've written a book about me? The goddess who most men don't dare acknowledge exists?"

He nodded vigorously, though it made his wheezy breathing heavier. "I did! And I have . . . so many questions."

She tilted her head, tail wrapping around her feet. She had never had anybody react like this before. "Questions? You realize that in about an hour you will be dead? I doubt you want to waste your energy."

The boy's eyes remained round with excitement and he licked his dusty lips. "You don't understand. You are my life's work." He paused to grimace at some unknown pain. "Talking to you is the peak of my career. I will die happy."

The cat looked pointedly around her and wondered how bad his eyesight was through those dirty glasses. "I've helped destroy your city. I've caused your precious library to be burned. Your friends are dead. Your nation will fall into chaos. You can't die happy."

The librarian looked around and pushed his glasses higher up his nose. "Well, it's a bit of a shame, isn't it."

She gaped at him, for once speechless. A bit of a shame? It was glorious, terrifying destruction! A witness to the depravity of human nature. A seismic shift in power.

She took a deep breath, closing her amber eyes. "You didn't leave the library very much, did you," she guessed. "Didn't have many friends."

He shook his head. "No, I was using all my energy to get to know you, you see. Besides, people are more interesting in books. In real life they just . . . " He made a vague motion with his hand, making him sway alarmingly.

A flutter of unease joined the warmth in her stomach, but she was curious now. "Well, what do you want to know?" It wasn't like he could pass any of it on.

He shifted closer. "What happens when we die?"

"You rot."

"No, to our souls?"

Oh please, not *those* sorts of questions. "Not my area. Next question."

He grunted as he dragged himself closer. "Can you appear anywhere in the world you wish?"

"Yes." She returned to licking one paw.

His grunting and shuffling and panting was starting to annoy her now. She couldn't heal, she had no practice or gift in that area, but she could stabilize his grating bones. She fused the breaks and was pleased when she heard his sigh of relief. She wanted this walking corpse to watch the sunset with her, after all.

"Thank you." He staggered to his feet and tested his leg. It barely bent at the knee anymore and was slightly shorter than his other one, but he seemed relieved. He hobbled forward a step before pausing to catch his breath. "What do you do when there are no battles?"

She firmed her lips. "Humans are always fighting. Always killing. Always destroying. It's who they are. They cover it with all these pretty illusions, but, deep down, they all worship me. They all hate and destroy."

He staggered to the wall beside her and leaned against it with trembling arms, looking out at the broken city bathed in red. It took him a moment to catch his breath and gain the ability to speak. "What motivates you to destroy things?"

Lea shifted, her tail swishing. This was becoming too personal. She let coldness flood her voice. "I enjoy it."

For once, Leif seemed to realize he was trespassing on a forbidden subject and changed. "Do you spend time with the other gods and goddesses?"

"Not if I can help it."

"Do you have a family?"

"No."

"Friends?"

She narrowed her eyes and her tail lashed against the wall.

"Aren't you . . . lonely?"

Lea, Goddess of Destruction, laughed. "How could I possibly have friends? I destroy everything I touch; that is why I exist."

"You haven't destroyed me."

"Well, you're dying. There's not much point."

They fell into silence for a moment, watching jagged, broken statues stretch through the ruins.

The librarian leaned heavier and heavier on the wall as his strength faded. "Do you like to be stroked?"

"I beg your pardon?"

"When you're a cat, do you like to be stroked?"

Lea thought about it for a moment. Whenever anyone approached her in her cat form, she bit or scratched them. Would it feel nice to be stroked as a cat?

Leif tentatively touched his fingers to her spine. When she didn't lash out, he smoothed down the fur all the way down to her tail. It felt . . . luxurious. Especially as she sat, watching the destruction before her in the sunset. After several strokes he scratched beneath her ear, which felt even better. When his fingers slipped to her chest and belly, she gave him a warning strike. "Not there."

"I'm sorry. Back and neck it is."

They sat in silence for a while, and Lea was calmed by the rhythmic strokes, leaning her head into them. A purr erupted from within her, and she felt content in a way she hadn't for years.

"Stroking does not get recorded in any books," she mumbled after a while.

The boy sounded so tired. "I'm not getting off this ledge. I'm dying, remember. I won't write any more books."

Lea considered this. She rather liked being stroked and having company as she surveyed her work. She'd never had an admirer before. No songs were sung about her. But apparently there had been a book. Part of her regretted inciting the invaders to torch the library.

Leif's strokes gradually weakened, and she could sense his heart rate increasing as it struggled to move his thickening blood.

"I think you're wrong, by the way." His words were almost lost in the evening breeze.

She bristled. "Wrong? I'm a goddess. We're never wrong."

"You said everyone deep down is made of hatred. Everyone wishes to fight and destroy. That everything covering that up is an illusion."

She looked down at the streets that had run rivers of blood fueled by hatred as strangers had killed one another. "I have seen it. I have seen what every man becomes when nobody is watching. When they have a sword in their hands and power over others, every person is a monster."

A slight smile curved his lips. "I believe that some things are stronger than hate. Some things that are inside every person. I wrote about it in a book."

She pinned him with a golden glare. "You have not seen what I have seen. You are young, naive. Nothing is stronger than hate."

He looked back at her. "I think you see what you wish. What you enhance and create."

The sun finally slipped below the horizon, and the shadows

merged like a black flood across all but the highest peaks of the buildings.

A tingle of excitement trickled through her as an idea awoke. "Let us have a challenge then. You will accompany me for a year and serve me. We will convince each other of the basis of human nature and whether destruction is all they deserve." She would see him destroyed by the truth and meanwhile enjoy his strokes.

He attempted a tired grin. "On one condition. I am allowed to write an accurate account." He paused as she narrowed her eyes. "Not including the stroking."

Lea Lectricheart nodded. "Fine." She puffed out her fur. "Include some songs too. Gloriously dark ones."

He nodded, though his eyelids were sagging.

"I think I will like keeping you," she murmured and reared on her hindlegs.

The goddess and librarian disappeared from the ruined library. For the first time, Lea saved a life instead of destroying it.

And it felt good.

ALICE IVINYA

Alice Ivinya is a USA Today bestselling author. She is also an award winning international and Barnes and Noble bestseller.

She lives in Bristol, England. She is wife to Sam, mummy to their toddler and owns the best dog in the world, Summer. She has loved fantasy all her life and loves dramatic stories with deep meanings behind them and happy endings. When she's not off galavanting in other worlds, she loves walking the dog and spending time with her church family.

Alicegent.com

MARIE REED

"Oyez, oyez, oyez!"

A loud cry snapped Callie out of her head and back to her surroundings. Somehow, she hadn't noticed when she'd entered the small village on the dusty dirt road she'd been walking on for hours. She had passed through the narrow streets of the town and entered the village square. A young man who appeared to be the town crier was walking up to a small podium near the center of the square. The surrounding villagers gathered nearby to hear his news. Callie lifted the hood of her cloak to shadow her face as she walked a little closer, but still kept distance between her and the crowd in the square.

The crier opened his scroll and started reading, "By order of King Benedict, all citizens are to be on the lookout for Callista Azuresmith, a fugitive of the crown who abandoned her post in the village of..."

Callie stopped listening, deciding to check the crowd instead. From personal experience, most people didn't pay much attention to any crier announcements, but calls-to-action like this one were always completely ignored. She'd held the post herself back home, and had hated it so much that she left without finding a proper replacement. She honestly hadn't realized that one sleepy little village going a few days without an official crier would be worth putting a warrant out for her arrest.

A few people in the crowd started wandering off, so Callie decided it was safe to follow them away from the crier. Unless they had raised the reward offered significantly, no one would be looking for her in a place like this. She'd seen a few poorly drawn wanted posters here and there during her travels, but a haircut and a false name when she was in public was enough to keep them off her heels for now.

She saw a sign for a general store down the street. Maybe she'd ask the shopkeeper a few questions while checking to see if he had any herbs in stock that could darken her hair. It wouldn't hurt to change her appearance a bit more. She was searching for a mage to teach her enough that she could get admitted into the Impassable Sorcerers, a group of unbeatable magic users who helped keep the nearby kingdoms and rulers in check. They were the real power in these lands, and once she was a member, she wouldn't need to worry about being arrested.

A bell on the wall rang as Callie pushed open the shop's door. A thin old man looked up at the noise, nodding to Callie before returning to his book. The large room was open and bright with sunlight streaming in through the clean windows. Callie pushed the hood of her cloak away from her face as she looked around the shop.

Food was in the back near where the old shopkeeper sat with his book. Baskets full of apples and walnuts sat on the floor. Filled burlap bags of various sizes sat on the shelves, while dried herbs hung from the ceiling. Callie walked to the back and browsed through the stock.

The walnuts will work better than herbs if I can find something to grind them, Callie thought as she turned back to search the shelves. She found a mortar and pestle that was small enough she could easily carry it in her pack, but large enough that it wouldn't take too long to grind the shells to make a dye.

The bell rang again as Callie was filling a small cloth bag with walnuts. She looked toward the door to see a small boy with dark hair and heavily-patched clothing clutching a piece of paper and a small purse.

"Hullo, sir," he said, raising his cap to the shopkeeper. He waved the paper in his hand. "I have a new list from Mister Gebbert."

Gebbert! Callie thought. *That's the name of the man I'm looking for!* She continued filling her bag, but angled herself to listen to their conversation.

Years ago, an apprentice mage named Gebbert had been banished from the Impassable Sorcerers. Callie was following rumors about an old hermit in the area, and this Gebbert was likely to be the same man. She hoped to find him and convince him to train her to help fix his sullied reputation.

"Well, bring it here lad." The elderly man sat his book on the table beside his chair and groaned as he struggled to get to his feet.

Callie saw her chance and took it. "No, don't get up," she said. She sat her items on the counter near the shopkeeper's chair. "I've found what I needed and have nothing important left to do today. I can help the boy collect what he needs."

"Thank you, lass." The old man lowered himself back into his chair. "These knees aren't what they used to be. You just let me know if you need help finding anything. Sometimes Tommy here brings some strange requests from the old hermit."

Callie turned to the boy, who had been standing quietly a few paces away. "Hello, Tommy. Do you need help looking for the items or reading the list?"

"Reading, ma'am," he answered nervously. "I'm not very good at it and Mister Gebbert's letters are mighty confusing sometimes."

"Well, I will help you, but only if you call me Allie." Callie smiled, giving the boy an alias she used often. "Do you want to go grab everything and bring it back here to the counter? I'm sure you know the store better than I do." Callie pointed to the first few items on the list, saying them aloud so the boy could go grab them. "How often does your master send you out on errands?"

"Oh, he's not my master, ma'a…Allie. Not really." Tommy wasn't so nervous now that he was grabbing things off the shelves. "My brother used to help 'im out with his shopping since he doesn't leave his land, but since my pa died a few years back, he works hard on the farm. Mister Gebbert always leaves more coin with the list than it all costs and I get to keep the extra money. Sometimes I get some candy or sweet buns, but I give the rest to Ma."

"I'm sure your mother appreciates all your hard work to help take care of your family," said Callie, continuing down the list as Tommy quickly found the previous items.

"Tommy-boy's a great help around town," the shopkeeper interrupted. "He helps me out here at the shop now that my granddaughter's off and married." He turned his head to speak to the boy directly. "If you aren't needed at home after you deliver all this, I have some crates in back that need to be unpacked."

Callie jumped in. "Tommy, I can deliver this for you as well if you want to get some more small jobs in today, as long as you don't think Mister Gebbert would mind."

The boy glanced up at Callie but was hesitant to agree.

"I'll even throw in a bag of taffy for you," she added. "You deserve a treat for being such a hardworking young man."

"I'd be awful grateful," he said, face turning a bit pink. "Ma said she'll need to replace my trousers soon and money's real tight." His pants were pretty threadbare and showing a large amount of his ankles.

"It's settled then," Callie grinned. She couldn't believe her luck. The boy smiled back and ran to collect the last things on the list.

Tommy drew her a map on the back of the shopping list with a small bit of charcoal he had in his pocket. "There's a rock near the road here," he explained around a large piece of taffy, "I leave the bundle there when I'm done. Hardly ever see 'im in person." He thanked her for the taffy and headed for the back room of the shop.

Callie hurried out of the village as soon as she gathered the bags. Finally, she was going to find someone to help her learn about her elemental magic. It was an inherited trait, but her father's family didn't do much with it. Back home he was a blacksmith, known for his stronger-than-average blades and tools. Fire was his most natural element, so his forge was hotter than most and the heat was more precisely applied.

His fame had earned him the name Azuresmith, as the flames in his forge burned bright blue. Hers were the same. She'd tried to teach herself about the other elements, but anything more than calling a strong breeze had been hard to learn alone. This was why traveling was essential. An uneducated mage would never be accepted into the Impassable Sorcerers.

She continued following the boy's directions and soon found herself near the large stone he'd mentioned. She looked out at the clearing behind the rock and saw a small cottage near the back end. Since she did need to actually speak to the old man, she stepped off the road and all but sprinted toward the cottage. Her heart raced as she thought about all the things she'd be able to learn from the former apprentice.

He must have been watching the road from the house, because a few minutes into her trek he stepped out the front door and stood in front of the house, tracking her approach. Callie sped up her pace even more, hope radiating from her body. Near the cottage she felt the chilling sensation of a spell wash over her, which made her even more certain she'd found the mage she'd been looking for.

Momentarily she slowed. Something bothered her about the prickly unease from the hazy outline of the spell she'd stepped through, but it was well done and she quickened her pace again, ready to learn from a true magic master.

"Hello!" she called when she was within comfortable speaking distance. "I met young Tommy in the store and offered to bring you your items, Mister Gebbert. I've been looking for a mage to apprentice under so I can learn what I need before I continue on to the Impassable Sorcerers."

The old man stared at her blankly.

"You are Gebbert, right?"

He inclined his head an inch.

I'll take that as a yes. She smiled, trying to look more friendly. "Great! So you can teach me. I would definitely be accepted if I showed them some of what you've been working on here."

Gebbert stood in the doorway for another minute, then blinked and walked back into the house, leaving the door open. Callie took this as an invitation and followed him. As she stepped through the doorway, Callie glanced around the room. A preserved rabbit's foot tied to a leather cord sat on a small table near the door. She closed the door, dropped her bags on the floor, and picked up the rabbit's foot.

Hello, said a strange, nasally voice in her head. *What did he promise you to get you inside the perimeter spell?*

Callie's eyes widened as she looked towards Gebbert, but he stood silently near the hearth ignoring her.

Oh, the voice continued, sounding amused. She glanced down at the rabbit's foot in her hand. *You didn't even stop to question it, did you? Poor, innocent thing. Pity Gebbert's trapped you here.*

"What do you mean?" she whispered, seeing the old man glare at her out of the corner of her eye. The door lock clicked behind her and her heart leapt into her throat. Callie inched to the open back door of the cottage, trying to work herself out of the corner she'd been forced into. She might have jumped into this plan a little too quickly.

There is an enchanted sundial here in the garden, the foot's voice explained. *He uses it to steal the life of anyone foolish enough to come onto his land.* The foot sighed. *Like I said, pity. I would enjoy having someone to talk to and Gebbert's too far gone. Now you're trapped, but soon you'll be dead, and I'll be alone again.*

Callie was halfway around the room now. She dropped the foot onto a nearby desk, a little disturbed that she was apparently hearing its voice directly in her head. She took another step towards the open door. Gebbert still stared at her blankly. *Maybe he's just been alone too long. He's just a little awkward around another person,* she tried to convince herself.

"I'm sorry, I didn't know you'd enchanted it. That's amazing! What else have you been working on?" Callie wanted to sound friendly and nonthreatening, but her voice was strained.

"You know the main one already, I presume," the old man grunted. It sounded like he hadn't spoken aloud for a while. "That gossip makes sure to tell everyone as soon as it can." He gestured to the rabbit's foot lying on the desk.

Callie shook her head. "No, I didn't really catch what it was saying. I was trying to figure out where the voice was coming from." She tried to lighten the tension with a chuckle. She felt like the walls were closing in on here, further trapping her inside the house. "Whatever it is, it must be impressive."

Gebbert nodded. "I've found the secret to immortality."

"Immortality! The foot did say something about a sundial. Is that what you use? Did you enchant it too?" Callie strode towards the back door. She was now to the point of rambling in her panic and needed to get out of the house. Gebbert stood silently, giving her that same blank stare instead of answering her. She kept walking the last few steps to the door. The openness of the sunlit garden called to her; the bright light glinted off the large sundial just a handful of steps from the back door.

As strange as he's acting, only a very talented mage would be able to create such an object. A sundial that grants immortality! I could still learn a lot from him, she thought. She paused her retreat and asked, "Could you teach me how it works? I'm sure something like that would get me into the Impassable Sorcerers."

She turned her head back to see if Gebbert heard her and jumped in fright. He had quickly moved much closer to her without a sound, still with that glazed-over stare. She darted over the threshold and into the garden.

The sundial in the center of the paved courtyard gave her the same unease she felt looking at the old mage, but at least she wasn't trapped in that small space with him and that creepy rabbit's foot anymore.

Gebbert stalked towards her, pushing her closer to the sundial. "The magic of the sundial only works for one. You will not take my immortality."

Well, that didn't last long. She could still hear the rabbit's foot from here in the back garden. *Did you have to be so pushy? You could have lived long enough to tell me about the outside world at least.*

Dark energy from the sundial coiled around her like a large snake. It was almost curious, slowly circling, testing her strength before it started tightening, claiming her as its prey.

"Look, I'm not after immortality. I just wanted someone to teach me about becoming a sorcerer!" She struggled to take a couple small steps away from the sundial, hoping Gebbert wouldn't rush at her before she could break its strong hold.

"Lies!" he cried, eyes suddenly wild as he threw flames at Callie. She jumped out of the fire's path and an apple tree burst into flame instead of her. The heat from the burning tree grew, branches and leaves popping as the wall of flame climbed higher. He staggered closer, hurling another fireball as he screamed, "You want my secrets! You will not have them, girl!"

Callie once again leapt out of the way and rolled for cover behind a short garden wall. "So, is that a 'no' on the lessons? I can leave and find another teacher," she tried. He ignored her and hit the brick wall with lightning when his flames failed to break through.

Callie distanced herself from the crackling electricity, blocking his view with her own wall of bright blue flame. Still fighting against the coil of darkness from the sundial, she pushed more power into the fire she'd created. The blue flames between her and Gebbert jumped higher, eagerly devouring the orange fireballs meant for her.

He switched his attacks back to lightning and she created a strong wind, using it to push against the sundial's tightening grip. The fire came to her naturally thanks to her father, but wind was harder for her to control and the gust didn't last long. She spun around the courtyard, forcing distance between herself and the cursed sundial as Gebbert lurched farther into the garden. Again, she focused on the wind and pushed hard enough that it all but blew out the flames separating her from her attacker.

She almost fell on her face when she finally broke free from the sundial's grasp. Gebbert stumbled moments after. *It must have him. Now is my chance!* She pulled the air to her this time as she jumped, aiming for a fallen tree too far away for her to reach without the extra push. She hesitated as she glanced at Gebbert from behind the smoldering tree, but saw the rage in his eyes as he pulled his arms back to hurl another attack.

Callie focused entirely on the wind, pulling as much into her outstretched hands as her power allowed. Then she pushed the swirling gale forward, sending a strong gust straight into Gebbert.

The wind threw him back against the brick surrounding the sundial, cracking the wall in the process. He struggled against the sundial's writhing grip as Callie recreated her wall of flame and forced him closer to the sundial. Gebbert grabbed its edge to pull himself to his feet. His eyes widened in shock when he realized what he'd done.

There was a bright flash of light as all color drained from Gebbert's face. "No!" he howled as he tried to pull his hand away, but it was too late.

His face and hands withered down to skin and bones. His body sank in on itself until all that was left was a hollowed husk. Callie's stomach churned as his remaining flesh started melting and she spun away. When she could finally bring herself to look back, all there was left of the old man was a pile of ash with bits of scorched fabric on the ground and a bright red handprint seared on the side of the sundial.

Callie spun slowly to look at the damage done to the garden. Stone pathways were cracked and blackened, trees knocked over and smoldering. She put out the last of the flames with a wave of her hand. At the outer edge of the garden, a fallen tree was propped up on what looked like nothing. She stepped closer, squinting at the slightly distorted landscape in the distance. The boundary spell stood firm.

"No!" Callie screamed and she collapsed against a section of garden wall that was still standing. "Why couldn't the spell die with him?"

I told you, the nasally voice of the rabbit's foot called to her from inside the house. *You won't be able to get away. The curse is too complicated for anyone to figure out. And sooner or later, you'll lose your mind and I'll be stuck here waiting for the next person to show up. Hopefully it won't be so long next time,* he sighed. *The last two years were really quiet.*

"I'm sure you can hold a conversation with yourself," Callie snapped, standing and walking back to the unharmed cottage. "If he created it, he must have written it down somewhere. I'm not staying here." She stopped suddenly. "Wait. How did he get his supplies? Surely he must have crossed the barrier."

Yes, the foot said, tone condescending as if he were speaking to a child. *He was able to pass through. It was his spell. He just preferred to stay here so no one would try to steal anything. Paranoid old man he was. 'Course, when you're sitting on a dragon's hoard of gold you tend to be suspicious of anyone. And I think using that sundial for so many years rotted his mind.*

"How did he make that sundial?" Callie asked.

He didn't. It was here with another man guarding it when he arrived. Their meeting went much like your own.

"So, I'm going to go crazy at some point and try to kill anyone who comes near?"

I don't think so. Gebbert didn't get too bad until about the fifth or sixth person he pushed into the thing. Usually travelers. He didn't want the townsfolk to get suspicious and stop selling him supplies.

"That's good then. I'll just make sure to stay away from it while I'm here." Callie grabbed the hermit's journal from the table and sat at the desk, pulled a few sheets of blank paper and a pencil closer to her. The silence only lasted a few minutes before the foot spoke up again.

Hello? Gold? No comment on that part? You could at least gossip with me now that there aren't any more pressing matters.

"Can't spend gold if I can't leave. Gold doesn't get me into the Impassable Sorcerers. Save the fortune gossip for later when I'm not trapped in this house."

You're no fun, the foot huffed. *That's all I even have to talk about. I've been so bored for so long...*

Callie tuned out the foot's complaining as well as she could and continued pouring through Gebbert's books, flipping through them quickly and then tossing them to the side. So far, she'd seen nothing remotely related to a boundary spell, and many passages were in languages she didn't recognize.

She searched chaotically for days until she had completely trashed the cottage.

At one point the rabbit foot's constant whining in her head annoyed her so much she threw it into the fire, not even caring if it could feel pain. Callie's actions were rewarded with laughter as the foot reappeared beside her in the room.

Really? The foot sounded like it would be in tears if it were possible. *You thought you could be rid of me so easily? That was the first thing Gebbert did when he realized what a failure I was. I was supposed to tell the future and help him make beneficial decisions. Instead, he created an indestructible companion and ignored everything I said.*

Callie sank to the floor defeated. Piles of books surrounded her. A few stacks had fallen over, spreading haphazardly across the room. "Now we can both be failures," she said. "I'm never going to get out of here."

Not if you keep this up.

"What do you mean?"

Did you really think that the answer would just jump out at you? Of course you won't find anything helpful if you're throwing books everywhere instead of actually reading them. If you had stopped to think...

"...I could have figured out how Gebbert grouped his books," Callie finished the foot's thought. "Now I'll have to search them all. After I pick them all back up."

All you really did was create a lot more work for yourself.

“I seem to do that a lot.” Callie stood up and started gathering the scattered books. “I'm wanted by the king because I decided to up and leave without warning, which makes traveling much harder than it should be. And this whole mess could have been completely avoided had I stopped before crossing the boundary spell.”

The rabbit's foot snorted. *You mean 'paid enough attention to notice there was a boundary spell.'*

“I'd throw you in the fire again for saying that, but I really should have known better,” Callie said. She paused with a book still in her hand. “You know, maybe neither of us are failures. Sure, it may take me longer to figure out the counter-spell and be able to leave, but I'll learn a lot if I go through all of these books. And when I do leave, you can yell at me if I try to do something without thinking again.”

You mean I won't just get left here in an empty house? Fantastic! You should look through that one first.

Callie opened the book she was holding. “This is all about illusionary magic! I'll be able to travel without worrying about wanted posters.” She smiled as she placed the book on the desk. She knew she had a lot to do to prepare for the Impassable Sorcerers, and now she was fully prepared to put in all the hard work necessary to make it there. She wouldn't just become a member of the Impassable Sorcerers; she would be the Commander.

Marie Reed is currently a stay-at-home mom of two who is still trying to figure out what she wants to be when she grows up. She fell in love with books of all kinds at a young age and devoured entire libraries while still in school. A dozen or so years later, she finally finished writing her first short story and is currently working on a full length novel. You can keep up with Marie's new releases on Amazon https://amazon.com/author/mariereed

and Goodreads https://www.goodreads.com/author/show/21713872.Marie_Reed

JO HOLLOWAY

I'll kill him. All I want is to be on my way home, for which I need Jacks, but of course my feckless protector is nowhere to be found. Typical. I know murder is wrong, but I bet people would understand. My reasons might be different, but my illustrious swordsman has earned the ire of plenty of other women besides me. I'm sure I'm not even the first to plot his demise.

"Whose murder are you plotting, Kelcy?"

I must have spoken that last thought out loud, because the bartender's question alerts me to my surroundings. I've entered the inn's tavern and should probably stop muttering my murderous thoughts to everyone nearby. "The usual. Have you seen Jacks?"

"Not since last night. By the fire."

That was the last I saw of him too, surrounded by a group of women, as always, waving me off with a promise that he'd be here in the morning. Maybe I'll kill him with my sewing needles; it would serve him right. Jacks was well aware we were leaving at first light. I swear, I should have fired him a long time ago, no matter that he's also my only friend.

In any case, I'm not about to search every available woman's home in this sun-forsaken town for him. "Did you see which lucky lady he left with?"

The bartender picks up another glass to dry, chuckling softly, but he has no answer.

At the end of the bar, a man lifts his drink in my general direction. "Kelcy Lustrousjourney." My name clearly amuses him. "Think Jacks might'a left with all three," he slurs. "Maybe if you let him under your skirts, he wouldn' run off." He tips his head back, laughing, and drains his glass.

I'm already digging a grave for Jacks in my mind. I can easily expand it to fit two. "Maybe if you didn't spend your nights drinking away every coin I paid you, Emir, you could find someone yourself. Go home, already." If that man didn't sell the best fabrics in all of Anterra, I wouldn't come here at all. No more crossing the Yellow Plain . . . sounds good to me.

Emir stands unsteadily from his barstool. "If it's a swordsman you need, got one righ' ere."

"Keep it in your pants, Emir." I wish I were home already. I have my new fabrics, and I have projects to start on and deadlines to meet. "You know what? Forget this. I don't need Jacks. I don't need anybody."

The bartender stops cleaning as a chorus of "*ooohs*" sound from the other patrons. "Kelcy, you can't cross the Yellow Plain alone."

"Sorceress'll get ya," Emir adds helpfully, as if I don't know what the fuss is about.

"I heard she cooks her victims and eats 'em," says one man.

"I heard she paints her skin in black ink to sneak up on people."

"Naked," adds a third, laughing.

My resolve hardens at their silly theories of the crazy sorceress of the Yellow Plain. This buying trip has already taken too much of my time, and I have work to do. Those suits won't sew themselves, plus my own bed is calling out to me from Winterset. From home. "I've never seen another soul when I cross with Jacks. I'm not sure the sorceress even exists."

Emir wags a finger at me. "Them people don't go missin' by their own choice, love. The Mist claims people."

I jut out my chin. "I'm not afraid of a little mist. Besides, I'm handy with a knife."

"Naw, you're handy with a sewing machine. I'll lose my best customer," Emir whines.

I've made up my mind and I'm not going to waste time here with stories meant to scare children. I leave the men debating whether it would be worth being eaten in order to meet a naked sorceress covered in ink. Clearly, we have different priorities.

Sure, the idea of going alone might scare most people, but I'm doing this. I am Kelcy Lustrousjourney; self-made, independent, and a master craftswoman. I don't need a guide or protector. I've never needed anybody but myself, and I can make this journey alone. It's not in my name for nothing.

I'm barely out of the stables before doubt sets in. It's Jacks's job to lead the hired lorcan and the stubborn beast knows it. Day broke fully while I was inside securing my belongings behind the pack animal's shoulder hump—another of Jacks's duties—and now that I have the light, I can't afford any more delays if I want to make it across the plain to Winterset before dusk. I certainly don't want to be caught in the Mist after dark.

"Come on," I urge the beast, pulling harder as the lorcan nearly stops.

Emir swaggers out of the tavern to watch me pass. "So you're a fool as well as a prude." I growl and tug the animal's lead, struggling to keep him moving, but Emir is unmoved by my obvious determination. "Pity. You were the best haberdasher on either side of the Yellow Plain."

"Still am," I say with a cheery wave and a big fake smile.

"Good luck, Kelcy Lustrousjourney. You'll need it."

I flip him a less friendly wave. My dramatic exit loses impact when the lorcan stumbles and nearly knocks me over with his broad head, but at least the animal doesn't try to stop again, and I breathe a sigh of relief as we exit the town's gate.

Before long, I'm the one wishing we could stop. The beast smells, and it's hot, but knowing I'm headed home keeps me going. Slowly, the sand turns to scrubby grass and a mat of green spreads ahead. By the first shrub, I register the change in light. Here, the sunlight fades to a filtered yellow and the blue sky turns grey. Soon, the sky is shrouded entirely in the mists. We're on the outer edge, but the lorcan grows anxious, snorting and shying sideways. I jerk the lead.

"It's only mist. Don't be stupid." Whether I'm talking to him or to myself, I'll repeat the words until we emerge at Winterset where my hearth, teapot, and sewing machine wait for me.

A branch snaps in the haze and the lorcan stops to stare. I can't see far, but I'm sure it's only a critter. Probably. When a huge rock looms out of the Mist, doubt settles in. I don't remember seeing it when crossing the other way with Jacks at my side. Getting lost and wandering too far into the Mist instead of skirting the edge is not good. Not good at all.

I pull out my compass—Jacks usually checks it, so I forgot. It looks as if I'm headed in generally the right direction, though. A small correction should have me on course. Even if I've angled a little too far into the Mist, it should only increase my time on the plain by a short amount.

Of course, the lorcan hates the idea of one instant longer in here. Another *crack* sounds in the Mist beyond the rock, and the beast spooks, knocking into me. The lead slips from my grasp as I start to fall. I scramble to grab it again, or any of the lashings wrapped around him. I can't lose that fabric shipment, or the only other living thing out here I can trust.

My hands fumble over the fabric and I grab for anything I can, desperate to hang on. The lorcan snorts, leaps, and kicks me in the thigh, sending me sprawling to the ground, and then he takes off.

Throbbing pain steals my breath, and I swear the plain itself gasps with me. My heart pounds.

I'm alone in the Mist.

I lay there a minute, fighting back tears and gritting my teeth against the pain in my leg. Then I sit up and survey my surroundings. I can't decide how far into the Mist I am, whether I should turn back or continue. Shivers crawling up my spine make me want to push on toward home, even though I've lost everything I came for.

Why did I come? Why did Jacks have to vanish on me like everyone always does? I wish . . . I wish I had one person to count on. But no, it's only me. It's only ever me.

I grab a clump of grass and rip it up by the roots, hurling it with a sharp cry of all my frustration. The root ball soars through the air to land beside a lump.

I peer at it. If I'm not mistaken, that lump is purple.

Testing my leg, I rise and limp over to where I'm overjoyed to find it's one of my fabrics. When I tugged at the bindings, I must have pulled them loose. Perhaps my knife fell out! I'll find whatever fabrics I can and carry them myself. Ha, I don't need Jacks *or* a pack animal.

"Who needs friends anyway?" I shout toward the hidden sky. Immediately, I regret it when there's a sound like an animal snuffling nearby. It's not smart to draw attention on the plain. My rushing pulse seems to have forgotten my earlier bravado about children's tales.

Thankfully, no sorceress strikes me down, and I head more quietly for the next colored heap. A breeze sways the grasses and swirls tendrils of mist around my ankles as I hurry on my throbbing leg. Finding the paisley I chose for Mr. Anglesway's vest, I smile. He's my best customer. I add it to my armload and move on to retrieve a charcoal tweed, a blue silk, and a few others. Then I spot a glint and rush over, hoping for my knife. Instead, I find my fabric shears. Not as helpful, but expensive.

Searching the haze for the next item, I see nothing. Following this haphazard trail, I haven't checked my compass once. Even the big rock is gone from my sight. I thought I was lost before.

I thought I was stronger than the scary stories, but now a very real fear sets in. I don't care if murder is wrong. If I live through this, I'm killing Jacks.

It's hard to tell time in the monotonous, dull light in the Mist, but I think it's growing darker, and I haven't found the edge of the plain yet. Once, I thought I spotted an area where the Mist thinned, but tangled shrubs blocked my way. One branch slapped me in the face when I got too close, and I heard a noise like a cough that sent me fleeing the other way.

I'm about to give up hope and collapse for a good cry when something looms out of the gloaming. It's too tall to be a tree. Too uneven.

Tall! That's what I need.

I can climb above the Mist and see where I am. Reaching the base, I drop my stack of fabric and look way, way up. If this is a beanstalk, then the Mist must have shrunk me because it's enormous. The trunk is the size of Emir's barrel chest, and branches twist in every direction. The leaves have a purple shimmer to them, like the mists have reshaped them and now they course with magic. Or maybe because the entire plant grew from magic.

Danger dances on spider legs up my spine. *Magic*. The rumors of the Yellow Plain sorceress might be true after all. The disappearances . . . all of it. I need to climb fast, get my bearings, and get out of here. I will my hands to stop shaking so I can tuck the shears into my skirt, and I grab the first branch.

Soon, my arms burn and my legs develop a tremble that won't quit. The branches are farther apart than they looked from the ground. I have to stand on my toes on the next branch to reach for anything above me, looking up as far as I can see. There's still only mist above me. I'm tempted to look down to see how far I've come, but I have a feeling I'd be disappointed. I can probably still see the ground.

My hand closes around a purple leaf, and I stretch all the way out to pull the attached branch toward me. The leaf tears between my fingers.

I lurch, one foot slipping from the branch beneath me, and I clamp my arms around the stalk. One foot dangles over nothing, and the other barely has enough purchase to keep me from sliding down. I can't let go, but I also can't move. Heart thudding, I try to suck in my next breath.

"What are you doing?"

I think I scream at the sound of the voice coming out of the Mist. It's hard to tell over my pulse thundering in my ears.

Branches slap into me as I tumble, beating my sore limbs as if the beanstalk is punishing me for ripping its leaf. Fortunately, the abusive branches slow my fall, but I still hit the ground with a hard thud. Or rather, I hit something. Breath grunts out of me at the impact, echoing like there are two of me, but the impact isn't as hard as I expect. Whatever is beneath me, I thank the blue skies it broke my fall.

A low vine is tangled around my ankle, holding me in place and sending a spike of fear through me that the beanstalk is trapping me here for something. Or for *someone*. Kicking and flailing, I fight to free myself.

"Stop that," yells a voice directly in my ear.

I freeze. There is only one person who could be out here. Sweet sunbeams, I'm about to die.

From under my hip, something twitches, and the vines untangle from my legs, dropping my full weight onto the lumpy object beneath me. No, not lumpy. Curvy.

"Ouch. Get off."

The voice is muffled under my wild hair, but my head snaps toward it, and I find myself looking directly into a pair of narrowed eyes.

I saw the sea once. It stormed our whole trip, until the last day, but I'll never forget the green of the water after a storm. That's the color looking up at me beneath dark lashes.

"Off. Now," she says.

Right. Shock has melted my brain. She's a dangerous sorceress. I need to run. I should pull out my shears. I scramble off her, but my wobbly legs don't seem to work. If I can't stand, what hope do I have of running? I'll be dead long before I can escape.

"Please don't hurt me," I say stupidly.

"*You* fell on *me*." She rises, pushing ink black hair over her shoulder and brushing dirt from her dress. It's light and flowy and not at all what I pictured for an evil sorceress.

"Will you kill me before you cook me?"

"What? Get up." She politely averts her eyes while I stand and straighten my clothing, and then she looks at me again, appraising me slowly. "You're an odd one, aren't you?"

"Odd in a good way? Or in a 'she looks too chewy' way? Because I bet I'm very stringy. Not tasty at all."

She stares. "They actually say I eat people?"

"Don't you?" Hope is a glistening thing.

"Of course not. That's disgusting." She lifts her eyes to the hidden sky, her elegant neck elongating.

"You're not covered in ink either."

"Why would I be covered—?"

"Or naked."

At that, she throws her hands up. "One time! Jacks caught me dancing in the rain one time, and he can't stop spreading that story."

"Jacks?" I can breathe again, but my heart is still pounding. "Jacks Goldenroot?"

She sighs. "Of course you know my brother."

"Your . . . brother? Wait. Jacks *knows* the sorceress of the Yellow Plain? All this time . . . He's your *brother*?" Oh, he is so dead.

She tuts, her mouth pursing. "Brave, noble Jacks, building my legend to line his pockets and impress the women folk."

"I pay him," I blurt. "What I mean is, he's my swordsman . . . sometimes a friend, nothing more." I don't know why I feel the need to clarify.

Her eyes widen, revealing their green as her mouth softens.

My heart thumps. "So you're not evil? Or mad?"

She scoffs. "I am neither of those, no. My brother does like to have his fun."

"I can't believe Jacks is related to the sorceress." I'm digging him up, resurrecting him, and killing him all over again in my mind. "Your *dear* brother was supposed to be with me today, did you know? Now I see why he takes so little care in his responsibilities. The scoundrel. He knows the sorceress poses no actual danger."

"I have a name," she protests. "It's Amber." When I don't immediately say anything, she sighs and waves a hand. "Known to my friends as the Amber Witch."

I jump when something nudges at my side, only to find my stack of fabrics being held out to me on one of the beanstalk branches. I gasp. "That was you? You moved the plants? You scared me."

She laughs, and the sound is like the bells of the Winterset tower —the clear, bright ring of home. "I had to do something. You kept going the wrong way," she says.

"How do you know it was wrong? Maybe I meant to go, um, that way."

"Toward the forest is always the wrong way." She looks serious again. "People don't return from the forest."

"I was following my compass," I say, pulling it out.

She leans close, her raven hair gleaming in spite of the low light, and she taps the compass hard. My stomach sinks when the needle dislodges, spins and wavers, and finally settles on a point forty-five degrees from where it had been pointing.

"Damaged when you got kicked," she concludes.

"You were following me even then?" I frown. "If you're not going to cook me or kill me, why not reveal yourself?"

"Travelers in the Mist tend to run from me."

For a moment, looking into Amber's lovely face, I'm unable to imagine why anyone would run from her. My confusion must show because she shakes her head. "Sorceress, remember?" She hands me my stack of fabrics. "Now be on your way, traveler."

I take them without looking away from her face. "Kelcy. My name is Kelcy Lustrousjourney."

Her eyebrows lift. "That's a mouthful."

"Goldenroot isn't much better."

"Fair." She begins to walk with me.

Her smile makes the corners of my mouth tug up. "I'm glad I amuse you. But if you're not the wicked sorceress people believe, then why stay here?"

"Someone has to keep you wandering fools away from the forest."

It's my turn to laugh. "I suppose you encounter a lot of travelers like me."

"Like you?" She turns to survey me with a gaze that lingers and warms my skin everywhere it touches. "No, Kelcy. Not like you."

A flush rises in my cheeks and I look away first. Before long, I find my eyes drawn to the ground she walks on. Studying the way her skirts brush the delicate bones of her ankle, I can't help but notice how the low groundcover rebounds from her steps looking ever so slightly greener and more lush that it did before she passed. Walking across the plain with Jacks is always a hurried and necessary affair. With Amber, the walk is peaceful. It's beautiful, actually, with swirling trails of mist winding around the bushes and the soft sound the breeze makes rustling the grass.

Eventually, I work up the nerve to speak again. "So you stay here alone?"

Amber walks in silence until I risk a peek at her again. She sighs. "As a witch, I'm immune to the Mist. Here on the plain, it won't affect you unless you stay too long. But deeper, where it grows thick . . . Like I said, people don't come back from the forest. I'm the only one who can stay and turn them away. My terrifying reputation, courtesy of our darling Jacks, helps with that."

A hollowness rings in her tone. Her self-appointed role helps so many people, most of whom will never know about it. None of them will ever know *her*. The thought suddenly strikes me as impossible. Intolerable, even.

"There." She stops and points.

I realize I can see shapes ahead and the glowing streaks of sunset in the sky. I recognize a ramshackle barn that sits at the edge of the Yellow Plain. Winterset is close. I'm nearly home.

I turn my back on it to face her. Amber's lovely face is set with a grim expression, one I recognize from my own reflection in the mirror each morning. My home is waiting, but is that truly what I can call my empty house? I have my work and my comforts, and I have myself. I thought it was enough.

My heart, which lodged itself in my throat long ago, finally releases to flutter in my chest. "If I were to . . . get lost again . . . you would find me?"

"Are you planning to get lost again?"

"Maybe I like to wander. Or maybe I"—I swallow and summon my courage—"maybe I'd like to see you again."

She smiles, and my gaze leaves her lips to find her sea-green eyes on me. "In the Mist?"

I nod.

With a flick of her fingers, blue herdsbloom sprouts at my feet. A trail of it leads back the way we came. Amber bends to pluck one of the spiky blossoms and holds it out to me. "You do seem like the type to get lost often."

I grin. "So long as it's a journey, I'm never lost."

And making her laugh, I've never felt more found.

JO HOLLOWAY

Jo Holloway is a Canadian author of fantasy books for young adults and fantasy-loving readers of all ages. *In The Mist* is a short story from the world featured in her upcoming series, *The Cursed Globe*. Her completed YA fantasy series, *The Immortal Voices,* features a unique hidden species known as the Pyx, the rare humans who can hear them, and the incredible bonds they form.

Jo refuses to choose between cheese and chocolate, but does hold a firm anti-soup stance for reasons no one understands. She loves animals, but traded in riding horses for riding a motorcycle. These days she can usually be found lost in a fantasy world, or out walking with her dog in this one.

Find out how Amber came to be in the Mist. Read her story, In The Dying Light, in WICKED WISHES, a YA Fantasy anthology benefitting the World Literacy Foundation. Pick it up here: https://books2read.com/wickedwishes

For a free book and a complete list of Jo's published works, visit johollowaybooks.com/books

ALEX STUBBLEFIELD

Death On Hollow Clouds

"Everyone's depending on you!" The mayor's words echoed in Darkbow's head as he climbed the steep path to the missing sorceress's home. Leonna was one of three missing persons cases he was working, and Mayor Glass was beginning to panic. In a place like Hollow Clouds, where not much happened, Darkbow was the closest thing they had to law enforcement. His hunting prowess was his main qualification.

Leonna's purple yurt was perched above the town on a rocky ledge. The stone path was lined with wind chimes and colorful glass baubles. Darkbow, his lithe figure well-suited to stealth, approached cautiously, crossbow drawn, but found no signs of forced entry. After making sure the premises were clear, he began a thorough search inside. There was a kitchen with a full pantry, dishes, a dining table, and chairs. Soft furs were piled together to make a plush bed in the sleeping quarters. A low sofa was built from a dozen or so separate cushions stacked against a wall. Darkbow turned over pots and pans, books and boxes, and finding nothing out of the ordinary, he took a seat at the table.

There he found an unfinished bowl of soup and a dirty spoon. Signs were starting to point toward a disappearance. Beside the bowl was a purple rabbit's foot strung on a silver chain. Sorceresses were known to keep talismans such as this to help them perform their magic spells. Darkbow puzzled over why the sorceress would leave her lucky rabbit's foot behind. Drawn to the object, Darkbow closed his fist around it, then everything went dark.

Darkbow landed with a squelching sound on a dark forest floor. Mushrooms the size of trees formed a canopy above him, blocking out most of the sun. The sweet smell of decay filled the air and Darkbow's nose. Condensation accumulated on the great umbrella-shaped underbellies of the fungi and dripped down onto his hair. Beads of dew formed upon his leather jerkin. There was no mistaking where the enchanted object had taken him—this was Hottentot Woods. It was infamously hard to track anything in these woods due to the rate of decay achieved by the overabundance of oversized mushrooms. It was a detective's worst nightmare.

Darkbow stood and surveyed his surroundings. His catlike eyes were keen in the dim light. He knew there had to be some sort of clue close by. Otherwise, why would the enchanted rabbit's foot have brought him there? Scanning the trunks of the nearby fungi he noticed some signs of disturbance. There was a smudge of dirt here, and a streak of slime there. Seeing something that looked like the impression of a handprint on the mushroom trunk to his north, he lurched forward to have a look. Unable to lift his feet from the ground, Darkbow fell forward onto his knees. It was as though a thick glue held his feet in place to the spongy soil below. He looked in disgust as he realized he was standing in a pool of yellow-green goo, and he was now sunken up to his ankles.

"Eck!" he exclaimed and tried to pull out one of his boots. As he tugged, the goo reached up its sticky tentacles and wrapped itself around his wrists. In horror, Darkbow watched the substance start to work its way up his arms and legs, threatening to engulf him. The more he struggled, the more the goo surrounded him. His limbs were glued down to his body, and his heart rate quickened. Soon, he was encased in the soft, putrid-smelling stuff. As it covered his face, Darkbow lost consciousness.

Darkbow awoke and the world appeared upside down. His head was pounding from all the blood rushing to it, and his arms and legs were trapped against his sides. Oil lamps glowed low and dim on a table below him. The light glittered off the handle of his crossbow which was leaning against the large workbench. He spotted his quiver of arrows on a table on the opposite side of the cavern.

Below him there was a table with strange objects on it. Murky glass bottles filled with unidentifiable contents, books and instruments stacked haphazardly together, and a series of different sized scales. There was also a cauldron so large that a man could fit inside if he were squatting down, or, indeed, cut into smaller pieces. Darkbow struggled against his bindings and felt the gooey substance close in on him even tighter.

"It doesn't help, you know," came a woman's voice. "To struggle." Darkbow strained his neck towards the sound of the voice. On the opposite wall was another shape suspended in the same green tentacles that held him. A braid of long, dark hair hung below an oval-shaped face with two violet eyes. The other captive was smiling at him, or at least, he thought she was. "It will just grip you tighter if you struggle," she explained.

Darkbow did his best to nod in response. "Where are we?" he whispered, his voice hoarse from disuse.

"We are in the lair of the witch Hippolyta. Trapped here by her trusty servants, unpleasantly known as slime molds," the purple-eyed woman answered.

"Mold? We're being held captive by mold?" Darkbow asked incredulously.

"Hippolyta is quite clever with fungi. She has enchanted these somewhat intelligent plasmodia to do her bidding."

"You seem to know an awful lot about our captor."

"Old schoolmate, I'm afraid. Unpleasant woman."

So, you're a witch, too? he thought. The woman was now familiar to him. In fact, there was no one else she could be besides the very person he had been tasked to find, the missing sorceress. "Leonna? I'm here to rescue you!"

She responded with a loud laugh. "Are you, now? What's your plan?"

"Well, I don't have one yet, but I'll think of something. The town is depending on me."

"Oh, yes, I recognize you now. You're Reggie's son. What do they call you?"

"Darkbow."

"I guess they would now that your father has passed on."

"Yes, I've inherited the title. Where are the others?"

Leonna's expression grew serious and sad. "I'm afraid it's too late for the poor shepherd and the schoolteacher. She gobbled them up yesterday."

Darkbow shivered. *Better find a way out of this before we end up like them,* he thought.

"Do you know anything about mold?" Darkbow asked.

"Mycology was never my strong suit," Leonna sighed. "However, luckily for us, I do have a plan."

"Oh, how's that?"

"You just have to relax." Leonna closed her eyes and let out a deep breath. She seemed to be drooping closer and closer to the floor, and then, finally, the slime mold holding her released its grip. Leonna fell to the ground with a graceless plop, and she was free. "Now you try," Leonna encouraged.

Darkbow screwed up his face and tried to relax his muscles as best he could. He could feel the tension around him subsiding, but then came a whistling sound from outside, chilling him to the bone.

"She's coming," Leonna whispered. Her demeanor was now alert and focused. "Darkbow, you have to relax. This is our only chance."

"How can I relax?" He writhed in his bonds, swinging violently from the side of the ceiling.

"Think of something that calms you. If you can get down, go straight to your crossbow. We'll need it."

"Can't you just cast a spell or something?"

"If only!" Leonna laughed. "No, Hippolyta has cast runes that prevent me from using my magic here. I would have left sooner, but I couldn't leave you behind, not after I saw the fate of the others. Plus, I saw that she brought your weapon in, and since I can't use my magic, you can help us escape." Leonna darted behind the large cauldron to hide.

Darkbow could hear the whistled tune growing louder. His heart was beating quickly, his pulse thundering in his ears. It was like the adrenaline rush he felt when he was on a hunt. Darkbow closed his eyes and imagined he was taking aim at a target. He slowed his breathing to calm himself. Then, suddenly—*plop*. He landed on the ground. Darkbow took a few hurried steps to his crossbow and hid. Unfortunately, he had no time to grab his quiver before their captor arrived.

From a large flap in the wall, a stout little woman appeared. She was bowlegged and pigeon-toed, and her skin was a sickly pale green. Stringy dark hair hung lankly against her wide, toad-like face, and she licked her lips constantly as though she was always thinking about her next meal. Hippolyta stomped into the room and busied herself at one of her work benches without looking up to where her prisoners should have been, as if her trusty slime molds had never let her down before. She was measuring various liquids and powders out on her scales and humming an eerie tune. The walls of the cavern quivered in harmony with her song.

Leonna crouched in waiting behind the enormous cauldron that straddled a fire pit dug into the floor of the cave. Darkbow could feel the tension in the air. Hippolyta began adding her foul ingredients into the belly of the bowl, and she brought it up to a roaring boil. While Hippolyta had her back turned, Leonna sprung up from behind the cauldron. She grabbed Darkbow's quiver of arrows and tossed it to him. The quiver passed over Hippolyta's head and into Darkbow's hands.

"Not so fast," Hippolyta croaked as she gripped Leonna firmly by the wrists. As Hippolyta and Leonna struggled with one another, Darkbow took aim, but he couldn't get a clear shot. Leonna was too entangled with the other witch. Darkbow watched as Leonna shoved Hippolyta back against the cauldron. She yelped in surprise, and Leonna broke free, pulling Hippolyta into a bear hug from behind, pinning down her arms. Darkbow assumed this was to prevent her from using any magic.

"Shoot her!" Leonna yelled.

"It's too risky," he called back.

"I can't hold her for long!"

"Let go of me," the toadlike witch shrieked.

"Do as she says," Darkbow instructed.

"No!"

"Let her go! I have a plan!"

Leonna hesitated then she released her grip on Hippolyta, jumping away from her as Darkbow raised his weapon. As his arrow pierced her right shoulder, Hippolyta let out a horrendous shriek. Still near the cauldron, Leonna hoisted Hippolyta up from the waist and tossed her into the bubbling brew!

Darkbow covered his nose with a handkerchief as a foul, green smoke rose from the deadly cauldron. They were both panting hard from the struggle which had just ensued.

"Nasty business," Leonna said, shaking her head. "I never liked her, but I didn't plan to kill her."

"Then why'd you throw her in?"

"You had only injured her. If she had enough time, she could have cast a spell and disappeared, or worse." Leonna peered curiously into the cauldron.

"You never told me; how did she get you here in the first place?"

"It was my fault, really. A few days ago, I noticed a strange new merchant visiting the market, selling charms. I was naturally curious about this potential competitor. So, after watching her for several days, I decided to approach her disguised as an average citizen.

"She was also disguised, so I didn't recognize her. But she told me more than she should have about her wares. For instance, their origins in the Hottentot Woods. I started to suspect her identity at that point and decided to buy some of the "lucky" rabbit's feet she was selling to study them.

"The translocation enchantment didn't take effect until later that evening when I had peeled away my disguise. Her spell brought me to the Woods just as it did you. Before I knew it, I was suspended upside down in her chambers."

"I was hired to recover you all alive, if possible. This will be a blow to the town."

"Such is your line of work at times, Darkbow, as is mine."

"I better be off to deliver the bad news to the mayor. Can you get us home with that?" Darkbow pointed to a rabbit's foot upon the workbench.

"Oh, yes, I think with a little fiddling, I can enchant this to get us back home." Leonna leaned over the workbench to inspect the "lucky" charm. "Now that the witch who cast the runes is dead, there should be no restrictions to my power here."

Darkbow watched as Leonna waved her hands in intricate movements over the rabbit's foot. After a few moments, she seemed satisfied.

"There. Now, take hold!" she said.

Once they were back in town, they delivered the bad news to the mayor together.

"Well, this certainly wasn't the expected outcome," Mayor Glass said, fiddling his bowler hat in his hands. "There's never been a murder in Hollow Clouds in its history! The only kidnapping was long before my time, but even that turned out to be a misunderstanding. My grandfather resolved it easily. Dangerous times we live in."

The news of the death of two of its citizens sat heavily upon the town of Hollow Clouds, and all residents wore black for mourning. The deaths were under such peculiar circumstances that many were not satisfied with Leonna's explanation. No one had heard of Hippolyta before. There had been no bodies recovered. How did Leonna get out alive? Under such scrutiny, Leonna packed up her purple yurt and prepared to leave town.

On the day of her leaving, Darkbow decided to visit and try to convince her to stay.

"They don't understand the difference between a bad witch and a good witch. Some of them lost a family member or a friend. I think having any witch around as a reminder is just too painful for the town right now," said Leonna.

"You've been nothing but kind to them!" Darkbow insisted.

"All the same, I think it is time to try my "luck" somewhere else." Leonna winked at him. "If you're ever in Hazeltown or Whitecap, look me up! News travels slowly over the mountains, so I should be able to make a little money before the rumors start to spread. I'll probably spend a little time in each place to see where business is better!" With a snap of her fingers and a puff of purple smoke, Leonna, her yurt, and all her belongings disappeared from the rocky ledge.

Darkbow stood and chewed his lip in thought as he looked over the town. Times were certainly changing. He was the first Darkbow in Hollow Clouds history to solve a murder mystery. They were bound to need his services now more than ever as the town discussed fortifying security and screening visitors at the gate. The mystery was solved, but his work was just beginning.

ALEX STUBBLEFIELD

Alex Stubblefield is a California based author with a full-time career in agriculture. From creative writing classes in school to journaling in her spare time, Alex has been weaving with words from a young age and continues to practice her writing skills in many areas of her life. When not writing, Alex enjoys snuggling her cats, tending her garden, and cooking up fancy meals with her fiance, Josh.

While she is working on her debut novel, *Las Hermanas Rodriguez*, her short story, Darkbow: Death on Hollow Clouds, featured in the fantasy anthology *Once Upon a Name*, will be her first published piece of fiction. Alex looks forward to bringing to life more stories in the future, and she hopes you will follow her writing journey on Instagram (@authoralexstubb).

SARINA LANGER

HAUNT OF THE NIGHT DOLLS

Inis Darkspark knew evil when she encountered it. As a warrior witch, she was also good at eradicating it. Its pull had drawn her to Fae's Crossing, but now she was here . . . the whole village felt on edge, but evil? There was something odd, almost pained, but her professional curiosity demanded she stay when, really, she wanted to leave.

She approached a farmer couple, judging by their pitchfork and the dirt staining their clothes—and hoped the pitchfork wasn't meant for her. She could easily defend herself, but she prayed it wouldn't be necessary. She had been trained to fight evil, not scared civilians.

Warriors were highly skilled; so were witches. But the latter were also often seen as unpredictable, and to combine the two was presumed dangerous, irresponsible. People were rarely reassured at the sight of her leathers, daggers, and pouches of poison—regular herbs and poultices, really, but she hadn't tried too hard to dispel the assumption. Being a warrior witch made her uniquely talented to deal with whatever monster the locals had trouble with. So, the villagers could frown all they liked, but they knew better than to provoke her outright. She'd never pick a fight, but fear of the unknown could make people irrational.

"Where is your inn, please?" Inis asked. She had been on the road for days. Even if no strange pull had drawn her here, she wanted to stay a night just so her feet could rest.

The man began to point down the main road, but the woman slapped his arm back down and hissed, "What are you doing?"

"The village could use the coin," the man argued in a whisper.

Inis had made it a habit to magically enhance her hearing when she entered a new place. It could be deafening in cities, but she'd learned to focus on the scared whispers and the racing heartbeats rushing away from her. She preferred early warnings when she truly wasn't welcome. Skilled as she was, she could only fight against so many people at once. She *could* rain fire on the world's largest city and burn everyone within, but that didn't mean she wanted to.

He glanced at the daggers on her belt. "Besides, what if she can help with the Night D—"

"*Don't* say their name. It's bad luck. And if she did help, she'd demand more coin than she'd spend, so we'd be poorer off, anyway."

Inis made a mental note for later. A little coin was better than none.

"Thank you," Inis said. "Have a good day."

She walked away in the direction the man had tried to point and feigned disinterest.

The inn wouldn't have stood out if it weren't for its weathered sign. The paint on the walls had faded almost entirely. No horses were waiting for their riders in its small stable. A shiver ran down her spine—an inn without patrons was never a good sign.

Inis entered. She reached out with her senses, half-expecting an ambush, but the only other people were outside or in their own homes. A man with bags under his eyes and a big dose of suspicion in them regarded her from behind the counter. His eyes fell on her daggers.

Inis sat on a barstool and placed five silver coins on the counter—the usual price for a gin with fresh berries. There was nothing like a refreshing drink after days on the road, except a bath, but she had a feeling she was out of luck for that much luxury.

Inis ordered her drink. "Where are your guests?"

The innkeeper scowled at her. "Not here. And we've no fresh berries. Plain gin will have to do."

She tried hard not to frown at his attitude. It was clear this village had fallen on hard times, and no inn survived long without customers. Of course he hadn't taken well to her question; she should have known better.

"The villagers seem on edge," Inis said. "Anything you need help with?"

He filled a tankard with gin. "You a warrior?"

Inis nodded. "And a witch."

Something shifted in his eyes. Over the years, Inis had grown used to the reaction.

The innkeeper growled something under his breath. "But I s'pose if you can help . . . Would be nice to have regular guests again. The neighbors can't afford to drink, since they've taken a hit too." He rammed his fist against the door behind him—to the kitchen, she suspected. "Boy! Come out here a minute."

A child no older than ten came out. His eyes widened when he saw her. "I've no food prepared, Pops."

"Doesn't matter," the innkeeper said. "Fetch Niall. This woman wants to talk to him."

The boy's eyes went wider still. "You mean she'll help us with the Night Dolls?"

The innkeeper rounded on the boy with his hand raised but caught himself. He let his tight fist drop by his side. "What have I told you about saying that name? They'll take you too if you're not careful."

The boy paled. "I'm sorry, Pops."

"Fetch Niall before she changes her mind."

Inis was too intrigued for that, but the boy bolted like his life depended on it. Given his father's reaction, maybe it did.

"My apologies, I forgot to introduce myself," she said. "My name is Inis Darkspark, warrior witch by trade."

He shrugged like he couldn't care less.

"Who's Niall?"

The innkeeper slid a tankard of pure gin over to her.

"Niall's our mayor, or as close to one as we get, anyway. We don't hold elections or anything fancy like that, but he takes much of the chores onto himself." He nodded at her. "He'll decide this too."

Inis sipped her drink. He was waffling just to fill the silence, but was he nervous about her, about the Night Dolls, or both?

Inis had never heard of Night Dolls before. There were plenty of monsters that could be summoned by name, but not without the right magical knowledge and rituals. She suspected neither from what she'd overheard so far. Even if the villagers had summoned the Night Dolls, they clearly wanted nothing to do with them. Unless . . . Could someone have summoned them in secret and was now too shy to take responsibility? Or maybe the villagers had agreed to the summoning but the result wasn't what they'd imagined? Magic often wasn't, especially for the inexperienced. Inis had lost count of how often she'd fixed the mess of someone too arrogant to ask for help.

Behind her, the door opened. The innkeeper didn't hide his relief. The mayor would either ask her to leave or to take care of the trouble plaguing his town. Either way, at least one of his problems would be solved soon.

"Ma'am?"

Inis turned around. "I hear you need my help?"

Mayor Niall nodded but didn't step nearer, like her presence alone was dangerous.

"Yes." He cleared his throat. "For weeks now we've had reports of hauntings. They must be stopped or we'll all go out of business."

Inis raised an eyebrow. "What kinds of hauntings?"

"All sorts," the mayor said, like it should be sufficient information. "Farmer Benneit had his pitchfork come after him, candles have been going missing, and the maiden Mairi felt watched out in the forest."

Inis slowly sipped her drink. Small objects like candles got misplaced all the time. She suspected the scared villagers were blaming supernatural causes for their own forgetfulness. It was hardly rare for young women to feel watched when alone and away from home, and it wasn't always unfounded paranoia either. The pitchfork was odd, though.

"Could I speak to this farmer? It'd be best to hear what happened from him."

But Mayor Niall shook his head. "The experience has left him mute, I'm afraid."

"And Mairi?" Inis asked. "You said she felt watched?"

"She ran here right away," the innkeeper said. "Told me of whispers in the bushes and . . . giggling." He paled like the very thought of giggling was wrong.

"Sounds to me like children were just having a laugh," Inis said. She needed the money, but she wouldn't waste her time.

"It does," Mayor Niall said, "except we don't have any who are young enough to match what she heard. She teaches the little ones and knows them better than their parents do. She'd have recognized the voices, and they'd never do her any unkindness."

Inis withheld a sigh. It wasn't unusual for adults to misjudge children—what child didn't love mischief?—but she wouldn't argue. She herself had always wanted children, but nature had other ideas. Still, she had observed many families over the years; all kids loved to play, even if they didn't all do it in the same way.

"Can I talk to her?" Inis asked.

The men exchanged a look.

"Afraid not," Niall said. "She was so spooked that she left town to visit her family."

Inis pressed her lips together in thought. "Is there anyone I can talk to?"

If not, she'd have to start her search by the forest where the young woman had felt watched. It wasn't much to go on.

Mayor Niall shook his head. "Everyone they've attacked is too shaken or has left. Besides, we're simple folk—we don't know how ghosts think. We'd have nothing of value to tell you."

"Can you at least tell me what the Night Dolls are? Do you know what they want? What do they look like?"

"What they want?" The innkeeper huffed. "They want to cause us suffering, that's what."

Mayor Niall held up his hands as if in apology. "They haven't told us why they're here. As for what they look like . . . we don't know what their true form is, but they've possessed other things than pitchforks. Mairi screamed something about dolls, and our candles seem to go missing at night. I'm afraid we don't know anything more."

Inis sighed. "How much can you pay? I have a lot of preparations to make since I can't question anyone who was attacked by them, and I've never heard of Night Dolls before. This might not be an easy contract."

The men exchanged another glance.

"We don't have much," Mayor Niall said, "but we'll all pitch in if you rid us of this danger."

Besides the feeling she'd had when she arrived, she hadn't seen anything to make her think there was any real danger here—at most, these Night Dolls had scared people a little—but she nodded. *We'll all pitch in* was usually short for *You won't get much from us, but we'll pretend to try*. However, the weather was turning colder. Any money was better than none.

"All right," she said. "Since there's no one I can talk to, I'll try the forest, but I may not be able to help if I don't find anything."

She downed the rest of her drink and made her way toward the forest.

Inis took her time walking across the field to the forest. The more she thought about this mystery, the more she became convinced the villagers were simply more superstitious than most. She doubted she would find anything worth investigating, but she had said she'd look into it. At least she'd likely be back on the road before nightfall—she preferred a warm bed to a hard field, but in this case, she preferred to find another town.

Inis stepped past the first tree—

And *pain* hit her. What she'd felt upon entering Fae's Crossing had been mere trickles of a larger ocean. The whole forest was . . . was . . .

Despair came over her. *You'll never be loved, never be accepted.*

Tears shot into her eyes. *You'll always be alone.*

This forest wasn't haunted. It was in pain.

Inis placed one hand on the cool moss and the other on the tree to ground herself. But the forest's anguish poured out of the rough bark and threatened to overwhelm her.

"Please," she said. "I don't mean to hurt you. I want to help."

She had been hired to stop the Night Dolls; Mayor Niall likely hoped she'd kill some demon and bring back its head as proof. But she hadn't known the full story when she accepted. She still didn't. But this pain didn't feel evil, it felt hurt, lonely. Afraid.

"Please."

Slowly, the pain receded and seeped into the soil and trunk, like the forest was calling back its flood.

Inis wasn't surprised Mairi had felt uneasy. If she'd felt just a fraction of what Inis had experienced, it was no miracle the young woman had fled the village. Inis also wasn't surprised everyone else thought the Night Dolls were some malevolent spirits. She was no closer to knowing what they were, though, or how giggling fit this pain. The two seemed too different to have anything to do with each other. Had someone gone mad in this forest, perhaps? She didn't know any spirits associated with madness, but maybe she was about to learn something new.

Inis took a deep breath in. She let it go into the soil with her whispered intention. "Guide me. Show me where it hurts."

From deeper in the forest, whispers came to her on the breeze. Inis spoke a quick protection spell and followed the wind. Throughout the years, she had followed trails of blood and innards, bone shards and pieces of skin. Wailing and screams. There was none of that in this forest.

Here, there were toys.

Covered in moss and worn by weather. Some hung in the trees like they'd been sentenced to death. Others peeked out beneath the branches and moss. She had thought the hauntings had an oddly childish feel to them, and the toys . . . Could the Night Dolls be children? Some of the toys looked too weathered and overgrown. Unless the children had survived on berries and a stream? But even then, wild animals would be a threat. Perhaps villagers had ventured this far, seen the dolls, and coined the name Night Dolls from them.

But Inis didn't believe it. She was still missing something.

She walked until the thickening forest gave way to fewer trees, a thin stream, and little treehouses made of branches and foliage. Clumsy ladders were attached to small openings. There wasn't one full wall between them, and an earthy smell clung to the place from the rotting leaves.

And around the tree trunks, toys and candles were arranged like graves.

Inis's stomach turned, but she held on to the new feeling she now sensed: hope.

"Hello?"

Rustling leaves answered her. Maybe Night Dolls only came out with the stars.

She knelt by one of the toys, a hand-carved horse, its painted details mostly flaked off. Three candles stood around it, but they didn't look like they'd ever been lit. Her eyes burned. If these were the graves of too-young souls, how could the candles not burn for them? Inis called small flames into her hands and gently lit the wicks one by one until their glow warmed the treehouse village.

The villagers couldn't have known they'd sent her after children. And hadn't they said there weren't any children young enough to match the voices they'd heard? But there was something the innkeeper had said to his son: *They'll take you, too, if you're not careful.*

Inis sat on the mossy ground and closed her eyes. If she could soak up all the anguish in this place, she would, but she feared there was no vessel large enough.

Something moved behind her. She opened her eyes. Slowly, so as not to scare it away, she turned around.

A fabric doll floated in mid-air. Its head was mostly disconnected from the seams and rested on one shoulder. One of its button eyes was missing, the other hanging by a thread. The fabric used for the mouth had unraveled, turning the once-pretty smile into a pained grimace. None of its stuffing showed and it looked hollow, like its guts had been torn out long ago.

"Hello," Inis tried again. "Do you . . . live here?"

"You lit our candles. Why?" The doll's mouth didn't move. The voice was that of a too-young girl, a stark contrast to the decaying cloth.

Inis's throat tightened. "Because someone should."

More dolls rose into the air from their mossy resting places. They were all in various stages of decay, but none were as tattered as the one who'd spoken. Inis guessed she was the oldest—not in age, but in time spent here—and had taken on a protective leader role.

"You're not like the others," the girl-doll said.

"What others?" Inis asked.

A cold gust shook the leaves and froze Inis.

"They want us gone," a younger-sounding doll said. Inis thought it might have been a boy. "They don't like us."

The pain in his voice broke her heart.

"Why are you all here?" Inis dreaded the answer. There was definitely magic involved, and she was beginning to wonder if it was a curse. Whatever the cause, she needed to know the details to work with it.

The dolls were quiet for a moment. Inis wondered if they didn't remember, or perhaps didn't want to.

The oldest doll spoke first. "They wanted a boy. Not me."

"I got lost playing in the woods. This place called me." A moment's pause. "They didn't come looking for me."

"Too many mouths to feed, Ma said."

"Not pretty enough for a dowry."

Inis's heart broke little by little as the dolls opened up. The villagers had been scared to even say their name, but the Night Dolls were just children. People feared what they didn't understand; Inis knew this all too well. They didn't understand why someone would want to be a warrior witch—an unthinkably dangerous, risky combination they couldn't wrap their head around—so they shut her out until they needed help and not a moment longer. The Night Dolls were victims of fear and ignorance, just like her.

"Were you from Fae's Crossing?"

The more weathered dolls didn't move.

"I sometimes think of a name, but I don't know what it means," a boy's doll said. "Whitewater."

Inis swallowed. Whitewater was far to the west.

"And these dolls," Inis said. "Are they your real forms?"

"You first," the leader doll said. "Why are *you* here?"

"Because the villagers fear you. They think you're evil spirits come to haunt them."

Giggling rustled the grass and creaked the branches.

"They're just pranks."

"How else are we supposed to play?"

"Silly adults, don't even know games."

"If they're scared, they won't bother us," the oldest doll said. "What will you do? I warn you; we can defend ourselves."

Inis smiled. "I don't doubt it." She did. "But perhaps I can help you stay safe for good." She was used to prejudice from most people, but these children didn't deserve it. They had suffered enough.

"Do you mean it?" a little girl's voice asked.

Inis nodded. "I'll do all I can to protect you."

All around her, the dolls dropped to the ground. Shimmering blue forms rose in their stead. The children's souls.

Inis didn't understand what had drawn them here or what made their spirits visible like this, but it was clear that this place was their safe harbor. Inis wanted to make it safer before she left.

She was sure of two things: this forest was a haven for lost children's souls, and the villagers were scared enough to want them gone. If Inis didn't return, they would find someone else sooner or later. How would the Night Dolls cope when warrior after warrior showed up to drive them out, or worse? What would they do if someone set fire to the forest?

Inis could use the villagers' fear in her favor. If they were too spooked by whispers and a possessed pitchfork to come near the forest, maybe they wouldn't need much more to keep them away entirely. Eventually, they might send someone else to investigate, but Inis was even more feared. She knew prejudice. Maybe she could use that in her favor too. If she didn't return, if she could make the villagers believe the Night Dolls had killed her or, better yet, possessed her and used her skills as they saw fit, then rumors alone might protect them. And if it wasn't enough, she'd leave a few traps closer to the tree houses just in case—invisible spells to feed the villagers' fears.

She just needed to be careful, or the villagers would simply burn the forest to the ground.

"I need time to prepare," Inis said. "Is there anywhere I can stay?"

The soul-lights flickered. One returned to the oldest doll.

"Any treehouse is fine," the doll said. "We don't really need them, we just feel . . ."

"Safer," another soul finished.

"They don't look very secure." Inis nodded to the nearest hut. "Are they enough for you?"

The first doll shuddered. It reminded her of a shrug.

"It would be nice to have a real home, but we can't do anything like that. The treehouses were already here when I arrived."

"So you don't know why they are here?" Inis couldn't help feeling disappointed. She had hoped for more answers. "There's old magic here."

It had to be old magic to have drawn the children here. Something had tugged at their instincts when their parents had abandoned them —it couldn't have been luck every time.

Another soul-light dropped into its doll and rose with its tattered body. "Mummy once said there was a witch here who took in naughty children."

Inis nodded. She hadn't been to this part of the world often and wasn't familiar with the local history. If that was all they knew, she'd have to make do.

"What will you do?" the oldest doll asked.

Inis looked around and pointed as she spoke. "I will create a magical barrier which will reinforce the pain I felt when I entered the forest. I will remain connected to it, so I'll know if any intruders pass. It should stop most people.

"I will also see if I can fix your homes, create a proper"—she bit back the word *graveyard*—"resting place. You may not need the tree-houses, but that doesn't mean you can't have homes." If she left this place more of a haven than she'd found it, she'd leave content. "Eventually, I've no doubt the villagers will come, either with someone else or carrying torches themselves."

Many of the soul-lights flickered.

"I won't let them hurt you," Inis said, "but I've no way of knowing how long it'll be before they come. It could be tomorrow, or it might be a year."

"Could you stay?" the oldest doll said. "We can make an exception since you're helping us. Please, miss."

Inis smiled in return. She could stay until she was sure that they were safe. After that, she didn't belong here. This forest was their haven, not hers.

First, she created the barrier around the treehouse village—invisible but heavy in the emotions it amplified—and did her best to improve the homes. She was no architect, but she repaired the roofs and walls as best she could with her magic. By the time she was done, the houses were far from luxurious, but they were whole. They spelled shelter. There weren't enough for all the Night Dolls, but they didn't mind sharing.

She also built a small resting area behind the treehouses. She coaxed forest flowers to the surface there. They left the candles at the tree trunks, and the Night Dolls stole a few more. Soon, the treehouse village looked and felt more like a home.

In return, the Night Dolls brought Inis nuts and fruits and sat around a fire with her at night. She caught rabbits and deer, and while the lost souls couldn't eat, they appreciated the warm smells and stories Inis told them. She had meant to make the treehouses a home for the Night Dolls, but the longer she stayed, the more it felt like home to her too. The souls didn't shy away from her or her profession. There was no end to their curiosity and awe. For the first time since she had chosen to become a warrior witch, Inis was herself without judgment.

And then, one night, she felt a tug on her barrier.

The villagers had come.

How long had it been since she'd reached Fae's Crossing? It had been easy to lose track of the days and weeks here. Inis was used to moving from contract to contract. Here, she had been focused on helping and soothing souls rather than killing beasts and breaking curses, and she enjoyed it.

The Night Dolls had grown excited when she'd revealed her plan.

"It's time." She asked the wind to carry her voice to every Night Doll so they'd go to their agreed stations.

Inis waited in the central treehouse. The oldest Night Doll stayed with her. Every candle was lit; when the villagers passed her chosen threshold on the mossy ground, the flames blew out.

Mayor Niall and the innkeeper led the others, but barely anyone had come. Some carried pitchforks, but by the unsure looks on their faces, she guessed it was more for their own peace of mind than out of aggression. None looked sure about this endeavor. Those who had feigned courage had lost it when the candles had blown out.

"See that?" the innkeeper said. "I said there's bad magic here! We can't fight something like that."

"We should have hired someone else," another villager said. "Maybe a witch to deal with the magic."

"We already sent Ma'am Darkspark," Mayor Niall said. "Perhaps there was nothing she could do and she has moved on."

The innkeeper huffed something about warrior witches being untrustworthy, and the villagers murmured their agreement.

Inis wondered if they recognized the candles as the ones that had disappeared from their houses.

"Let's get this over with, then," Mayor Niall said.

"Must we?" one of the men asked. "I don't see a witch. You must be right, she's probably left."

Inis whispered a spell to make the leaves rustle A few branches fell to the ground.

One of the men jumped; another gasped.

"I don't think we're welcome here."

"Of course we're not welcome here," the innkeeper barked. "Told you. This whole forest is cursed!"

The group walked toward the treehouses. To anyone the Night Dolls didn't want here, they appeared as dilapidated as Inis had found them.

"Ma'am Darkspark?" Mayor Niall called. His voice was loud enough, but the tremble in his words betrayed him.

"Now," Inis whispered to the oldest Night Doll.

All around, a single candle lit beside every tree . . .

And by every candle, one Night Doll rose into the air.

"*Leave*," they whispered. "*Leave*." Over and over again, until their voices were a chorus joined with the breeze. Some of the younger ones giggled when the villagers paled and stepped back.

"Maybe we should find another mercenary," Mayor Niall said.

Inis smiled to herself. From what she'd seen, they couldn't afford it.

But if they did find someone willing to work for little to no money . . .

Better to ensure they wouldn't try.

Inis had painted her face with mud and covered her hair and clothes in moss. With magic, she made herself appear translucent and floated down the rope ladder. The innkeeper pointed at her, his face ashen, and took a step back. The villagers didn't see the Night Doll right behind her, but they would hear her.

"This one is ours now," the Night Doll said. More giggling from the younger ones joined a whispered chorus of *ours, ours*.

Most of the villagers ran. Mayor Niall and the innkeeper stayed, looking nearly as ghostly as she did.

"We will leave your village alone," the Night Doll whispered, "but you will leave us alone too. If not . . ."

Inis flicked her wrist and kept it at a slightly painful angle to make it look like the Night Doll was controlling her. Around the tree-houses, the forest lit on fire—a well-controlled illusion.

"Leave us, or your houses will burn."

Inis and every Night Doll fell to the ground. The candles extinguished, but Inis kept the illusion of the burning forest alive.

"Should we . . . take her with us?" the innkeeper asked.

Mayor Niall had already retreated several steps. "You heard them: she's theirs now. Do you really want to anger them?"

A whispered *noooo* rustled through the leaves.

"Right then," Mayor Niall said. "Let's leave."

The moment Inis felt their feet cross her barrier, the Night Dolls rose and cheered. Inis dusted herself off and picked the moss out of her hair with a smile.

"And they really won't come back?" a young boy's doll asked.

"I don't think they will," Inis said. "As long as you hold up your end. No more stealing candles, and no more playing tricks on them."

"Will you come back to help us if they come again?" the oldest Night Doll asked.

Inis nodded. "If I can and if I hear about it. Or . . ." She bit her lip.

Would she be asking too much? "I could stay. I could tell you stories and keep you safe."

The oldest Night Doll cleared her throat. "I suppose we could allow that."

And so, Inis Darkspark stayed, and the villagers didn't bother them again. Whenever one ventured too close, a few candles would go missing from their drawers—a reminder of burning forests and whispered threats. And while they kept their distance, Inis stayed with the Night Dolls: her own family of lost-soul children.

SARINA LANGER

Sarina Langer is a dark epic fantasy author who lives with her partner and daughter (read: their cat) in the south of England.

She's as obsessed with books and stationery now as she was as a child, when she drowned her box of colour pencils in water so they wouldn't die and scribbled her first stories on corridor walls. (A first sign of things to come, according to her mother. Normal toddler behaviour, according to Sarina.)

In her free time, she reads magical stories with dark plot twists, plays video games, and goes on nature walks. She has a weakness for books on writing, tarot cards, and pretty words (*specificity*, anyone?).

If you liked her short story and want to read more, you can get her dark epic fantasy e-book *Rise of the Sparrows* for free: https://books2read.com/u/3yEEd6

And if you *really* liked her short story, you may even want to join her mailing list for free books and monthly updates: https://www.subscribepage.com/sarinasbooks She'd love to have you on board.

BEKAH BERGE

The first bite could make or break a dish.

It would take more than cooking with finesse to win the illustrious cooking competition, Salty Sweet. To win, that first bite would have to be extraordinary. Unique. A flavor profile filled with nostalgia that blended seamlessly with talent—a slice of perfection.

That was the goal.

Salty Sweet was a three-part cooking competition hosted by the Troll Brothers: Toby, Terry, and Tegal. Every year, ten of the best cooks in the kingdom were invited to exhibit their culinary skills and have a chance at winning the grand prize: a trunk of gold.

Though not actually brothers, the intimidating trio collectively owned several fleets of ships and controlled much of the trading in the kingdom.

Everyone knew of the Troll Brothers and their wealth.

Everyone also knew that they enjoyed only one thing more than gold.

Food.

"Ten seconds remaining!" shouted Perry, the competition's announcer. His nasally voice set my teeth on edge.

Focus.

Don't forget the garnish.

I really needed my hands to stop shaking.

"Seven seconds!"

Very, very carefully, I tipped my spoon and slowly drizzled the yuzu compote onto the savory rice custard. The tangy sweetness of the fruit would complement the richness of the dish well.

"Four seconds!"

I inhaled deeply, stood up straight, wiped the edge of the plate clean with my cloth, then took a step back from the table.

"Time! That is time, everyone!" shouted Perry. "Please grab your signature dish and place it beside your name at the judging table."

I left my assigned cooking station and joined the other nine cooks as they each placed their dish on the table. Pride filled me as I set mine down. The seaweed and salmon rice custard was something my nana used to make for me as a young girl. She'd called it a "hug in a bowl."

The moment I'd been invited to compete in the annual Salty Sweet cooking competition, I'd jumped on the opportunity. My family's tavern, the Hollow Hail, wouldn't survive the next few moons unless I won the prize money—a trunk of gold that would change my life.

I needed to win . . . or the tavern would be shut down for good.

"Interesting choice for a signature dish, *princess.*" Axel de Cozmos put his dish down beside mine, and I immediately felt the hairs on the back of my neck stand up. He'd made a fresh slaw—lightly dressed, of course—positioned elegantly atop buttery cod, with some kind of creamed turnip on the side.

The smell of his dish made my mouth water.

I cursed under my breath.

"How many times have I told you not to call me princess?" I fired back, glaring at the unbearably handsome cook. Tan skin, dark hair, and warm brown eyes, with hands scarred from cooking. Same as me. We'd known each other since childhood, eaten at each other's taverns, and been in a ridiculous rivalry ever since I'd taken over ownership of the Hollow Hail.

"Norenia." He winked. "Is that better?"

"Only slightly." For reasons known only to Axel, he'd begun calling me princess *after he*'d caught me having a heated exchange with my sugar supplier. It wasn't my fault I'd had to be stern with the merchant. He'd tried to sell me sugar for twice the amount that he'd charged the male cook down the street.

Words needed to be exchanged, and I informed him that should he try and swindle me again, I'd report him to the merchant guild.

"Attention!" Perry shouted loudly enough to make me jump. My cheeks burned with humiliation as I realized I'd been standing there like a fool, staring into Axel's eyes. "All cooks are to line up. The Troll Brothers have arrived and are eager to taste what you've created for them today."

"Nervous?" whispered Axel. His warm breath tickled my ear, and I suddenly had the insane urge to giggle.

Good gods, I hated this man.

Loathed him.

Despised him.

And yet, I melted every time I remembered the taste of the browned butter sauce he glazed his lobster cakes with . . .

No.

Concentrate.

"I *don't* get nervous," I lied, straightening my spine as I clutched my hands behind my back.

The judges would begin the tasting soon.

The Hollow Hail was my family's tavern, and it had been in the family for generations. Sadly, a tragic sailing accident had changed everything. Two years ago, I'd suddenly found myself orphaned at the age of eighteen and the sole owner of our tavern. I'd done my best to run the place, but the expenses piled high and then higher still.

I needed help, but I couldn't afford to pay anyone a livable wage.

I was stuck.

And I was desperate.

Of the nine other cooks in the competition, I'd only met two of them: Katya from The Wishing Well, and Axel. Katya had an excellent fish stew, and her tavern always put on great music.

"Of course not, *princess.*"

By all the gods, I could strangle this man.

"I know you've become accustomed to others groveling at your feet," I hissed through my clenched teeth. "But you will find no such behavior from me." I held my head up high and basked in the mild breeze coming in from the nearby sea. The competition was taking place in the town's park, where there was plenty of room for passersby to stop and observe.

"Wouldn't dream of it." Axel snorted. "How about we make a deal? When I win, I'll make you dinner at my tavern. But if you win, you make me dinner?"

"Ha!" I rolled my eyes. "You're assuming I even like your food."

"You ate at my tavern last week."

I bit my lip and remained silent because, blast it all, he was right.

I loved his food.

Bastard.

The three trolls grunted and shrugged their way through each of the prepared dishes. It was difficult to discern if they liked or hated a dish, because nearly every emotion they showed seemed to be neutral.

I imagined this was why they had become so successful in their businesses—they were impossible to read.

There was a great deal of tension once the trolls finished tasting the dishes. They turned around to discuss our fates, and I closed my eyes, anxiously hoping, I would make it to the next round. Everyone knew the first round was the signature dish, but after that? It was anyone's guess. Rounds two and three changed every year.

The trolls turned around, and I held my breath.

Please gods, let them pick me.

Though twice my size, the trolls were shockingly dainty eaters. And their expertly tailored black trousers, vests, and overcoats complemented their swamp-green skin.

Deep breaths.

"Excellent dishes, one and all," said Toby, the littlest troll, who sported not one but seven gold rings, one on each finger.

"You should be proud," added Terry, the tallest of them.

"But only five of you can continue on," finished Tegal, the only troll I'd ever seen with spectacles. He honestly seemed rather charming.

Until suddenly, those spectacles landed on me.

Sizzle and Pop

A mystery basket.

Along with Katya, Axel, and me, there had been two others lucky enough to make it to the second round.

"Begin!" shouted Perry.

Inhaling deeply, I opened my basket and froze. What in all the gods' names was I going to make with minotaur meat, purple endive, a jar of pickled eggs, and pineapple?

After tapping my fingers on the rims of the basket for far too long —I was wasting precious time—I decided that there was only one answer to a basket like this. I was going to be making dumplings.

I spared a glance to my right and bit my lip to stop the laughter that threatened to spill free at the look of shock on Axel's face. Of all the repulsive ingredients in the realm to be given, a jar of fish eyes was definitely up there. It was going to be next to impossible for him to make that ingredient shine.

Hustling over to the outdoor pantry I grabbed a jar of flour, a variety of fresh herbs, a few sweet onions, black garlic, jalapeno, honey, rice vinegar, a loaf of bread, and sesame oil.

I hurried back to my station, organized my ingredients, and then grabbed a bowl to put the slab of minotaur meat in. I'd never tasted minotaur meat, but I imagined it to be tough. I would need to mince the meat finely if I was to have any hope of it cooking properly within the dumpling.

Once that step was complete, I dabbed at the sweat on my brow with the back of my sleeve. My heart was racing as I snuck a peek at the trickling grains of sand slipping down the hourglass. There was no chance these dumplings would cook all the way through unless I moved faster.

I placed one of my black skillets on the iron grill resting above the open flame. I quickly stoked the fire to ensure it was nice and hot. I tossed a hunk of butter onto the pan while I chopped onions and black garlic. I divided up the onions and garlic, throwing half onto the skillet and half into the bowl of minced meat.

It sizzled and steamed. The aroma of onions and garlic sautéing in hot butter was positively delicious.

Snatching the pineapple and placing it onto my cutting board, I quickly sliced it up and added the large chunks of pineapple to my mix of sautéed onions and garlic. Next came salt, pepper, a few slices of jalapeno, and a cup of hot water. Steam hissed. I added a touch more salt to my broth before turning my attention back to the filling.

Unsure what else to do with my purple endive, I decided to chop it up and add it to my meat mixture. That would have to do. I started in on the pickled eggs, then paused as I realized I needed coconut cream to really bring the dish together.

Racing back to the pantry, I nearly collided with Axel as he stood up and whipped around with an enormous catfish in his hands.

He cursed. "Announce yourself next time, *princess.* I almost knocked you out with a fish."

"As if you aren't secretly trying to find a way to sabotage me," I fired back, sidestepping him as I searched the pantry shelves for a jar of coconut cream.

I hoped I wasn't going to have to cut open a fresh coconut.

I did not have time for that.

"Now, why would I need to sabotage you if I'm so confident I'm going to win?" Axel grinned.

"Perhaps because sabotaging me gives you great joy."

"Careful, *princess,*" Axel's velvety voice was soft as a whisper. "Your insecurity is showing." He winked and then took off back to his station.

I clenched my fists and glared at him.

The nerve of that incorrigible man!

My heart was racing for all the wrong reasons.

What was I doing?

Oh . . . yes, that's right. Coconut cream.

Focus.

My eyes snagged on a jar of coconut cream hidden behind a bushel of carrots. I grabbed it and hurried back to where my broth was simmering nicely over the flame. A quick taste led to a dash of more salt.

Tossing in a handful of flour, I drizzled the coconut cream over the dumpling's filling and began mixing it all together by hand. Once I was satisfied with the consistency, I shifted my attention to arguably the most important part of any dumpling: the dough.

"Hands up!" shouted Perry. "Cooks, please step back from your stations."

My heart hammered with confusion as I dutifully stepped back from my station. I glanced at the hourglass that was now sitting on its side.

What in the five hells was going on?

My gaze locked with Axel's, then Katya's down the way.

Everyone was baffled.

Perry cleared his throat and placed a jar on a clear spot in the pantry. "Let's make things a little more interesting, shall we?" His grin was downright vicious. "Inside this jar are five pieces of folded parchment. Each bears the name of one of our competitors. You will each step forward and pull one from the jar."

Oh no.

"One by one, you will have the opportunity to choose a single ingredient from the pantry to gift to cook whose name you've drawn." Perry smirked. "This is your golden opportunity to cause as much chaos as you'd like. Choose wisely."

This was absurd.

I cut a quick glance at my simmering broth, while I waited for Perry to call me forward. Hopefully whichever cook pulled my name from the jar wouldn't give me some heinous ingredient that would effectively ruin my dish.

"Norenia, please step forward," said Perry.

Gold.

I was doing this for gold.

Wiping my hands on my apron, I hesitated for the briefest of moments before plunging my hand into the jar and pulling out a piece of parchment. I ignored Perry's jovial smile and turned back to my station.

I unfolded the parchment and smothered the chuckle that threatened to rip free.

Axel.

Yes!

The gods were smiling down on me for once. I had drawn Axel's name and could barely contain my excitement. Let's see what that arrogant bastard could do with sea cucumber—the one ingredient in the realm that made me squeamish.

"Excellent. Now that everyone has drawn a name, let's reveal who you'll be sabotaging!" Perry laughed.

The hair on the back of my neck stood up when Axel turned toward me and smiled wolfishly.

My stomach tightened.

I cursed.

"The time left in the hourglass will begin once more when you have all delivered the new ingredient to the person you're sabotaging," said Perry.

"You know, *princess.*" Axel stepped away from his station and sauntered toward me. "I saw an ingredient earlier that I know you'll just love."

My nostrils flared as I scowled at him. "Funny you should say that." I raised an eyebrow and tilted my head to the side. "I was thinking the same thing." I held up my piece of parchment with his name on it.

Axel's eyes flashed.

"Fair enough," he replied as we stood there glaring at each other while the other three cooks sped toward the pantry.

"Fair enough," I repeated. His captivating eyes held me hostage for far too long. I needed . . . to . . .

His hand reached up, and I swear I held my breath as he plucked something from my hair. He took a step closer, too close. I could smell the lemon and garlic he'd been cooking with on his hands. "You had a piece of endive in your hair," he said softly.

My face flamed with humiliation when he dropped the endive into my open hand. With another aggravating wink, he took off toward the pantry, and I sucked in a sharp breath.

Focus.

I shook my head and raced after him, hoping he didn't get to the sea cucumber before me.

The last few pieces of sand slipped to the bottom of the hourglass.

Perry shouted for everyone to step away from their stations. The second round was officially over, and my dumplings now rested in a flavorful broth, accompanied by the ingredient Axel had given me: tarragon.

It was a deceptively simple ingredient.

For those unfamiliar with the herb, one might decide to mix it into a dish with some rosemary and thyme. However, tarragon was not to be handled carelessly. The pungent herb could easily overpower a dish and destroy it. The flavor profile of tarragon began and ended with the heavy taste of fennel. Something that would not blend well with the flavors I had already created in the broth.

So what in all the gods' blasted names had I decided to do with such a vile herb? I'd ground it into a fine powder and added it to the minotaur meat. Did it work? Well, seeing as I hadn't had time to actually taste my dumplings, I was going to find out if Axel had successfully sabotaged me when the judges tasted my dish.

Should be fun.

The five of us waited in various states of terror as the judges began tasting.

Somehow, Axel had made both the sea cucumber and fish eyes blend seamlessly in his dish, and the judges couldn't stop fawning over his *sheer perfection* blah, blah, blah.

How unfair for the gods to bless him with good looks and a brain.

"Norenia, please come forward."

My dish had been saved for last.

I placed black ceramic bowls of steaming dumplings in front of each Troll Brother and waited for them to scold me for my use of the tarragon.

The trolls made noises, whispered to each other, tasted some more, and then without another word, thanked me for my dish and dismissed me.

Spinning on my heel, I closed my eyes and cursed spectacularly in my head. I was going to lose the tavern.

I clasped my shaking hands behind my back and stood behind my station while I waited for the inevitable.

"Very interesting dishes," said Terry.

Even while sitting, he was taller than me.

"Though some were more enjoyable than others," added Toby.

"But only two will move on to the third and final round," finished Tegal.

I held my breath.

"Axel de Cozmos," announced Toby.

"Norenia TeTrayzure," said Terry.

Oh, my gods . . .

"The two of you have been invited to cook in the final round," said Tegal. "As for the other three, thank you for participating in Salty Sweet."

Wow.

I bit my lip as I glanced over at Axel—of course the man had to be grinning from ear to ear.

"Axel. Norenia." Perry rubbed his hands together in excitement. "You will have half an hourglass to create a dessert worthy of our judges. But here's the catch."

My stomach dropped.

"You will only be allowed to use three ingredients in your dessert." Perry grinned. "Begin!"

Not a moment to be wasted, I sprang into action.

Axel and I nearly collided once more in the pantry while we snatched up three ingredients for our desserts. Only one dessert came to mind when I thought about creating something simple, yet complex: a piping hot cup of chocolate. I would be using an old family recipe, but this dessert was the absolute highlight of my menu at The Hollow Hail.

Rich, decadent dark chocolate melted into a warm bath of sweet coconut milk. Half a vanilla bean pod would give it some much needed balance. The trick with the dessert was never to let the mixture boil. Burnt chocolate wasn't going to win me a trunk of gold.

Good gods, I was so close to winning.

So close to being able to save my family tavern.

I would be able to afford more help.

I would be able to focus solely on cooking the food while others served it.

This gold would change my life, and the only thing standing in my way was Axel. But I could do this . . . I could win. I was good enough to win.

Scraping the delicious vanilla beans from the pod, I added them to my coconut and chocolate mixture, then continued to stir the rich decadent dessert vigorously.

The texture needed to be silky smooth.

"Final moments! Final moments!" shouted Perry as he held the hourglass high above his head.

How was it already time?

My heart raced as I quickly poured the mixture into three small glasses.

"Time is up! Step away from your stations!"

I blew out a long breath and stared at my dessert. It was simple, perhaps too simple. But I was proud of it. If this dish lost me a trunk of gold, then so be it. At least I had stayed true to family tradition and made a dessert that reminded me of home.

This dessert was my heart and soul.

Axel and I brought our desserts up to the table where the Troll Brothers sat. Compared to my dessert, Axel's looked elaborate—a bright pink mousse with a dusting of pink crumbs. He must've used beets. For only being allowed three ingredients, his dessert was fancy . . . and smart. I would expect nothing less from him.

Clasping my shaking hands behind my back, I stood next to Axel as the trolls began tasting our desserts. Just as they had in the previous two rounds, the trolls remained stoic as they made noises and spoke softly to each other.

When all three heads, bent closely together, began nodding . . . I knew a winner had been chosen.

Deep breaths.

I had done my best.

"It has been an honor to taste your dishes today," said Tegal.

"This year's competition has been filled with immense talent," added Terry. "Both of you should be very proud of your cooking."

"But there can be only one winner," finished Toby.

Oh gods, oh gods, this was it.

Please, please pick me.

I closed my eyes.

"We are delighted to announce that this year's winner of Salty Sweet and the recipient of a trunk of gold is . . . " said Terry.

"Norenia TeTrayzure!" shouted all three trolls at once.

My eyes flew open, and my jaw dropped.

I won?

I won.

Oh my gods, I did it!

My hands covered my mouth, as tears filled my eyes and my heart squeezed with joy. Strong arms suddenly surrounded me, and I realized Axel was hugging me and whispering "well deserved" into my hair.

"Your dessert was exquisite," beamed Tegal.

"Comfort in a cup," added Terry.

I was speechless.

Axel released me, and I quickly wiped the tears that cascaded down my cheeks. I couldn't believe I'd won.

The Hollow Hail was saved.

I did it.

Axel gave me a true genuine smile and said, "You owe me dinner."

BEKAH BERGE

Bekah Berge fell in love with all things mystical at a young age. Her love of stories led to her writing her first book in her early twenties, and she's never looked back since. When not scribbling down fantastical tales, she enjoys traveling, gardening, vegan baking, and brewing the perfect cup of tea.

She also suffers from a rare chronic pain condition called CRPS (Complex Regional Pain Syndrome) and to learn more visit: CRPSBookshelf.com

Her latest novel, Needlework, follows a group of four musicians as they vie for a spot on the coveted main stage at the illustrious Olive Branch Music and Arts Festival.

Instagram: Bekah.Berge

LYNDSEY HALL

BARONESS OF BLOOD AND BONE

THE SUN SANK LOW OVER THE ETERNAL CITY AS TULLIA ARTFULBEAU sharpened her blades, ready for the night's festivities. As Baroness of the Northern Wolves, Tullia had a reputation as the fiercest alpha in the empire. She'd hate to disappoint her loyal fans.

A wicked grin curved her red-painted lips as she tucked the knives into sheaths at her waist and strapped around her arm and thigh. She slid Lucky Number Five into her boot. You never knew when you might need to toe off your boots and cut yourself free from your bonds using only your feet.

It wouldn't be the first time.

Or the second.

"The lunar eclipse is starting soon, Baroness." Octavia, Tullia's second-in-command, stuck her blond head around the door. Like her alpha, she was dressed head-to-toe in leather, a veritable armory of weapons decorating her body like jewelry.

"I'm ready," Tullia said. "Let's ride."

In a matter of hours, she'd know the truth about her mother's death and would finally be able to take her revenge. But first, she had to make a quick stop at the Crescent Club.

Numbering just eight, the Northern Wolves was the smallest pack in the Eternal City, but what they lacked in size they made up for in attitude. Tonight would be the first total lunar eclipse in years, a night for celebration among the wolf packs. And lupine festivals tended to devolve into violence at the best of times. As Tullia's father had always said, better a knife in your hand than a knife in your back. He had lived his life by that rule until the day his own brother had killed him—a knife in the heart, as it happened—and taken over as alpha.

Tullia had been forced to live under her uncle's oppressive rule for five years until, at eighteen, she'd challenged him for control of the pack, and won. By cutting his throat with Lucky, that knife in her boot.

"Time to go, wolves," she called to the rest of the pack as she strode out of the side chapel she'd commandeered as her office in the derelict church they called home. She strutted to the door, heeled boots clacking on the crumbling stone floor. "We don't want to be late to the party, now do we?"

A chorus of whoops and howls went up from the pack members who'd been draped over the rotting pews drinking bottles of red wine. Felix and Cassius appeared to be playing a card game on an upturned crate, a small heap of gold coins in front of each of them, while Valentina applied another layer of black lipstick in a silver compact mirror.

"Move it, you vermin!" Tullia barked. The wolves finally dragged themselves away from their pregaming and followed their alpha outside to where their sleek, black motorbikes waited.

Tullia straddled her bike and kicked it into life, engine roars filling the air as Octavia did the same beside her. As head members of the pack, they rode together in front. Safety in numbers, some might think. More like double trouble. They'd been known to cut down an entire gang of would-be attackers between them before the others had even put down their beers.

Tullia slid the visor on her helmet closed and revved the engine before tearing out of the graveyard, followed closely by the rest of the Northern Wolves.

"Artfulbeau," the doorman at the Crescent Club sneered when Tullia strode up the steps.

"There should be a Baroness in there somewhere, Magnus," she purred, strolling past him into the dark, smoky room. Incense filled the air and music pounded from speakers along every wall. The heat inside the club was intense—sweat had begun to bead along Tullia's collarbone before she reached the bar.

"I'm here to see Atticus," she shouted to the barman over the noise. The man frowned, looking her up and down. Tullia bristled. Clearly, he was new here.

"What's it about?"

Tullia's jaw clenched. She hated being interrogated by lowlifes who belonged under her boot, eating the dirt she walked on. "Business."

The barman gave her a skeptical look but lifted the bar for her to step through. As she passed him, she caught a scent that seemed at once familiar and foreign. A shifter then, but not a wolf.

When Octavia moved to follow, he held out a hand to stop her, but Tullia grabbed his arm, long, red nails digging in. A snarl tore from her throat and she bared her teeth at the barman. Nobody touched her wolves without invitation.

"She comes with me."

Silence fell when the door to the back room closed behind them, and Tullia's ears thanked the moon and stars above. She hated club music.

"Baroness," Atticus Wintersale crooned from where he sat, draped across a black, velvet chaise longue, his silk robe gaping to reveal a chest as pale as milk. "To what do I owe this great pleasure, Artfulbeau?"

Tullia rolled her eyes, there was no need for the amateur dramatics. She knew Atticus despised her, and she felt the same about him. It had always been that way between the wolves and the vampires. But this wasn't a personal call.

"I'm here to pay my debts."

"My favorite reason for an unexpected visit! Come, sit down. Bring your friend." He patted the end of the chaise longue, lips curving to reveal elongated canines. Instead, Tullia pulled up two padded chairs for herself and Octavia. No way was she getting closer to Atticus than she needed to.

She took a silk, drawstring bag out of her jacket pocket and held it out between them. Atticus set down his drink—a thick, dark-red liquid in a glass with a cocktail umbrella—on a mirrored-glass table.

"Thank you for letting me use these." She placed the bag in the vampire's outstretched hand without touching him. The thought of his cold, clammy skin made her shudder. She supposed it was an occupational hazard with the undead.

"Thank you for returning them," he murmured, tipping the finger-bones he had lent her out onto his palm and stroking them reverently. "I trust everything went to plan?"

"We'll soon find out." When the earth moved between the moon and sun in less than an hour, and the world was cast in blood red light, they'd know if Tullia had found what she was scrying for.

Since the day she'd entered the world, all Tullia had ever known was blood. It was time to find out the truth and take her revenge on those who had murdered her mother and destroyed her family. She took out a second pouch that jingled with coin as she dropped it onto the table in front of him.

The vampire's lips curled up at one side. "Your gold's no good here."

Tullia bristled, the hair on the back of her neck stood on end and her inner wolf snarled. "Then, what's your price?"

Atticus tucked the pouch of bone fragments into the pocket of his robe and gave Tullia a long look. "A favor. I want you to owe me, Baroness."

Tullia filled her lungs with blessed oxygen and ran her hands through her long, dark hair. It'd take several washes to get rid of the smell of incense.

It was a minute before the remaining members of the pack appeared in the car park—probably finishing their drinks and peeling themselves away from potential paramours.

They didn't have long to get to the real party. Wolves tended to prefer to be under the open sky during lunar events, and that was exactly where they were headed. To the Grand Arena.

The paved streets of the Eternal City were packed as Tullia and the Northern Wolves made their way to the arena. The air stank of a thousand sweaty bodies, the heat from the day rose off the stone floor and made Tullia's hair stick to the back of her neck.

They'd had to abandon the motorbikes in an alley when they'd reached the base of the hill—they'd be quicker on foot from here. The closer they got to the crest of the hill where the stone archway stood, the more eyes turned to Tullia. Shifters and even a few humans nudged their friends or grabbed arms and pulled people aside to allow her to pass.

It's good to be the Baroness, she thought.

Inside the arena, the Northern Wolves found a spot near the center of the sandy oval and settled in to wait for the lunar eclipse to begin. Leather jackets were dumped on the ground, Felix and Cassius began to spar playfully, tanned biceps rippling under matching tattoos of a wolf's head beneath a crescent moon. Octavia and Valentina sat cross-legged, taking turns to stab the ground between the other's fingers as fast as they could without drawing blood.

Tullia's stomach roiled with nerves, even as the hair on the back of her neck stood up, electricity coursing through her. This was it.

She dropped to her knees and dug her fingers into the sand, her back arching as a howl ripped from her chest. The rest of the pack joined in, their voices entwining with Tullia's until all she could hear was the sound of her people filling the arena and the night sky with a beautiful, primal chorus.

They didn't shift, it wasn't necessary in order to absorb the moon's power. All she needed was this, her hands anchoring her into the solid ground, a choir of howling wolves lifting her soul to the sky.

"Tullia." She barely heard the voice at first, soft as it was. But then it came again, closer, more insistent, and she opened her eyes.

She scrambled back as the ghostly apparition reached out a hand to her. A beautiful young woman in a long, black dress was standing just a few feet away from her, dark hair cascading over her shoulders.

Tullia would recognize that face anywhere, not only did she have a photo of her mother in a gold locket that always hung around her neck, but the woman in front of her could have been her own reflection.

Everything was bathed in a red light, making the world appear drenched in blood, as Tullia slowly got to her feet and approached her mother's spirit. The eclipse would be over in moments, she had to do what she had come here to do. She needed to know the truth.

"Who was it, Mama? Who killed you?"

Her mother's eyes shone with sadness as she gazed at Tullia. The light began to shift, and panic rose up in Tullia's chest. They didn't have long. She had to know the answer, and she wouldn't get another chance for years. Maybe never. It had to be now.

"Who did this to you?" Her voice was low and dark, her words rushed as the eclipse drew to a close and the reddish tinge that had turned the sand bloody, the way Tullia imagined it had looked the day her mother was killed, softened and paled.

"Tell me," she ground out, desperate now.

The vision of her mother faded with the red light, but before she vanished completely, her mouth formed one word. A name that Tullia knew all too well.

"Atticus."

Tullia's mother had been a noblewoman, the wife of a very powerful man—Senator Quintus. But that hadn't stopped Tullia's father from courting her mother with a single-mindedness only a wolf could possess.

When the senator had discovered that his newborn daughter wasn't actually his—Tullia supposed the shifting may have given her away—he'd had her mother killed. Slaughtered, more like.

Tullia kicked in the door to Atticus's back room and stood in the doorway, chest heaving.

Atticus didn't move or take his eyes off the thing in his hand. A knife, she realized, as he spun it with the point balanced on a fingertip.

"It worked then?" He mused.

"Why? Why did you lend me the bones if you knew what I'd find?"

The club owner sighed. It was the sigh of an old man, much older than his years. "Because I'm tired, Tullia. Tired of the secrets, tired of the lies. Tired of this half-life."

Tullia felt as though the wind had been taken out of her sails, but she had come here to avenge her mother, and avenge her she would.

First, she needed to know one last thing.

"Why you?"

Atticus set the knife down next to his empty, blood-smeared cocktail glass. "Good question. I crossed the senator and he didn't like that. Before this, before I was . . . what I am, I wanted to make a difference. I was young, naïve. I campaigned against one of the senator's policies, held rallies. I even got some traction. People liked me, if you can believe that." He chuckled darkly, but Tullia could see there was no humor in it.

"I had one too many drinks one night, celebrating my popularity in this very club. I took a wrong turn on my way home, ended up in a dark alley I didn't recognize. The next thing I knew, I woke up in the middle of the arena, and I was so thirsty. *So thirsty.* I couldn't think straight, it was like—well, it was bloodlust. And there she lay, your mother. Beautiful, pure, and I don't know how . . . It all happened so quickly, but I must have blacked out. I remember coming round, lying on the sand. And she was dead."

A sob tore from Tullia and she bit her lip, her fists clenching at her sides.

Atticus glanced up at her face, there was real remorse in his eyes, and it gave Tullia pause.

"I would never have hurt her if he hadn't had me turned, if he hadn't locked us in that arena together before I'd had a chance to feed. She'd been nothing but kind to me, despite me being her husband's biggest rival. I have regretted what happened every day since, Tullia, you must believe me."

"I don't believe a single word out of your filthy mouth," Tullia roared, but it didn't ring true. She could see that Atticus was telling the truth, that he felt terrible about what had happened.

No, this was the final act of vengeance she needed to commit. After this, her mother's spirit could rest peacefully, and she'd be able to let go of all the anger and pain she carried inside every day of her life. She had to kill Atticus Wintersale.

In a flash, she'd drawn Lucky from her boot and was on the club owner, blade pressed to his heart.

"Tsk, tsk. That just won't do, Baroness." Atticus wrapped a hand around Tullia's and gently guided the point of her dagger up, away from his heart, to his neck. "There's nothing vital inside there now, you know that. You'll have to take my head off if you want it to last."

Tullia frowned. Atticus's own knife lay just inches away to his left, but he didn't move to grab it. Only pressed her blade into his own throat, eyes boring into her, cold and empty.

"Why are you doing this? You could fight back, call for your guards. Why would you let me kill you?"

Atticus let go of her hand and sighed. "Because it's over, Tullia. I'm ready to die. And it's only right that it be at your hand. You killed Quintus, and you killed your uncle, it was inevitable you'd find me someday."

Tullia froze. "My uncle? What does he have to do with this?" He'd killed her father, so she had returned the favor. She avenged the wrongs done against her family. That was all.

Wasn't it?

Atticus raised his eyebrows. "You weren't aware? It was Darius who betrayed your parents to Quintus. He'd had his eye on your mother for years before your father seduced her. I thought you knew, I thought that was why—"

Tullia shook her head. It was too much to take in, Atticus's words were clouding her judgment and she needed a clear head. That was what all of this was for, all of this violence and vengeance. To lift the weight that had been on her shoulders, the immense pressure that pushed down on her some days, making it hard to breathe.

She took a step back and stuck two fingers in her mouth, whistling to her pack. Atticus's eyes widened.

"What are you doing? Tullia, you owe me, remember? You owe me this." His voice rose, whiny and irritating. She couldn't listen to another word from this pathetic creature.

"I owe you nothing."

Octavia and the other six members of the Northern Wolves burst into the tiny back room, filling the available space. Atticus cowered on his chaise longue, a whimper escaping his lips as Tullia turned to leave.

She hesitated, casting one last look over her shoulder, and said to the pack of wolves descending on her mother's murderer, "Make it quick."

And then she strode out of the club and into the cool night air, leaving Atticus's screams behind, passing the eviscerated bodies of Magnus and the barman as she went.

This was how it ended for everyone who crossed the Artfulbeau family. In blood and bone, ashes and dust. They would all know what happened when you betrayed the Baroness of the Northern Wolves.

They would know her name, and they would fear her.

LYNDSEY HALL

Lyndsey Hall lives on the edge of Sherwood Forest, one of the most magical places in England's history, and the inspiration for her debut novel, THE FAIR QUEEN. She grew up surrounded by books, and loved to write from a young age.

She loves to travel and try her hand at new things, but is most at home when curled up in a chair with a cup of tea and a good book, usually accompanied by at least one dog. She's fortunate enough to share her home with two cherished humans and two beloved dogs.

Find Lyndsey online here:
https://www.lyndseyhallwrites.com

Find out more about THE FAIR CHRONICLES here:
https://mybook.to/TheFairQueen

D.M. TAYLOR

SULTANA OF THE DEATHLY STARS

On the night her mother brought her into the world, Nessa Sagehammer was abandoned. The icy stillness that welcomed Nessa that blistery winter evening had ushered out her mother.

"Leave this room," the midwife said, holding the crying baby Nessa. "Allow Isa the decency of a private passing."

Isa's husband was well aware of his wife's abilities, even in death.

Many years later, one stormy night brought the young Lady Nessa to her cliff where she often screamed at the sea.

It still consumed Nessa with rage-filled grief that Isa had abandoned her, and she knew where to find her mother. She recounted the story she'd been told again and again about the night she was born.

"Each night, your mother became the sea. And as far as your father was concerned, regardless of her death, this night was to be no different," her midwife would say. "Arran resigned himself to give her back to the sea, where she might live on and love him from afar. And he'd always know where to find her."

"I know this part," Nessa replied. "He carried my mother through the blinding snow until he'd trudged frozen and numb to the shoreline."

"Exactly." Her midwife would tap Nessa's nose with a loving gesture. "There he found a small boat and laid Isa within. The water beat against the shore, a relentless demand for its Lady Isa to return."

Nessa often asked to be told this story, and her favorite part to recite was the ending. "He remained as the icy water refused to freeze over in wait for Lady Isa, and he did not leave until it claimed her."

Nessa pulled herself from her misty meditation as a thunderous boom accompanied the pounding rain. Far past her little cottage nestled within the forest, Nessa could still make out the silhouette of her father's castle. The constant reminder to Nessa that he didn't want her. He hadn't once seen Nessa since the night she was born, and he lost his Lady Isa.

As the waves lapped against the headland and further soaked her sweeping emerald dress to her body, Nessa fell to the ground consumed by her tears.

"Why?" she cried out to a singular star shining through the stormy skies. She waited for the star to respond. That star, *her star,* had been looking over Nessa for many years.

The girl had started sneaking out around her tenth birthday. The older she became, the more often she'd slip away into the night.

Her nighttime adventures eventually led her beyond the forest's edge, to this narrow headland jutting from the coastline. Here she'd dangle her legs from the side of the cliff while lying on her back, talking to the same bright star shining overhead.

"I wonder if anyone will ever want me," she said to her star. Her eyes fixed on its steady location; she swore it beamed a pulse brighter. "Did you just answer me?" she asked, hunched on her elbows. "I must be imagining it."

Night after night, Nessa found that star, even when every other constellation moved with the changing seasons.

"You must love me, as all of the other stars have left this sky. Only you remain." And after a time, she came to expect her star's subtle responses. In many ways, her star became humanlike to Nessa.

"I waited all day to sing your favorite song to you," she told her star one summer evening. For the first time ever, Nessa watched her star dance across the sky. "Oh!" she exclaimed. "I didn't know you could do that."

As the years passed, Nessa told him of her loneliness and longing to be part of a family. He'd listen and wish to have her as his own. This star too was alone and banished. He too knew this wish.

But that stormy night, as she looked to her star for comfort while rain pelted her skin, a small creature brushed against her leg.

Startled, Nessa whipped her head around to discover almond-shaped eyes glowing in the darkness.

Shrieking, she rose from the ground into a run. "Bright star, please help!" she begged.

Rising high over Nessa's head, she watched in dismay as the green hue of those eyes appeared to float.

How big is this monster? she wondered in terror. Squinting to get a better look, she couldn't be clear if she was seeing shadows or the large outline of something massive.

Nessa retreated into the nearby trees, which granted her coverage from the storm. She hid under branches that she'd woven together on an earlier—much less perilous—escapade.

With measured breaths, Nessa was careful not to give away her location. Though she continued her maniacal search in the dark for those glowing eyes.

Nessa wished she hadn't chosen to come into the storm to swear at the open sea, cursing her dead mother. It was then she heard a woman's voice booming through the dense air.

"Nessa, come out!" the woman commanded. "There is no reason to worry."

Nessa had been alone most of her life. She hadn't learned to trust anyone outside of the midwife. And she didn't have a reason to obey the strange voice.

"I'll come to you, my dear," the voice said.

Her lids squeezing shut, Nessa swallowed hard. The tips of her toes met the soft, wet fur first. As the creature brushed along her bare feet, her eyes flew open to behold what had come with the woman. It was the same creature she'd noticed on the cliffside.

"Look at me, I am nothing to fear," she said. "Your mother, Isa, sent me." The woman's voice came nearer. "She heard your crying."

A deep purr rose from the creature accompanying the woman. It brought Nessa a calmness she'd never known. Nessa ached to pet the creature. But her vision hadn't yet adjusted in the dark forest.

At once her pupils settled onto the animal, and Nessa discovered the creature was nothing more than a cat. Its black fur was soaked from the rain. The cat came closer to Nessa, and its emerald eyes fixated on Nessa's face.

"Your mother says you are ready to receive your gifts, young Nessa," the cat said.

The girl stared, absolutely stunned, her mouth hanging open. The cat sat on its hind legs and stretched open a glorious set of wings that glittered under the moonlight. Nessa peered beyond the winged animal, past the trees.

She contemplated running from the tree stand, but although the rain had slowed it was still falling onto the rolling hills beyond, so she was compelled to stay in her shelter.

Nessa looked back at the winged cat, unsure if she had tricked herself into seeing something altogether wrong.

The cat now soared to a nearby tree and perched on a branch. It spoke to Nessa.

"Are you ready for your gift, dear?"

Nessa blinked into the vast space now between them. She stared as the cat flapped its wings in unison with a rapid succession that instilled fear into Nessa's chest.

She didn't want what this cat was offering.

"Is this witchcraft?" she whispered to herself.

Cats didn't talk, and they certainly didn't fly.

Still hiding beneath the branches she'd once spent hours weaving together, Nessa recognized that her long red locks of hair suddenly became lighter and her arms tingled from tender brushes of love she'd craved her whole life.

Soon she was eye level with the black cat, who now studied her with intense approval.

"Nessa, I am your muime," the cat said as it flapped its wings. It lifted itself from the tree branch and beckoned Nessa to follow it with her eyes. Nessa became aware that she could instantly be anywhere the cat could fly.

"I wasn't aware that I had a godmother," Nessa replied.

The cat ignored Nessa's comment. "Pay attention girl!" her muime scolded. "I have revealed your gifts. It is time you try them."

She glanced down at the newness of her body. Nessa found that she had shifted from human form into the branches of the trees surrounding her.

Upon each thought of a location in the forest, Nessa became what she pictured in her mind's eye. She looked to the coastline and became the lowest-hanging branches that dipped low to the water's edge.

As she peered at her reflection in the moonlight of the now-dry skyline, Nessa saw that her red hair had become a mix of the most delicate twigs jutting from the tree and dancing leaves.

She'd never been so glorious. Nessa wanted to share her newness with the familiar bright star overhead. She looked up and sang out to him.

"Can you recognize me?" she asked.

The cat glided onto one of Nessa's outstretched branches.

"That star is named Al-Jabar," the cat said in her silky voice. "He's the Sultan of the Deathly Stars." The cat, now on four paws, walked along Nessa's thinnest branch. "You shouldn't speak freely to him."

"Why not?" Nessa asked.

"It is said that whenever he comes too close his radiance smothers nearby life, turning it to dust."

Nessa's branches swayed with a breeze that swept up from the sea's current.

"That was your mother," the cat warned. "She watches over you to be sure you don't get too close."

Again, Nessa looked up at her star. Nessa was certain her muime was wrong.

"I've been close to him for many years. He's never brought me any harm," Nessa said.

The cat resumed its seated position. "How very interesting." After a long moment, Nessa's muime went on, "It is said that true love can release him from his prison."

"How?" Nessa asked.

"He must explode into a supernova that he may fall away within the dust and be reborn from the ashes."

Nessa begged her godmother, "Please, Muime, help me release him."

"If there is no true love between you two, the supernova will consume you with its raging fire." The cat's tail swung back and forth like a mad pendulum. "The forest will burn," she said. The cat's warning heard, Nessa spotted the tallest tree in the forest. And in that moment, Nessa embodied it. She lifted the longest of her century-old branches, arms outstretched to her sultan star.

"I am yours and you are mine!" she cried out.

The black cat landed on Nessa's head this time, her paws pressing firm into the treetop.

"Young one, you have until the sun rises with your star. In the morning, you must return to your human shape. If you do not, your branches will burn from the heat your deadly star consumes in its rotation with the sun."

Nessa remained through the night in the old tree, having never gotten this close to her star before. She was sure that she'd find a way to release him from his prison.

Before dawn the cat returned, purring into the soft stillness the last minutes of the night offered.

Her muime was gliding between the leaves of Nessa's hair and swooped below to the sturdy trunk upon which it grounded her. The cat scratched its spine along her legs.

"My dear," the cat purred, "the galaxies have regarded the two of you tonight." She padded on her paws. "They have granted your wish."

"My wish?" Nessa inquired.

"You may be with your sultan, but he will not look the way you recognize him."

Nessa pulled herself from the treetops and found that she was level with her godmother, below the canopy. Her dark rich bark was softening into the skin she'd been born into, and her heavy red locks once again fell across her cheeks.

"What will he become?" she asked the cat.

"They've said you'll know him when you see him," the cat answered.

And just as the orange glow along the horizon hinted at its grand entrance, a burst of light showered the highest point of the early morning sky where Nessa had last located her star.

Until then, Nessa had never seen a shooting star. In the moments following her return to human shape, Nessa kept her gaze on the nova disappearing into darkness.

At once she became overwhelmed with the double loss, and once again ran to her cliff. But this time in desperate search of her sultan.

She wished her flowing green dress, which now blew in the breeze, was the lush leaves that had carried her up to him. With the fire of sunlight creeping above the water's edge, Nessa first noticed the distant image of wings flapping. Morning beckoned and her star was no longer. The soaring creature caught her attention as it flew toward her.

She wondered yet shook the foolish idea from her thoughts. Her sultan would not come to her as a bird. Still, she waited as it closed in on her location.

Much too late, Nessa realized she had been mistaken. It wasn't a bird at all. It was a reptile, and it too had glorious wings. Stricken with fright, Nessa understood she was standing on the narrow strip of coastland that a dragon had chosen for its landing.

She looked around for her godmother, who appeared to have abandoned her. Stumbling backward, Nessa tripped on a rock and fell to the ground. Above her, the dragon circled, fire seeping from its nostrils.

Concerned for her beloved forest, Nessa didn't dare run inside so as not to lead the dragon and its fire within its boundaries. Instead, she lay still and looked at the beast above her.

The rhythm he created in his flight brought a stillness to Nessa. She'd become transfixed by the dragon's infinite loop. Intoxicated by the calm the dragon induced, Nessa observed his orbit for a long moment, until she recognized her bright star within the dragon's eyes.

In an instant she was on her feet, calling out, "I am yours and you are mine!"

Just as the sun finished its rise above the horizon, Nessa had proclaimed her love. The dragon swooped onto the headland, bowing deep before Nessa.

An orange fire consumed the beast, leaving behind her sultan. His bronze skin gleamed in the golden sunrise. His dark hair fell to his shoulders, and Nessa couldn't take her eyes off of his beautiful face. She could not look away from the dark concentrated circles of his eyes, where she still found the energy of the stars. Nessa brought her hands to her mouth, her joy overwhelming.

"Al-Jabar?" she asked. He bowed deeper.

"Lady Nessa?" he asked in return.

She ran to her star. Al-Jabar embraced her. She was no longer alone, and he was now free.

Every evening after sunset Nessa goes into the forest, becoming the trees. Her sultan flies off into the night sky, breathing fire. She sways in the wind while he burns the stars that orbit too close. Before dawn, they unite to welcome a bursting new sunrise on the horizon.

D.M. TAYLOR

D.M. Taylor is a writer of science fiction thrillers. She has a constant desire to be at the beach or as close to a combination of: water, sand, and sunshine as she can. You can tell by looking at all of the freckles she has collected as evidence.

If she's not writing in her tiny cottage by the lake, then it's not summer. The rest of the year, she's writing on her couch under blankets near a giant bay window. On the less romantic days of writing, and let's be real--most of them, her pages come together while waiting in a car for one of her kids--as part of her chauffeur gig.

Her gravitational pull to science fiction developed throughout her teacher training; where she concentrated on science education. Graduating from Michigan Tech with an Applied Science Master's Degree jump started her geeky interests. An obsession of time travel pushed through her romantic notions of the world and the easy fear she holds of anything frightening. Together, these elements created a writer of: sci-fi thrillers who sprinkles in a bit of slow burn romance.

Accruing in her head is a checklist of places to travel, items to accomplish, and book ideas to write.

She regenerates from deep conversation, laughter, and dancing.

Instagram, Facebook & TikTok: @authordmtaylor

M.S. WEAVER

TEN YEARS AGO

"Correena—where are you?" A girl's voice, shrill with anxiety, echoed through the forest.

With a flutter of wings, a raven landed on a low-hanging branch. Looking down with its one good, beady yellow eye, it let out a loud, echoing croak.

"Shh." A tiny, dirt-streaked face glared up at the raven from beneath the leaves. "Maeve will find me if you keep doing that."

Clutching her small wooden bow in one hand, she crawled out of her hiding spot, yanking her long hair loose from where it got stuck on a few twigs. Leaves rustled a few feet from her, and she halted. Two eyes the same color as the warm golden honey her papa always brought back from his hunting trips to the Darkwood forest, peeked out from behind the dense green foliage.

A young boy's face soon followed; his finger pressed to his lips. He was older than her, even older than her sister Maeve. A broader than usual nose flared as if he was scenting the air like a nervous deer. Sunlight painted streaks of fire through his shoulder-length brown hair, but that wasn't what captured her attention. It was what curled back into the copper strands that made her jaw drop.

"You have horns," she whispered, clapping her hands, her bow forgotten at her feet.

She had only seen horns like that once before when her best friend, Blaine, had dared her to sneak into the Great Hall. The skull was mounted high against the wall behind the chief's chair. The teachings of her elders meant the horns revealed the boy was the enemy. But to her, he was strangely beautiful, like all the other wonderful creatures that roamed the forest.

The boy smiled and stepped closer. "Yes, and you have dirt on your face, Little One."

"I am not little. I am seven," she said, raising her chin

The odd boy chuckled, and she balled her fists. "It is not funny. That glowing thing your eyes do is funny." She scowled, scrunching her nose. "What is wrong with them?"

"Nothing," he replied, reaching for a strand of her unruly pitch-black hair, and tucking it behind her ear. "It happens to my kind when we find our mate."

"Mate?" She peered into the lush green surrounding them. Her papa had taught her that some animals had mates and that they stayed together for life. "There is another one of you here?" Her eyes glistened with excitement, and she closed the distance between them. "Does she have horns as well?"

He gently held her shoulders and stared into her eyes, grinning. "No, she will only get her horns once we are bonded, but she is still too young for that."

The scar on her wrist pulsed and she pulled away, rubbing at the rough patch of dark, scaly skin. The mark of the devil, the villagers called it. And the only thing that could spark fear in her burly papa's eyes.

A branch snapped, announcing Maeve's hasty approach, and the raven flew to the boy with a scratchy squawk, landing on his shoulder. In the same moment, the yips of the hunting dogs sounded in the distance.

"I must go." He pulled the hood of his black cloak over his head, covering his horns, and bent to pick up her bow. "Will you meet me here tomorrow? I can teach you how to hunt, and I have a friend who is excellent at stalking."

Correena hesitated, biting her thumbnail. She really wanted to learn, and lately her papa had been spending all his time training Blaine and the older boys.

"Okay," she agreed, then asked, "what is your name?"

"Lokheth."

Now

Lokheth

I scraped the dry blood from beneath my fingernails with the tip of my blade as I watched her slow, stealthy movements. A lock of her midnight-black hair blew across her cheek. She wiped it away with the back of her hand, leaving behind a streak of dirt. I almost smiled. A lot of things had changed in the two years I'd been gone, but not that. She was still as wild as ever.

Something stirred in the undergrowth a few feet from her. She froze. Dark blue eyes locked onto her prey. Little did she know that she was mine.

My fingers traced the thin silver line that ran from the top of my brow to just below my cheekbone, then they dropped to the space above my heart. The scars that littered my body were a constant reminder of what happened when our two worlds collided.

Rising to my feet, I pulled the hood of my black cloak lower over my face, jostling the raven perched on my shoulder. He ruffled his feathers and looked at me.

"Go," I ordered, my eyes never leaving their target. He took off with a loud squawk and the corner of my mouth lifted in a grin.

It was time.

Correena

I knelt at the base of the ancient, gnarled oak. Dropping the dead rabbit and my worn satchel next to me on the reddish-brown leaves, I snuggled deeper into my faded green cloak. There was a chill in my bones that had nothing to do with the changing seasons.

"Hello, Mama," I whispered, and reached out to trace the grooves of the intricate symbols Mama had carved into the bark when I was small. There was one for each of us—her, Maeve, me . . . and Father. My fingers curled into a painful fist right at the edge of his symbol. A single tear broke free, and I let it fall. There was no need to pretend. In these stolen moments there was no one to see the cracks in my armor. But it was how I survived.

"Maeve sent me to fetch water earlier." I kept my voice light as I cleared away the dead flowers from the hollow between the oak's roots. "Isabella and Matilda were there. Isabella's aim is improving. She nearly got me in the eye this time." I squirmed at the memory of her warm spittle striking my cheek. To her, I was not just the village outcast, shunned and vilified, I was the one who held the attention of the man she wanted.

If only she knew what I would give to escape Blaine.

I kissed the fresh flowers and arranged them in the hollow. "Blaine's father came to see Father last week." I felt no emotion as I said it. I'd cried it all out in Maeve's arms after the men had gone. "He even brought one of the elders with him. As if Father would have refused the proposed marriage. He stopped caring about me a long time ago."

The leaves to my left moved, a glint of yellow scales catching my eye. Inhaling sharply, I froze with my hands in midair. The snake slithered closer, and I blew out a relieved huff as I noticed the small emerald set between its eyes.

"Nagini, you scared me." I could have sworn the snake smiled, and knowing her, she probably did. Creeping up on me had been her favorite game since we were children, and she was good at it. "You heard?" I asked and pulled my satchel closer. Inside were fresh clothes, a soft fur blanket, flint, and spare arrows. Everything I needed to survive on my own.

Nagini waited patiently while I hid the satchel and slid into my lap after I settled my back against the tree. This had been our routine for the past two years since—

I swallowed the lump in my throat.

"I miss him, Nagini." It was barely a whisper, but she heard me and angled her head to nuzzle my cheek. "I wish I could have traded places with Mama." My tears flowed freely now. Dying from the fever would have been merciful compared to existing without the man I loved each day.

A raven landed on a branch across from me and I hastily wiped my tears with the sleeve of my cloak, sniffing loudly. The bird hopped down to a lower branch and observed me with a tilted head. One eye was a dull, milky gray. My mind went numb with shock as I recognized the cocky bird…surely there couldn't be two of them with such a distinct disability?

Memories flooded me of the day, two years ago, when I had been torn apart, body and soul.

Aged fifteen, living through brutal and bloody war between humans and Fae, death was no stranger. Neither was cruelty toward one the village believed was hand-picked by the devil. But nothing could have prepared me for the day it all came to our door.

Mama had come down with the fever. Papa fetched the healer, but there was nothing a human could do. With despair, I watched the illness overtake her, weakening, diminishing, stealing her life force. So, I went to the only being I knew who would do anything for me.

I hadn't known that I was being followed by a heart that had turned as black as coal with jealousy and obsession. They'd found us, wrapped together as my mate held me close. I watched as all the love my papa had ever felt for me vanished from his eyes. They turned cold, hard, like the black ice at the top of the mountain pass in the depths of uncaring winter.

If Lokheth Flinthorn had been a huntsman from another village, I believe Father would have accepted him. But he was not. He had broad black horns that curled into his long copper-brown hair, razor-sharp canines, hooves for feet, and magic coursing through his veins.

He was a Faun.

A Fae.

The enemy.

Before I could explain, an arrow had whistled through the air. Vines twisted around me, taking me to safety. But Lokheth bellowed in pain, and I hit the ground hard as the vines he'd conjured to protect me faltered.

There were shouts, the glint and ring of steel. As I struggled to my feet another whooshing sound split the air.

Blaine's heavy body had collided with mine as he tackled me to the cold, squelching mud. I fought with teeth and nails, but his large hand grabbed hold of my hair, painfully turning my head towards the chaos. Lokheth was kneeling on the unforgiving ground, one hand wrapped around an arrow shaft embedded in his chest, the other extended towards me. Reaching. Pleading. Blood ran down his cheek and dripped from his chin as he screamed my name, his uninjured golden eye remained fixed on me.

I'd begged. Pleaded as Lokheth's body swayed and tumbled backward into a motionless heap. My heart shattered. Blaine roared with laughter; his glacier blue eyes filled with glee as he watched me break.

His words had crawled into my ear and filled my muddled mind. "The elders suggested we purge the devil from your soul," he'd lowered his voice to a deep growl, so close to my ear I could feel his hot breath branding me, and I shuddered. "But I want to watch the flicker of hope fade from your eyes with each passing day as you realize you belong to me, and there is no escape."

Lying beneath him with his wet lips trailing down my jaw towards my clenched mouth I learned an important lesson—it was not horns and teeth that defined a monster.

As I tried to push Blaine off, my scar hummed, my mind cleared, and something inside me stirred.

It was rumored that demons commanded the Deathbringers. The serpents whose venom was lethal to humans and Fae alike. I was a rare exception, a strange anomaly that had survived the bite as a child, enduring a lifetime of scorn for my ability. *My blood. Could it save Lokheth like it had saved me?* Everything that couldn't be explained was considered dark magic or demonic by my people. And what was darker and more powerful than blood?

I slammed my forehead into Blaine's nose and slid my palm across the blade at his side, cutting deep. Crawling a few feet, I yanked the arrow from Lokheth's chest, praying I didn't cause more harm by removing it, and pressed my bleeding hand to the wound, feeling a surge of something unexplainable convulse through my arm and into Lokheth. Then an ear rattling thud throbbed from my temple, and I'd toppled into shattered light.

A warm touch on my shoulder brought me back to myself and I blinked up at a wide-eyed, flushed Maeve. A part of me was still tangled in the memory, my body sluggish. She pulled me up and I felt Nagini slither into the hidden pocket of my cloak.

"Maeve, what—"

"A regiment of the king's army, all bloodied and bruised, marched into the village after you left." She gasped for air and shook her head when I tried to talk, rushing through the rest of her story. "I overheard Blaine and Papa speaking after they returned from the Great Hall. The army had run into a group of Fae warriors, led by a huge Faun with a scar across his eye, at the edge of the woods."

My heart tumbled into my stomach, a weight pressing down on my head as the corners of my vision blurred. *Could it be?*

Maeve shoved a linen-wrapped bundle into my numb hands. "Here. Papa and Blaine are searching for you. I placed bread, water, and dried meat in there. It is not much, but it will hold until you are far enough to slow down and hunt."

"Maeve—" I began, but she shushed me again, pulling me into a bone-crushing hug.

"I couldn't protect you the last time," she sobbed, "but I am not failing you again."

"I love you," we said simultaneously.

She released me. I grabbed my stuff and ran as if all the hounds of hell were on my heels.

LOKHETH

Correena was running.

The air was coated in her fear, and it drove the protective beast inside me to the edge of insanity.

I had been separated from my mate for two long years. Two years filled with war and bloodshed. And the desperate need for the one I couldn't reach, separated by the runes around her village.

I thought I'd died that day in the forest when her father shot me with a venom-tipped arrow. But I had woken in a cave, surrounded by yellow scales and two familiar emerald eyes that promised me I would see the girl I loved again. So, I waited. For two endless years.

I stopped and sniffed the air. A growl built in my chest.

Correena was being hunted. I'd smelled that rival scent so many times on her before that I knew exactly who the hunter was.

He was about to experience the wrath of a Faun protecting what was his.

CORREENA

Sweat flowed in small rivulets from my hair and down my spine. My lungs were on fire, pain bit into my side and my heavy feet stumbled over fallen branches and uneven ground as I dodged endless trees, but I couldn't slow down for a moment of rest if we were to escape. Blaine was a formidable tracker, and I was his favorite prey.

A soft hiss came from my pocket over the sound of my ragged breathing. Poor Nagini was having a rough ride and I hoped she wasn't too battered.

Spindly shadows pulled along the leafy ground when I finally took a break.

Nagini slid from my pocket, shaking her head, looking a little dazed. Collapsing onto the soft grass and scattered leaves beside her, gulping down air into my starving lungs, I smiled, a small line cracking my mouth. Nagini nestled up to me as my smile turned to a burst of carefree laughter. The weight that had been pressing on my chest for years lifted. I giggled and huffed through my tears, the sounds echoing in the trees around us.

Nagini was watching me, and I smiled. "Our plan worked, Nagini. I am free." I wasn't safe or with the one I loved, but I trusted her when she promised this was the first step to reuniting with Lokheth. She was not only Naga, but a Jinni after all.

I dragged my satchel closer to take a sip of water and my scar pulsed. There was danger nearby.

Nagini coiled and hissed, and I shot to my feet. Despair ripped a hole through my soul. What did I have to do to be free of the shackles that chained my destiny to the man I loathed?

I tried to reach for Nagini. A meaty hand wrapped itself around my throat and wrenched me backwards. The pain in my windpipe was nothing compared to the fear as I crashed to the ground. The air whooshed out of my lungs; I struggled for breath, my fingers clawing at the hand that forced me down into the dead leaves.

The cold blue of Blaine's gaze broke through the blur of tears, and icy tendrils wrapped around my heart as the pressure on my throat increased.

My life was over.

"I warned you what would happen if you ever tried to run from me." Blaine's voice was arctic.

My lips trembled and my eyes sought out his in a wordless plea.

Nagini sank her teeth into Blaine's forearm, and he cursed. Loosening his grip on me for a moment he grabbed her behind the head and flung her away.

I heard the dull thud as she collided with the trunk of a tree, and I moaned.

He pulled back the sleeve of his shirt with a grin. Thick strips of leather covered his arm and beads of venom oozed harmlessly from two tiny holes. "You don't fight against fanged beasts without picking up a few tricks along the way."

"It is good she missed," I managed to choke out. "She probably would have died from biting such a vile creature as you."

He snarled, hatred radiating from his narrowed eyes as he backhanded me, pain shooting through my jaw and neck. My head lolled to the side, stars filling my vision from the force of the blow. But I did not care. I would rather he killed me here than drag me back to hell.

I spat out blood and looked back at him and laughed. It sounded cold, hard, and slightly insane.

"Is that all you've got?" I mocked.

Blaine gave an unearthly growl and grabbed the front of my threadbare shirt, almost tearing one side completely off in his fury. "You will learn your place, woman!" he screamed into my face. "And when I am done with you, you will know the only place you belong is beneath me."

I lifted my eyes to the vibrant orange, gold, and pale red that tainted the spotless white clouds. I hung onto the beauty painted in the sky and retreated into myself. It was just me and the love I held for my Faun.

My eyes closed as calm stole through my body, my muscles going slack. They could never take this from me, no matter how hard they'd tried in the past. "Do your worst."

There was a thud like the sound of distant thunder, and Blaine's weight was gone.

I blinked, trying to make sense of the blurred shadow that had swept over me, taking my tormentor with it.

Sitting up, I gaped at the two bodies rolling on the ground in a tangle of limbs and flying fists. The one was Blaine and the other—a giant Faun dressed in leather pants. His broad chest was plated with bones woven together by vines and his long, braided copper-brown hair was in a loose knot at the back of his head.

I didn't need to see his face to know who it was.

My heart overflowed with joy, and it spilled down my cheeks.

He'd finally come back for me.

Cold fingers brushed the scars criss-crossing my exposed shoulder, tracing them down my back. Nagini's emerald eyes in her half human form showed her sorrow, ripping my heart in half. The joy I'd felt mere moments ago, drained from my soul.

"Oh, Correena..."

I blinked away the tears. I would not go there, not now. "Help me." Together, we gathered the torn pieces of material, tying and knotting it as best we could. I pulled my tattered cloak tighter and rose to my feet.

All those days and nights I'd dreamed of escaping, I'd refused to think about what my father and the elders had done to me after they'd brought me back from the forest. But there was no ignoring it now, and dread crawled into my heart and made itself at home.

I'd survived more torture than most people could imagine in a lifetime, but if Lokheth rejected me now, it would kill me.

I could not think. I could not breathe.

Blaine's taunting words as I'd hung from the village torture pole, humiliated, almost naked, my flesh a bloody mess, rebounded through my mind. "Who would want a scarred, broken piece of trash like you? You should kiss my feet for even looking at you without losing my meal."

Pressing my clenched fists to my forehead I tried to push the memory out of me, but it was carved into my flesh forever.

A thundering roar came from the adversaries. Lokheth stood above a battered and bruised Blaine, who was crumpled at his feet. Turning to me, our eyes locked. The words tore from me in a sob, "I can't—"

I turned and ran.

But I didn't get far.

Strong arms wrapped around me from behind and pulled me into a broad chest.

I thrashed and squirmed, but Lokheth held on, murmuring soothing sounds that meant nothing and everything. Eventually, I grew tired, going limp with exhaustion and sadness. He picked me up without a word and walked back to where we'd left Blaine and Nagini.

The sound of Blaine cursing reached my ears before I saw him. As we emerged into the clearing, I looked up from the crook of Lokheth's neck to find him dangling from Nagini's strong tail. Her lip curled in disgust and anger at the creature in front of her, his face turning red, and he flapped his arms like a bat.

"Now what am I going to do with you?" she said, flipping her long golden hair over her shoulder. The unsuspecting could be lulled by her breathtaking beauty. But the Fae who had supported me through the toughest two years of my life had another side. The glint in her eyes was her tell: she was deadly if provoked.

She turned to us with a smile and motioned with her hand. "You are just in time for the show. Take a seat."

Lokheth sat down with his back to a thick tree trunk and placed me in his lap. I tried to wriggle free, and his arms locked around my waist. "Please, Correena," Lokheth's voice was rough and deeper than I remembered, yet soft and gentle. "You are the only thing keeping me from killing him with my bare hands. I just need to hold you, to know you are real and not a figment of my imagination, or I am going to lose it."

"Did you show your precious Faun—" Blaine's eyes zoned out for a moment as blood dripped from his busted nose and disappeared into his hair, "the monster hidden beneath all those layers of cloth?" He angled his crimson face towards me, the veins on his forehead prominent and pulsing. "Because no mating bond is strong enough to keep him at your side after he sees that."

I shrunk in on myself and Nagini slapped Blaine so hard his head rocked to the side, blood smattering the leaves beneath him.

"What do you know about love, you filthy piece of slime." Nagini was shaking. Anger radiated from her in waves, and I wished I could dissolve in it.

Lokheth moved his calloused hand to my chin, and I could feel the question burning like a white-hot flame between us. I just couldn't bring myself to answer. What if Blaine was right?

"I have decided on your punishment, Human." The ominous tone in Nagini's voice spelled trouble. Lokheth tenderly cupped my cheek. With his powerful arms cradling me and his warm musky scent filling my nose, he felt like an impenetrable shield.

Nagini extended her hands toward Blaine and a glowing orb of golden light formed around him. He screamed, his eyes wide in terror and I knew what he felt at that moment. But I couldn't muster a shred of compassion for the man who had made my life a living hell.

"Blaine, son of man, you will become that which you hate. From this day forward you will be Fae. Your only cure, redemption."

The orb pulsed, expanded, and exploded into blinding light. Lokheth moved his hand to cover my eyes. When I could finally see again there was just a bundle of clothes on the ground below the spot Blaine had hung.

The material stirred and a much smaller Blaine emerged from beneath his shirt.

"What did you do to me, Witch?" he yelled.

"It is Naga, actually," she said, then cooed. "Aww, you look adorable as a dwarf. I think I shall call you, 'Grumpy'."

With a battle cry that sounded more mouse than man, Blaine charged Nagini. She swerved out of the way with a coil of her body and cackled when he stepped on the hem of his shirt and fell face first into a pile of steaming dung.

Despite myself, I had to fight the smile pulling at my lips, but it quickly disappeared when Lokheth lifted me and stood up.

"We need to talk." He clasped my hand tightly as he pulled me deeper into the forest, and with a rolling stomach, I looked back at Nagini.

"Trust in your love," she whispered to me, smiled, and flicked her tail, sending a spluttering Blaine flying through the air.

I rubbed my sweaty palm against my thigh and swallowed, trying to keep my stomach from clawing up my throat.

Lokheth didn't say a word as we walked. He didn't even look at me and I couldn't keep the tears from running down my face. My love for him was the only thing that had kept me sane throughout everything I'd had to endure. But would it be enough when he saw what I had become?

He stopped next to a stream and turned to face me.

"Why did you run from me, Correena? I can smell your fear and it is enough to choke me." He stepped closer, lifting his hand to my face only to drop it again. "Is it me?" he asked, sadness welling in his eyes as they scanned my face for answers.

"No, it's..." I couldn't find the words.

Running his hand down his face he looked over my shoulder, his voice tired. "You are afraid of me."

I closed my eyes. I couldn't bear to see him like this. For two years I'd yearned to be back in his arms. To hear his voice and tell him how much I loved him.

"I am not afraid of *you*," I said, opening my eyes again. Closing the distance between us, I cupped his face with both my hands. "I am afraid of *losing* you."

He gasped and pulled me to his chest. "You will never lose me, Correena. I love you and I need you more than I need air to breathe."

He threaded his fingers through my hair and planted a tender kiss on my forehead. "There is nothing on this earth or the heavens above that could change the way I feel about you."

Trust in your love. I repeated Nagini's words in my mind and swallowed before stepping back.

"You need to see why Blaine called me a monster."

I kept my eyes on him as I loosened my cloak and it dropped to the ground. I needed to see his reaction, even if it ripped my heart from my chest. My fingers fumbled to untie the knot keeping my torn shirt together and the muscle in Lokheth's jaw rippled. But he didn't say a word. He didn't even blink.

I turned my back to him but looked over my shoulder the moment I'd let go of the material, dropping it to my waist to expose my back.

My heart pounded. This was it.

Anger flashed in his eyes and he balled his fists, but there was no disgust. No rejection.

"May I touch you?" he asked softly, and I nodded.

Lokheth ran his fingers along the raised ridges of marred flesh, and I finally closed my eyes. Just for them to fly open again when he pressed a feather-light kiss to the scar on my shoulder.

He slowly turned me back to face him and pulled his vine-woven shirt over his head, revealing a multitude of silver, red and purple scars across his chest, arms, and back. My eyes traced the maze of pain through a haze of tears. My fingertips grazed the scar above his heart resembling the one on my wrist—dull gray and scaly. *What a pair we made.* Both marked by death, yet miraculously surviving.

Lokheth kissed away my tears with a tenderness that kept them falling and I buried my face in his neck. He pulled me in deeper until I could no longer tell where I ended, and he began.

"These scars don't change who we are, and they certainly don't make us monsters. That title belongs to the ones who inflicted them upon us," he said into my hair. "You are perfect to me just the way you are."

I lifted my face, and he lowered his until the tips of our noses touched. "And together we will be whole again."

The moment our lips met I knew; I was finally home.

MS WEAVER

MS Weaver is a storyteller from South Africa. She lives on a farm with her husband, three children, a cat, dogs, and a bunch of other animals. Her home has been a haven for a wide range of creatures, from orphaned lambs to an enormous python who thought he could make a meal out of a porcupine. All this madness leaves her with little time to write, and that is why most of her stories come to life during the silent hours of the night.

If you want to take a peek at her fantasy world filled with myth and legend that will make a shiver run down your spine, follow her on Instagram. https://www.instagram.com/sneakymewriter

R.S. WILLIAMS

Ella

"Where have you hidden it?" The commodore slammed his hand down on the table as he spoke, but Ella didn't flinch. She smiled at him, and his eyes narrowed. "You won't be smiling when we are done with you, Captain Shadowboar," he continued.

"I haven't hidden it." Ella's cheek stung as the commodore's backhand hit her. She looked up at him as she continued speaking. "It's been in the same place all along. I was simply on my way to collect it."

The man sighed. "If you don't tell me where it is, Shadowboar, I will have to force you."

Ella laughed to herself, not fearing the hand coming for her a second time. She shook her head, loosening a few strands of her brown hair and crossed her feet, allowing the rope around her ankles to slacken. "If my own father doesn't scare me, what makes you think you do?" She raised an eyebrow. "Do you know why they call me Shadowboar, Commodore Thorne?"

Ella twisted her wrists until they were free enough that she could conjure dark clouds above them. A small storm brewed in the interrogation room. Commodore Thorne looked up as his mouth fell open.

"What the—" He looked back at her, and she grinned. "You're a Stormwitch." He drew his sword and placed it below her chin. "Stop this, now."

She leaned back, revealing more of her neck. "You haven't got the authority to do that. Besides, if you kill me, how will you find the crown?" Ella chuckled.

The commodore removed his sword and yanked open the door to the small room. He yelled at the guards, "throw her back in the cells. Maybe another night without food and water will loosen her tongue."

"Doubtful," she muttered under her breath. *I want only what I came for.*

The guard untied the rope at her feet before they both grabbed an arm and marched her out of the room. As she passed a few of the cells, their occupants shouted obscenities and begged to be let out or for her to be put in with them. For a split second, she thought the guards would do it and ruin her plans. However, they escorted her to the cell at the very end. *Just where I wanted to be.*

One of them opened the door while the other man-handled her inside. Ella smirked as they slammed the door closed and walked away. Once she was sure they were both gone, she looked around. It was hard to see in the dark, but she felt the presence of someone else in the cell. Ignoring it for the moment, Ella stood on the small bench and looked out of the barred window. The sight of her ship on the horizon was exactly what she needed. It looked so tiny compared to the bay. She tried to count the distance to the shore from the jungle below.

"You won't get out."

Ella spun on her heels toward the voice from the corner.

"Have you tried?" she asked. She stepped down and placed a hand on her hip. The person in the dark stepped forward into the moonlight, his handsome features illuminated. "Of course not. You're still here."

He raised an eyebrow. "You seem to know who I am."

My additional bounty. The prince without a home.

"Of course, I do. Though I am curious: how did you end up here of all places?" She yanked at the bench by the window.

He sank back into the shadows. "A poor decision and misplaced trust."

The faint sound of whistling filled the air. Ella dove forward and pulled him to the floor. "Get down!"

"Hey!"

An explosion blasted the wall.

Ella kicked at the rubble on her leg and scrambled up. "We better get moving before—"

"Shadowboar!" the commodore's voice rang out.

"Too late. Listen, stray," she said and helped her cellmate up. "You have two choices: come with me and earn your freedom or stay here the rest of your miserable life." *Please make this easy for me.*

The commodore's hands fumbled with the keys as he tried to find the right one to fit the lock. "You're not going anywhere."

Ella grabbed her cellmate's arm and shoved him to the edge of the crumbling wall. "Sadly, Commodore, as much as I enjoy your company, I have a crown to collect." She took out her necklace and kissed the jewel for luck, then bowed. "Jump." It wasn't the smartest decision she had made, but she trusted her plan and the trees below them to break their fall.

Once they'd recovered from their rough landing, Ella gestured for her cellmate to follow. "Come. This way."

"What? I'm not going with you." He stepped back from her.

Ella rounded on him. "I did not just get myself captured and tortured to find you and let you go." She grabbed him by the wrist and twisted it. "You're coming with me. I only need you long enough to collect my money. Then you'll be free to go."

He frowned, folding his arms. "Ah, so that's all I am. A bounty."

"Listen, lots of people want you. My father—God knows why—your father, and the governor to name a few." Shouts from above made Ella look up at the sky. "Right now, you have little choice. It's either me or back to your cell with the commodore's men." She flicked her wrist, and the storm clouds gathered above.

"Neither sounds ideal. I suppose, at least with you, I won't be in a cell." He held out his hand. "I'm Renwick."

"Fantastic. Now, which way to the crown?"

Renwick shook his head.

"Don't try to play coy with me. I know you know where it is. You're the only lead I've had since my father asked me to track it down. So tell me where it is or I will tie you up and leave you for the commodore's men."

"A hundred paces that way, but you won't be able to take it." He pointed through the trees past a signal rock.

"Watch me."

Ella looked back every few steps, making sure they weren't followed, until Renwick stopped her. He nodded toward the right and then disappeared through the trees. Following him through, she stepped into a small clearing outside a cave. *No one would have found this if they didn't know where it was.* There stood a statue Ella could only assume was the sea god Poseidon.

The crown in the statue's hand was imbued with the magic to control the seas, a power given only to the Foy royal family. Until one of them had abused it. An earthwitch who'd cared for the statue had infused a protection spell into the limestone. Ella hoped her magic would counter the spell, knock the crown to the ground, and allow her to take it.

"I wouldn't," Renwick said as she reached for the statue's arm.

Three officers stepped into the clearing.

"Well, well, boys. Commodore Thorne will be impressed with us." A grin spread across the officer's face. "Hand it over. The commodore wants the crown."

She scoffed. "Sure. Take it if you really want it, though we wouldn't recommend it. It's cursed." She scrunched up her nose and stepped back.

The first officer stepped up to the statue.

"Mason," said the second officer. "She wants you to take it. What if it is cursed?"

Ella cocked her head as they squabbled and used her magic to feed the storm.

The officer ignored his comrades and reached forward. As his finger touched the golden crown, a crack of lightning came down. *Perfect timing.* The two officers closest to the crown jumped back and landed on their backs, while the third shielded his eyes. The crown flung from the statue's grasp and landed on the ground beside her cellmate's feet.

Dashing forward, Ella scooped up the crown before Renwick could and grabbed him with her free hand. Her fingers tightened around the crown, and the pull of the ocean guided her back.

"Do you have a plan?"

Ella rolled her eyes. "Yes, I do. Now be quiet and follow me." Turning back through the trees, she felt a sharp sting across her cheek. Something trickled down. As she wiped it away, a dark stain appeared on her cuff.

Renwick yanked his arm away from her. "This has all been fun, but . . ."

"But what? The only reason you're out of prison is because I got you out. I could have gone into any other cell, but I chose yours."

"No, the officer chose it."

"Did he?" Ella stepped out onto the beach where her ship was in full view. "Or did I work it so the officer thought he chose the cell?"

Renwick sighed again. "You have what you wanted. Let me leave."

"And where will you go?" She stopped and turned to him. "I have one of the only ways off this island. Once again your choices are the commodore or me."

"You make a pretty terrible captain."

She narrowed her eyes. "At least I have a ship. You're an exiled prince without a single piece of land to rule." His eyes widened. "I told you, I know who you are. Renwick Foy, the prince with no home and the blood of the sea."

He tried to swipe the crown from her. "That is dangerous."

"Only in the wrong hands," Ella said softly. "Can you trust me?"

The prince looked behind them. The shouts of the commodore's men were getting closer.

"Well? We haven't got all day, Foy. Can you trust me?" Ella held up the crown. The power of the sea flooded her body, and she smiled.

"I don't have any other choice, do I?"

Renwick

He watched Ella singing atop the piano while one of her crew played a tune. For a pirate captain, she had the voice of an angel. He supposed that came with being a stormwitch, manipulating the air to make it sound better. He could see the magic rippling around them.

His eyes darted to the door. Would he be snatched up again?

"Drink." One of the crew slammed another mug of ale down in

front of him, and he jumped. "Celebrate! We are home and you are alive." He took a swig of his own drink. Half of it ran down his face into his beard. "Drink!"

Renwick picked up the mug, raised it in acknowledgement, and took a sip. The music stopped, and Ella plopped herself down next to her crew mate.

"Teddy!" Ella swung an arm around the man's neck and clinked their drinks together. "Where does the crew want to go next?"

Teddy's eyes landed on Renwick and frowned. "Foy, what's the matter with you?"

"Wondering why I am still here."

Ella swung around in her seat and leaned forward so her lips brushed his earlobe. "I may have need of you yet, prince." She giggled and leaned back. "You, after all, are very valuable." She finished her drink and handed the empty mug to Teddy.

"Are all pirates this greedy?" Renwick leant forward. "Or are you considering keeping me all to yourself?"

She cocked her head to the side, a grin spreading across her face. "Depends on who makes the better offer." She adjusted her seat. "I already have trouble choosing. I could sell you back to your father, who exiled you, or to Admiral Levens, though I doubt he'd give much of a reward to have you back rotting in a cell. Then there's my father, but I'm not sure I want to give him what he wants." Her eyes flickered to Teddy for a moment. "But then, there's King Vernon . . ."

Renwick shivered at the mention of the tyrant.

"He might pay well for your head. Though I'm not sure I want to see that pretty head roll." She flicked her hair over her shoulder and stared deep into his eyes.

Renwick opened his mouth to speak as the door to the tavern banged open and the whole place went silent. Though tempted to turn and look at who commanded this much attention, he couldn't peel his eyes away from Ella. The captain sighed and shook her head. Behind her, Teddy's eyes widened; he dropped his head and hid behind her.

"Ella," boomed a voice. "Did you bring what you were sent for?"

"It's safe." Ella stilled, her jaw tight.

The crew bowed their heads. Something Renwick had only seen people do when in the presence of the king.

"I don't see why the location matters until payment is settled," Ella said.

Renwick turned his head slightly. His eyes fell on the man who strode forward. *He's too graceful to be a pirate.*

The man stopped in front of her. "Ella. I will ask you only once more. You will not see a cent of the money if you do not tell me where the crown is."

She looked up at him and sighed. "And your question?"

"Why did you not bring it with you?"

Renwick gulped. The five people near their table froze, some held their ales up to their lips without drinking, their gazes transfixed on the conversation.

"Because I've decided I want to keep it. Your bounty is worthless to me when I have the crown. You do remember it can control the sea?"

The man raised his hand as if to strike her. The hairs on Renwick's neck shot up. Before he had a chance to think, he stood between the man and Ella. His chair had toppled over from the speed he rushed forward.

Ella chuckled. "You should move."

"He shouldn't raise a hand to a woman." Renwick gestured towards the man. *What on earth am I doing?*

The man cocked his head to the side and eyed Renwick as if he were nothing more than a gnat. "Interesting find, Ella. Tell me, why did you bring this . . . stray back with you?" He leaned to the side as if to look at Ella, but his eyes remained fixed on Renwick. He wanted to move, but something held him in place. "It's not every day that someone stands up to the Pirate King."

"Captain Peyton, please don't play with my toys." Ella stood and forced Renwick down into a seat.

"Yet another thing you try to keep from me, sweet daughter."

Daughter? Will I ever learn to keep my mouth shut?

Ella's smile disappeared into a frown. "Don't call me that. Now finish your business and go back to your own party. This one is mine.

How many times do we have to go over the same argument? The Dark Peon is my tavern; you have The Jackel."

The Pirate King brought his face inches from Ella's. "I own this island. As its king, everything is under my control. When someone doesn't pay their due, I get twitchy." His hand tightened around the handle of his pistol. "No matter who they are."

Ella held out a hand, preventing him from getting up. The room grew darker as shadows crept forward from every corner.

"Time to leave, Father."

A rumble from the darkness rattled her crew, who gathered closer to the fire.

The Pirate King sighed. "You have a choice, Ella. Bring me the crown or we will sell Prince Foy to his enemies." The Pirate King laughed and turned to the door. "I'll get more for him alive, but I'll happily take him dead." He walked away but stopped at the door. "You have two days."

Once the Pirate King was gone, Ella turned back to her seat, caught Renwick's eye, and gestured for him to move over. The darkness she'd conjured shrank with every passing moment. Music and conversation resumed as she sighed and looked at him.

"You're an idiot." She slapped him across the face. "Don't ever do that again. I can handle myself. Captain Peyton knows that all too well."

Renwick blinked hard. The sting of her touch disappeared. "And I thought my father was the worst. Does he try to hit you often?"

She laughed. "It's not the first time. He's not exactly father material."

"You can't sell me or the crown."

Ella gestured for him to come closer. Renwick frowned but obeyed. Her lips almost touched his cheek as she spoke. "You, Renwick Foy, do not get to tell me what to do." She sat back and smiled as they locked eyes. "See, the thing is, both the crown and you are important. I can't let one go without the other."

Renwick leaned back in his chair. She knew. "So . . . I'm stuck with you?"

"For the moment." She eyed him over her ale and smiled as she sipped her drink.

This is the only chance to find out what she knows. "And what exactly do you plan to do with the crown?"

"Use it. With my magic and the sea's power, no one would be able to challenge me." Ella rolled her eyes. "I can see the questions rattling around in your brain. So, hurry up and ask them or shut up and enjoy your evening."

"Do you know why Admiral Levens captured me?"

"Because you're a Foy. Legend has it your family descends from a sea god, though no proof has been seen for nearly a hundred years." She rested her elbows on her knees. "Coincidences don't exist. My father was looking for the crown, one of five items made out of orichalcum." *She definitely knows.* "I don't particularly want him to have it, so I presented it as a test to prove myself. Then I'll take it away from him at the very last moment by challenging him for his title of Pirate King."

One of the crew closest to them dropped their ale and turned away.

This woman was a mystery. No doubt formidable and able to kill someone with her magic, yet Renwick had the feeling there was a softer side to her.

"And where do I come into it?"

"You are an added bonus. My father had a lead on the crown. When that led nowhere, I learned of you: an exiled prince and a Foy no less. I knew it couldn't be a coincidence." She put a hand on his leg and squeezed it as she stood.

He bit his tongue.

Pacing casually, she continued. "You are the key to my father's plan. I need to keep you far away from him."

Legends should stay buried. Renwick leaned forward as she moved away from him. "You're a clever woman."

"I'm the daughter of a pirate king and a princess from across the oceans. *Clever* is hardly the word to describe me. My father taught me how to fight men twice my size and chop them into little pieces, while my mother . . ." She lost her balance for a split second. He reached out to steady her, but she batted him away. "I'm fine. It's time for me to get some rest. No doubt my father will have something planned for the morning." She held up a hand stopping him from saying whatever words were on the tip of his tongue. Renwick watched her go. As the door closed behind her, he could've sworn he saw something move in the darkness.

The doors to the tavern opened once more.

"Hello, son."

Something hit Renwick on the back of the neck, and the world went black.

Ella

Ella stirred from the pain in the back of her head. As her blurred vision focused, she saw the familiar sight of a ship deck and the flag of the Skystorm; its crew carrying out whatever tasks had been asked of them.

My father's ship.

Next to her, Renwick was snoring. She nudged him with her foot. When he didn't respond, she kicked him. "Foy, get up." He waved an arm and rolled over. "Renwick," she hissed. "We have a problem. Wake up."

"What's the matter now?" His eyes widened as he looked around. "How did we get here?"

She gestured around them with tied hands. "Considering this is my father's ship, I can only assume it has something to do with his plans for you, though I didn't recognize the men who attacked me."

The Pirate King appeared on deck and strode towards them.

"Ah, Ella, you're awake. I trust they didn't hurt you too badly?"

She frowned as another man came up behind her father. He seemed vaguely familiar. *The one who stopped me on the way out of the tavern.*

"King Athel," her father said. "Lovely to make your official acquaintance."

"I'm sure you could have done it under better circumstances," Ella said as she struggled with the binds on her wrists. She looked to her father. "What exactly have you agreed to now? It seems a daughter cannot even trust her own father. I presume you stole my crown as well?"

The Pirate King laughed. "We will be rich, my dear: money, an island for you to rule, your independence from me, and control of the seas." He gestured, and two men grabbed her and Renwick by the arms and lifted them.

Renwick shook his head. "You cannot do this, father."

"It is done." King Athel held up his hand, and Renwick closed his mouth. "We will find Poseidon's Tomb, and we will open it. It should be easy now that I have the crown."

Renwick struggled against the man holding him. "You don't understand. It's not a gift; it's a curse! Why do you think our ancestors hid it?"

Ella scowled. Her blood boiled at her father betraying her, his only daughter, for the mere promise of land and money. *Bloody pirates.*

The ship rocked as it stopped.

Ella turned away from her father and fiddled with the ropes. They loosened. She slipped a hand out, ready to strike.

"Oh, Renwick, my son. Calm down." King Athel turned to Ella's father. "See, this is what I have to deal with. At least you can control your child."

"*Control*?" Ella's anger flared. "You think Captain Peyton controls me?" She laughed and pushed back into the man holding her. She reached for his sword but missed by a fraction. Two more men moved forward and grabbed her. The sky rumbled above as she struggled against them.

"Father," Renwick said. "We won't help you do this."

"We thought you might say that." King Athel tutted. "We don't have time for your childish notions. We have arrived at the Isle of Dryad, and the tide is low enough that we can enter. You two are coming whether you like it or not." He turned to the Pirate King. "You said she would play nice." He waved his hand at the sky.

Ella allowed the men to maneuver her after the kings across the gangway onto the island's stone path. No one spoke as they crossed through a rock-formed doorway leading to a staircase. She frowned at Renwick as he muttered something to himself. Whatever his father was doing, whatever the gods had planned . . . she wasn't sure she wanted to know.

It got colder as they descended into a cavern. Inside, numerous small pools of water were filled with coins, goblets, broken swords, and other treasures. One of the crew reached for something, but the king smacked his hand away.

"Touch nothing until I tell you."

"Ella," Renwick hissed as the crew moved past him. "Grab the sword hilt."

She looked around her. "Can you be more specific?"

"The gold one, there by your foot."

The man holding Renwick's arm pushed him forward.

The room began to shake as Renwick and Athel got closer to the largest pool in the cavern. A pedestal rose from beneath. Once in position, the tremors stopped. Renwick shook his head.

King Athel held out his hand. "The crown."

"Father, don't."

Renwick yanked his arm free from the man holding him and walked forward. "If you ever cared about me, do not do this. It's not what you think."

King Athel flicked his hand at his son. "Poppycock." He took the crown out of a bag and placed it on the pedestal.

A green glow filled the cavern. The rockface behind the pedestal fell into the water, revealing a carved emblem of the sea god.

Ella kicked the man to her right behind the knee, and he fell. She pretended to trip, landed by the pool Renwick had pointed to earlier, and grabbed the gold hilt. Though why he wanted half a sword, she didn't know.

"Come now, Ella, what exactly were you trying to do?" her father said. "Did you think I hadn't planned for an escape attempt?"

Two men picked her up and turned her to face him. His sword was in his hand and his crew poised, ready to move on his command.

She eyed his sword. "I'm not a scared little girl anymore, Father. You cannot intimidate me."

"Awfully confident, aren't you?" Athel shook his head and scoffed. "Look around you, my dear. There's nothing you can do."

Ella grinned. "You'd be surprised. My mother taught me well."

King Athel looked between her and her father and gulped. "Enough!"

She took a deep breath and broke free. Ella pulled the air in the cavern toward her and pushed it back out, knocking everyone but Renwick and herself to the ground. She made it to the prince and untied his hands before anyone could regain their footing.

"Here, whatever you wanted this for." She shoved the hilt in his hand.

"It's missing something." He grabbed her arm and yanked off her necklace.

"Hey! Now is *not* the time to admire my jewelry." She faced her father. "Oi!"

Renwick placed the jewel on the sword's hilt.

Only, it wasn't a sword.

The wind rushed into the cavern, and the sound of trickling water filled her ears. The small pools were emptying and heading to Renwick.

"That's my boy," King Athel said, wiping the dirt off his trousers. "I always knew you were special." He stepped up to Ella's side and tried to push her out of the way.

She slapped his hand off her arm and scowled.

Renwick's eyes glowed green. "You, Athel Foy, are not worthy of my blood." The water solidified into a trident.

Ella wanted to move but hesitated. "Renwick?"

He turned to her. This time, her feet moved and she stepped back. "You have nothing to fear, Ella Shadowboar. The crown is yours. Take it and go." His eyes landed back on King Athel.

She hesitated, but when Renwick nodded, she understood that whoever or whatever was using his body wouldn't harm her. She reached for the crown only to pull her hand away as her father's blade came down.

"Not until it's open."

Renwick lifted the trident and banged it on the ground once. The entire room shook. All but three of her father's men ran out, leaving the odds in her favor.

"I don't think we have a choice, Father." Ella grabbed a sword from the floor and pointed it at him. "Now get out of the way."

"I always wondered if it would come down to this. Me fighting you."

Ella shook her head. "You never wanted me. As soon as my mother died, you left me with anyone who you could charm to take me." She cleared her throat and continued, "Honestly, I'm glad. I never wanted a father like you either. Now get out of the way or I will cut you down."

Her father lunged for her. Ella dodged and used her magic to bring the storm inside. The light grew darker, making it near impossible for anyone other than a stormwitch to see.

Taking advantage of the darkness, she tapped her father on the back. He turned away from the crown, and she picked it up. The room shook as the slab of rock rose from the ground to cover the tomb again.

"No!" King Athel roared in the dark.

Lightning streaked all around them and highlighted the people left inside the cavern. Ella snuck up behind one of Peyton's men and jabbed her sword into his back through his chest. She put a hand over his mouth to stifle his gasp.

As she turned to the second man, something hard hit her on the back of the head. She stumbled and tripped, expecting to land on hard ground . . .

But what she hit was soft and warm.

"Renwick?"

"Your magic is fading. Put on the crown and I will get you out of here."

"Who are you?"

He smiled. "Apologize to Renwick for me when he is free. I rarely possess mortals, though it's a little easier when they are my offspring."

Ella nodded, too stunned to say anything. Once Renwick let her stand on her own, she placed the crown atop her head and ran out of the cavern. She heard her father's cries as Renwick raised the trident and brought the entrance down. Dust and rubble filled the air, making her cough. As it cleared, she saw Renwick sitting on the ground against a rock.

"Renwick? Are you okay?"

"Hmm?" He was dazed, so she slapped his cheek. "What? Oh. It's you."

"It's me. Are you . . . you again?" Ella scrunched her nose, and he nodded. "I was told to apologize to you. Though I don't know—"

He placed a hand on hers and used her to stand. "Poseidon possessed me. He apologized for doing it without my consent." He tapped the crown on her head. "Poseidon has chosen you to rule the seas. You with the crown and me with the trident. What a pair."

She smiled, her heart expanding. "Come on, you lunatic. Let's go commandeer the Skystorm."

R. S. WILLIAMS is a fantasy author from Somerset, England who lives with her husband and two cats.

She started writing in her late teens and grew up on a steady diet of books and tv shows feeding her imagination. When she's not writing or reading, Rhianne enjoys watching far too much Netflix, playing video games and going for walks.

To find out more, sign up for the newsletter or follow her on Instagram @authorrhiannewilliams

Find Rhianne online here:
www.authorrhiannewilliams.com

Find out more about THE KANE SAGA here:
https://books2read.com/u/m2RWv7

DANI HOOTS

PROVE ME WRONG

I wouldn't let them define me.

Staring up at the world tree Yggdrasil, its massive branches containing worlds that only the gods could traverse, I made my decision. I wouldn't give up—I would never give up.

For the past few weeks, I had been gathering supplies for the trip —a seax, food, water containers, a set of clothes, picks to climb with, and a tent, just in case I could find a flat spot to make camp for the night. I stared up at the large roots that Svartalfheim surrounded, wondering how far it went up as it made it past the clouds and sky. On a clear day, I could barely make out where the trunk started. No one knew what it led to, although some said it led to other worlds.

And that was why I had to go—to find the truth, not only for my people but also for myself.

"Arian! Don't go! Even if there are other worlds, it will be impossible to climb that high," my mother pleaded. I turned to find her crying, as she had been for the past few days.

"I need to know the truth, Mother. I need to know who I am."

She shook her head. "He'll never accept you. He'll never consider you his child."

I let out a little laugh. "He? Will you finally tell me who my father is?"

My mother pursed her lips but didn't say another word. She knew this was why I wanted to make the journey..

I knew my father wasn't a dark elf, living here in the DreadHighlands, full of fog and shadows. I didn't fit in. My hair, not dark like my brethren or my mother's, was a fiery red and orange that shone whenever light touched it. My eyes were the color of the sea on a stormy day and not dark like the night sky similar to my mother's. Our skin was also not the same hue—theirs a minty gray while mine had a pinkish tint to it.

My mother did everything she could to help me fit in, and I never felt as if I weren't welcome in her arms, but sometimes I could see it in her eyes when she looked at me—as if I reminded her of my father. So I had to find him.

And then I would know myself.

I gave my mother one last hug. "I love you, Mother. Thank you for letting me be who I am. If I find him, I promise I'll make my way back and tell you my whole adventure."

She squeezed me one last time, then quickly looked away, knowing I had made up my mind. Others from our village on this side of Svartalfheim stood in the distance, curious if I would keep my word and leave. I nodded to them, then turned back to the roots that lay before me.

"Here goes nothing."

Tightening my hair band, I stuck my pick into the smooth root that had a diameter larger than some houses we had. With the other pick, I moved up and began to ascend the glorious tree.

Many had tried to climb the tree, but most came back only days later to report it was impossible. Others never came back. The elders of the village claimed that the climbers died from lack of food, but I liked to believe they survived and found another world, living out their lives there. If that were the case, however, I wished they had made their way back home so we could have found out the truth. I knew there had to be other worlds out there—worlds full of life and creatures from all the stories that we had been told as children.

How else would one explain why I appeared so different?

There were no other dark elves or other beings in Svartalfheim that looked like me. I had visited countless villages over the years while training to climb this tree, and I had found no one. Since my mother didn't want me to go, she could have told me if my father was someone not from a different world, but she never did that. She knew I had to go and find the truth.

Even with my hours upon hours of training I performed by climbing rocky cliffsides over the ocean, running up and down mountains, my body grew tired as I ascended the roots with my picks. Although some areas were flat and I could traverse without climbing, the ground was slippery from the moist air, and I had to be careful. Since I could feel the smoothness of the roots before I left, I had brought shoes with small spikes in them, but even with those, it was a hard terrain to conquer. I could understand why many decided to turn back after a few days. But I wouldn't do that—I wouldn't give up.

I had made it to the cloud layer and could barely see where I was going—only gravity indicating which way was up and down. Although I had quite a few layers of wool and furs on, the coolness was beginning to make my sore joints even achier. I imagined this was where many people turned around to head back as I felt cold, shaken, and alone.

But I had to press on—I had to keep going.

Night came, and I was able to pin my hammock into the side of the tree. It was dark, and I clutched my blanket, hoping that there was nothing in the darkness that would find me there. I felt vulnerable, as there was nothing to keep me hidden from the beasts that were said to climb up and down the tree.

In the legends I heard from the elders of our tribe, there were creatures that could traverse from the topmost leaves to the very bottom of the roots. I had spent many nights waiting to see if I could spot such a creature, but I never once saw one. Other legends claimed that only the Aesir and Vanir could travel between realms via the Bifröst, a rainbow bridge that could be summoned when needed. They were both different types of gods that were said to protect the people of all the lands and keep order. Centuries were said to have passed since any god had visited Svartalfheim. However, some stories suggested that they could disguise themselves as one of the dark elves.

So, perhaps, they were among us. We just didn't know it.

I had mentioned this to my mother, and she always ignored the question. I had a feeling it had to do with my father. It was why I knew I could find something about him if I traveled up Yggdrasil, otherwise why wouldn't she tell me the truth? He had to be up there —I just knew it.

As quietly as I could, I pulled out a piece of dark elf bread. It was a bread that didn't have much taste, but it was thick and did not spoil so easily. I had brought five loaves with me, each able to last at least a week. It had all the nutrients I needed to keep on climbing. I nibbled on it, listening carefully to see if anything was out there, but all was silent.

More days passed, and I never thought I was going to make it out of the layer of clouds. It was like fog—eerie, cold, and damp. I had made it past all the roots and was now only climbing the trunk. There were no easy ways to stop, so I had to only climb as far as my muscles would allow, then set up my hammock to rest for a bit. I spent many hours crying, wondering what I was going to do. I couldn't turn back as I didn't want to abandon my journey, but I also didn't want to die alone. My food was dwindling, although I was still able to absorb moisture to use as drinking water.

One day, as I was taking a break, staring out into the vast nothingness, I heard a caw in the distance. I clenched my entire body, hoping it wasn't some massive bird that was going to swoop in and eat me in one gulp. As the cawing grew louder, I saw a black figure come out of the pure white mist. It was a raven. The bird swooped down and landed on the metal pick that held up my hammock.

Seeing another living creature after so many days made me smile. "Hello, creature. What are you doing here?"

It cawed again and watched me carefully. I didn't know where it had come from or what it was doing. Was this creature from another world? Was it going to lead me to where I needed to go?

"I am called Arian Artuflnose of the DreadHighlands. It's a pleasure to meet you." I held out my hand as if the bird were a person, then quickly realized my mistake. "I'm sorry. I'm used to talking to other dark elves. I guess you don't have hands to shake with."

The bird cocked his head, then cawed again.

I glanced around, wondering if I had anything to offer him. I was on my last few bites of bread. "I don't have much, but you can have a little piece of bread if you wish."

The raven swooped down and took the bread. Instead of going back to its perch, it flew up into the white mist, out of sight. I was about to give up hope when I realized something.

It had flown up, not down. There had to be something up there.

Gathering my things as quickly as I could without losing my balance, I started up the trunk again. I pushed myself harder and harder, not wanting to stop when I believed I was close to where I needed to be.

Over an hour passed, and I felt as if my arms were going to fall off. As I swung the pick into the wood, something felt a bit different. It felt as if the wood were a rock.

I placed my hand on the surface, and it was indeed hard and smooth. I reached up and felt the edge of a cliff.

I had arrived in a world beyond my own.

Pulling myself up, I found a land not covered in fog but full of life. I had stepped out of the misty clouds and onto land adorned with yarrow, grass, plantain, clover, and much more for as far as the eye could see. In the distance were large trees. The sky above me was a reddish orange as the sun began to set. I collapsed onto the ground. I had made it—I had finally made it.

My body surrendered to how tired it was, and I found myself asleep within moments of finding this world. When I woke, the sun was in the sky, and I felt something furry nuzzling my cheek. I opened my eyes to an orange, friendly face.

It was a fox.

We had foxes in Svartalfheim, and many were hunted for their furs. I always felt bad for them, as they were such cute and delightful creatures to watch. From learning all about animals from one of the best hunters in my village, I knew it was a male.

"What are you doing here, little one?" I asked.

It ran around me a few times, letting out a laughing screech. I laughed with it as I glanced up at the sky.

It was rare for the sun to shine this bright in Svartalfheim. Usually, it was dark and dim with many days of fog and rain. I had never seen anything quite this bright.

"Are we in Asgard?" I turned to the fox, who simply stared at me.

Of course the fox couldn't speak. I sighed. "Well, let's get some water and food, shall we?"

The fox followed me over to a small stream that led into the forest. I filled my water sack and washed my face. The fox knelt and drank a bit of the water. As he did that, I searched around for some food. There were some bushes on the tree line full of berries. Having no idea whether they were poisonous, I grabbed a handful and went back to where the fox was.

"Do you eat these?" I asked him as I handed him one of the berries.

He ate it in a quick bite and grinned at me. Apparently, they were not poisonous. I went back to the bush and ate as many as I could. They were sweet, and some were a bit sour, but they were all delicious—much more delicious than the bread I had been eating.

As I sat down on the edge of the stream, I glanced up. It seemed that there was still more to the tree than this place. I could spot branches from the forest that went up into the sky and kept on going. I sighed.

"This isn't Asgard, is it? This is some other world. Well, no matter. I made it this far, and I'm not giving up now."

The fox seemed to nod. It was as if it were my companion and wanted to help me on this quest. I gave the creature a pat on the head and scratched behind his ear.

"And what should I call you? How about Refr?"

It gave a scream of approval. I grinned.

"Well then, Refr, how about we head into the forest?"

Refr was up before I was and darted toward the tree line. I quickly scooped up my things and ran after Refr. The beginning of the forest was quite open and easy to make my way through the foliage, but as Refr led me deeper inside, the thicker everything became.

Soon I couldn't see the bright sky but was reminded of my home. Moss and lichens hung from the trees, branches appearing gnarly and grotesque. The brush became denser, and I could hardly see Refr any longer.

"Wait, Refr!"

But it was too late. He was gone.

I clutched myself and glanced around. I didn't know which way led back to the stream or which way was the next section of Yggdrasil. I didn't want to be alone—not anymore.

"Refr!"

"Are you looking for someone?" a voice behind me asked.

I jumped and spun around to find an old man with a walking stick, staring at me with his one good eye. His other eye was as white as snow. He wore a long gray cloak, hiding his clothes underneath. I wasn't sure who he was or what he wanted. Was he a person of this world?

"I, um, there was a fox I met today. I didn't want him to leave me is all. I guess it doesn't matter. It was silly to think a fox would want to travel with me."

As I said that, a raven flew down from the trees and perched on the man's walking stick. It cawed as the man petted its head.

"It's not silly to have an animal companion. Creatures of the forest are loyal to those they believe in."

As I watched the raven, I realized it was the one I had fed. "I just met that bird yesterday. Is it your raven?"

He nodded. "Indeed he is. He told me about a young dark elf who was climbing Yggdrasil. You have traveled quite far. Tell me, young one, what do you seek?"

I didn't know what I should tell this person, as he was but a stranger. However, something about him made me feel as if I could trust him. "I seek the truth. I am searching for my father, whom I believe is an Asgardian or part of the Vanir." I pulled down my long red hair. "I assume he has the same fiery hair as I do."

The corner of the man's lip almost went up in a grin. "I see. And what makes you believe he was a god?"

"Because he would have had to travel the Bifröst in order to go to Svartalfheim."

"But you made it all the way to Midgard without the help of the Bifröst. Perhaps he did the same."

I shook my head. "No, someone would have told me they saw him do that. My father had to have left without anyone knowing it."

The man laughed. "You are a bold one, Arian. You are indeed correct. Your father is in Asgard right this moment. Perhaps your fox friend can show you the way." He nodded behind me.

I turned to find Refr. He leaped into my arms. "Refr! I'm so happy you're back." Then it occurred to me. "How did you know my name?"

I turned to find the man was gone. I glanced all around, but there was no trace of him. As I stepped where he had been standing, I found a metal amulet lying on the ground. I picked it up and examined the runes. It appeared almost like a compass of some sort. As I held it, it began to glow.

Refr shifted in my arms, and I placed him on the ground. He began to scream and run around in circles.

"Do you know what this is?"

Refr nodded and started to run again. I hurried after him. This time he ran a bit slower so I could keep up. The amulet glowed brighter and brighter until we made it to a clearing.

I couldn't believe my eyes. There was a rainbow of colors glistening in the air that almost appeared like I could touch it. I reached out and found that it was indeed solid even though I could see through it.

"Is this . . . ?" I whispered.

Refr chirped and then jumped up onto the rainbow.

I peered up and gasped. This was the Bifröst—this was how I was going to get to Asgard.

Holding the amulet tight, I knew there was only one way to find out if my father was truly a god. I began to climb.

It was true—I was a demigod. I could use the Bifröst.

Refr jumped ahead of me, showing me the way. With every step, my heart beat faster and faster. I would finally see him—I would finally meet my father.

Hours passed, but I didn't stop. I was almost there—I could feel it. I didn't want to stop. I didn't want to wait. I never looked back, only forward. Forward to my destiny.

The light of the universe grew brighter as I came closer. I raised my head to Asgard—the world of the gods—knowing that was where I belonged. It was where my truth was of who I was, who I needed to be, and who I would be.

With my first step into the world, I felt as if time had stopped. I felt the power awakening in me, the knowledge of my existence, my energy, and my destiny all swirling together as one. I would be worthy of this place. I would be worthy of my fate.

A man with red hair and a red beard was standing at the top of the bridge, peering out at the universe. Stars and nebulae stretched as far as the eye could see. The land under my feet was similar to that of the rainbow bridge in that it was solid but was colorful and transparent. I stared in awe as I had never seen anything so beautiful.

Refr stood next to my leg as the man began to step toward me. His crystal-blue eyes watched me as he twirled a large hammer in his hand. He wore clothes like that of the men in our tribe—furs, leather, and cloth made of hemp. As he came close, I felt every muscle in my body tense.

This was him—this was my father. I could feel it.

"Who are you to step into Asgard?"

I straightened up. "I am Arian Artuflnose, demigod of the Dread-Highlands. I have come to claim my birthright as the child of Thor."

The man went wide-eyed, then laughed. "You are no child of mine."

I shook my head. "I will prove myself to you even if it is with my dying breath."

The edge of Thor's lips curled up in a smile. "Fine then." He held out his hammer. "Prove to me your worth. Prove to me you can carry Mjölnir, and everything of mine will become yours."

And that was where my destiny began.

DANI HOOTS

Dani Hoots is a science fiction, fantasy, and young adult author who loves anything with a story. She has a B.S. in Anthropology, a Masters of Urban and Environmental Planning, a Certificate in Novel Writing from Arizona State University, and a BS in Herbal Science from Bastyr University.

Her hobbies include reading, watching anime, cooking, studying different languages, wire walking, hula hoop, and working with plants. She also loves mythology and has a YouTube channel called Mythology & Folklore w/ Dani Hoots where she talks about different figures in mythology and tells old folktales. She lives in Arizona.

Instagram: https://instagram.com/danihoots

Free Book: https://dl.bookfunnel.com/crulacn4p7

BETHANY HOEFLICH

THE KILLER COUNTESS

"For the last time, I'm not killing your mother-in-law for you."

Slack-jawed, Henry stared at me, blinking his froglike, watery eyes as if he couldn't believe I had said no. Again. "But, you're a killer," he spluttered.

I gritted my teeth. These plebeians had grown far too comfortable with the idea of casual murder for hire, but then again, the Deathly Backwaters would do that to a person.

"Your point being?" I reclined in my plush velvet chair—a gift from the magistrate for ridding the sewer of a dozen water drakes last month—and propped my booted feet onto my desk as I contemplated murdering him instead. Ice flowed through my veins as I sensed his life force—sensed how easy it would be to snuff it out. I closed my eyes and balled my hands into fists. Before I could respond to the forbidden magic awakening in my blood, I grabbed my chipped porcelain teacup and gulped down a mouthful of lukewarm tea, hoping that would stifle the temptation.

It didn't.

Henry continued, "Killers kill people."

"Even killers have standards, and I'm not going to do your dirty work for you. If you want her gone so bad, do it yourself. Next!"

He shuffled away, no doubt cursing me under his breath. He'd be back next week, and I'd tell him the same thing I always did. Even if his mother-in-law hadn't paid me off years ago, I still wouldn't kill her. Her blackberry tarts were a delight.

I stood and crossed the too-small room to the lone window that overlooked the marsh, taking in a deep breath of the thick, sulfurous air that made everything smell like rotten eggs. Just another day in paradise. Another day reminding me of everything I'd lost. I would have given anything to be free of this wretched place where my life consisted of trading lives for coin.

Footsteps on the wood floor alerted me to another hopeful client.

I glanced over my shoulder and froze. My heart thundered in my chest as blood rushed to my ears. The man was taller than me by a head with stubble that coated his jaw and hair so brown it looked black in the shadows of my hut. Even if he hadn't been wearing expensive clothing, the way he carried himself screamed of wealth and privilege. Every pickpocket in the Deathly Backwaters would be salivating.

His face was so familiar it hurt.

Before he could open his traitorous mouth, I growled, "No."

His brows creased. "You don't know what I'm offering."

I crossed my arms. "You could offer me a palace in Khaldiris and a hundred servants to wipe my butt and my answer would still be the same."

"But—"

"Not interested. Next!"

"Lina . . ."

"I go by Delilah now. Delilah Lucenthart, Countess of the Deathly Backwaters at your service," I said, letting enough of my former accent bleed through to be mocking. Just another change that happened five years ago, and it served as a reminder of everything he'd stolen from me. "I'd say it was a pleasure to make your reacquaintance, Edward, Duke of Lennon, but I'd be lying."

Holding my defiant gaze, Edward reached into the pocket of his overcoat and withdrew a bulging pouch. He weighed it once in his hand before tossing it onto the desk. Skeptical, I loosened the ties and fought to stifle my gasp at the glint of gold. For a moment, I forgot to breathe. My hand acted on its own accord, snatching the pouch and wedging it down the front of my dress, before he realized he'd drastically overpaid.

His expression turned hopeful. "You'll take the job?"

"Your gold just bought you a total of five minutes to tell me about the job, at which point I'll decide if I want to take it and how much it will cost you."

"You're just as ruthless as I remember," he said, eyes narrowed, though a smirk played on his lips.

I shrugged and sat down, crossing my legs at the ankles and arranging the skirt of my dress before tucking my blonde braid over my shoulder. "That's business."

He stared for a long while. "You look good."

"Are you going to waste your five minutes showering me with compliments? Because if so, I have no objections."

He sighed. "I need you to dispose of a reaver."

I burst out laughing, arms holding my middle to keep me from falling out of the chair. When I glanced up at him, his face was grave. "Oh, you're serious." I wiped my eyes with the back of my hand. "Well, thanks but no thanks. Exile is one thing, but I don't have a death wish. Now, if you had a flight of windsprites, or a deranged horned-bear . . ."

Edward pulled a letter from his pocket and held it up. "The king is offering you a full pardon in exchange for this service."

I zeroed in on that scrap of paper and stilled. With the gold and my freedom, I could go anywhere. I could start over with a new identity, and as long as I kept my magic hidden, no one would know the difference. I allowed myself a moment to imagine what it would be like to walk down the street and have people look at me without fear. It was too good to be true.

"What's the catch?"

"No catch." Edward tucked the letter back inside his jacket. "His Majesty is simply . . . motivated."

"Oh, this is too good . . . The reaver is at the palace?"

He nodded.

"Then that makes my decision easier. It can eat him for all I care, and it can have you for dessert. Have a nice trip back to the city."

After a long moment, he turned to leave and take my one chance at freedom with him. I should have known my fate was sealed the second he'd pulled out that pardon.

"Wait . . ."

He looked back at me over his shoulder.

I sighed. "When do we leave?"

"Immediately. I have a coach waiting outside the gates."

"Very well." I grabbed my leather satchel and stuffed it with spare clothes. I didn't bother with weapons beyond a dagger—they'd be useless against the reaver.

With a questioning look, Edward led the way out of my hut. I blinked as my eyes adjusted to the sunlight. He picked his way through the dirt streets, placing each boot with care to avoid the mystery stains.

I couldn't resist needling him. "The dried blood and urine smell add a touch of charm, don't they?"

He stopped suddenly, and I turned to him. His face was pale and drawn in revulsion. He shook his head slowly. "I didn't realize it would be like this."

"Oh, what? Did you think I'd be pampered, sitting around in pretty gowns and braiding my hair all day while suitors paraded through to visit the demon girl?"

"I—"

"Let's go before I change my mind." I tightened my grip on my bag's strap, bumping against his shoulder as I led the way.

He followed in silence. I might have thought he'd fallen behind if it weren't for his familiar footsteps and the occasional gasp. Yeah, I remembered what it had been like the first week I was here when I couldn't sleep without a blade in my hand. To be fair, that hadn't changed.

There was one rule in the Deathly Backwaters, and that was to survive. The prison city was surrounded by inhospitable stretches of land, each mile packed full of deadly creatures. Most people chose to stay put in the city rather than wander out. A knife in the back was a quicker way to die than being eaten by something.

Still, a handful of people tried to escape every year—usually the new people, dropped off every few months after judgment day. The lucky ones came back with most of their limbs intact.

We had nearly reached the gates when I heard footsteps behind me, and I tensed for a fight until a tiny hand tugged on my arm. A child looked up at me with wide brown eyes. Her stringy hair hung limply to the middle of her back, and it took me a moment to recognize her beneath the layers of dirt and grime. I crouched down. "What is it, Abby?"

"Granny Lois. Please." Tears filled her eyes as she pressed a doll into my hands. Payment.

Knowing that was the only doll she owned, I resisted the urge to hand it back to her. Here in the Deathly Backwaters, people didn't accept charity.

"What is it?" Edward asked.

"We have a detour to make before we can leave. Come on."

"But . . . we need to go."

"Then by all means, go. I don't *need* to help you with the reaver, now do I?" I smiled sweetly, knowing I'd keep his gold regardless.

He gritted his teeth. I would have smirked, but the weight of my duty pressed on me. This was the reality of being a death mage.

It was nothing but a curse.

The Deathly Backwaters was far from a bastion of wealth and beauty, but Lois's house was even more run down than the rest. Rusted nails poked out from salvaged wood, and the rough clay that had been slathered in between the slats was now dry and crumbling.

"Wait out here," I told Edward.

He frowned, looking like he would protest until the stench of unwashed bodies and filth hit him. He took an uncertain step back. "What are you going to do?"

I looked down at the doll clutched in my hand and whispered, "What I'm paid to do."

He gripped my upper arm and leaned down. "What's that supposed to mean?"

"What do you think it means, Edward?" I tilted my head back so he could see the truth in my gaze.

Fury crossed his face. "You're going to kill someone. An old woman." When I didn't respond, he said, "I was right then. You *are* a monster."

He released me as if he couldn't do it fast enough. As if I were something dirty to be discarded. After five years, I couldn't believe that still hurt.

"You're right." I didn't bother to explain. It would do nothing to change his mind and only waste my breath and time. If seeing me as a monster helped him sleep at night, then so be it. My lip curled. "I *am* a monster. I'm the monster you hire when you can't escape the monsters in the dark."

Then I spun on my heel and marched inside.

When I came back out minutes later, he wouldn't speak to me, wouldn't even look at me, but I could feel the disapproval coming off him in waves as we walked silently to the gates that marked the boundary of the Deathly Backwaters.

Could I stand traveling with him to the palace? I briefly considered overpowering him, stealing the pardon, and taking my chances in the next city. It was only two weeks to the nearest border. Then I saw the guards. Most looked at me as though I was a powder keg about to blow, and the closest held up a syringe.

I planted my feet. "Is that really necessary?"

"King's orders."

I would have loved to tell them where the king could shove his orders, but right now, that carriage was the only ticket out of the Deathly Backwaters, and if my magic needed to be suppressed in order to get out, I'd deal with it. I held out my arm without another word, jaw working as the needle pricked into my skin and fire replaced the cool stream of magic. This wasn't the first time I'd had my magic suppressed, but it's the first time since being dropped off at this hell hole.

My own mother had been the one to drug me throughout childhood. She'd told me my magic was dark, evil, and if anyone found out about it, they'd take me away.

She was right.

I hadn't believed her, so when I'd gotten a chance to skip my dose, I had.

I just hadn't realized it would cost me everything.

Refusing to show a reaction to having my magic harnessed, I lifted my chin and climbed into the carriage.

Edward sat on the bench across from me, angling his body to be as far away as possible. I tried not to be offended. Most people reacted the same way when they realized I was cursed with death magic. It should have been an automatic death sentence, but because of my former station, the king was loath to execute me. So, he'd shipped me off to this backwater to languish. Many might have assumed it was his particular brand of mercy, but to me, it was a clever way of keeping a leash on someone he might have further use of.

"Tell me of the reaver."

Edward jumped in his seat, but he quickly got a better hold of himself. The look he shot me was venomous, but perhaps his sense of duty overcame his personal dislike. "We aren't sure where it came from. It worked its way through the city, leaving a trail of bodies behind, until it found its way into the castle. The king and his family secured refuge inside the western tower."

"Leaving the rest of the castle unprotected and at the mercy of the reaver?"

"Would you have preferred him to lay down like a martyr?"

Well, yes. I couldn't deny the thought of him getting his comeuppance was pleasant. "I'm assuming the western tower is warded."

"The protections are old and . . . deteriorating."

I couldn't stifle my smirk. "What a pity the king has such a prejudice against mages."

"For good reason!"

"A boundary mage would have been convenient to have in his pocket, no?" I raised an eyebrow at him. "Too bad they fled the country."

He sighed. "In retrospect, his policies might have been a bit . . ."

"Idiotic?"

"I was going to say shortsighted." He scowled. "He's still your king."

"What makes him my king, exactly? A king has a responsibility to all his subjects, not to just the ones he doesn't fear."

"And would he have been right to trust you?" His gaze turned probing, and I knew he was remembering that day in the garden.

I turned to look out the window, all the fight leaving me. "We'll never know now, will we?" I murmured.

The constant crunch of wheels on the dirt road lulled me back into the memory. It had been a warm spring morning when our estate was in a tizzy over the Duke of Lennon's arrival and the official announcement of our betrothal. It was an odd thing to marry a boy you grew up with, but as with all arranged marriages, I had no choice. "Better the kind boy I knew than a cruel stranger," Father had said. My mother had been too distracted by the flower arrangements and invisible dust on the candelabras that she'd forgotten to give me my dose of medicine that morning.

I wasn't going to say anything. What could it hurt? Plenty of mages lived in the village nearby, and nothing bad happened. Sure, the king didn't approve, but he left them alone save for the dangerous few.

I'd been daydreaming about the type of magic I could wield when it was freed. Light magic, plant magic, water magic . . . all were a beautiful fantasy in my mind.

The morning passed on, and the maids had already dressed me and curled my hair. I could feel the icy magic pulsing beneath my skin, and with each rapid heartbeat, I grew more excited.

The Duke arrived an hour early with his retinue. I gathered my skirts and hurried to the back of the gardens where I knew he'd be waiting by the pond. He sat on a bench with a book in his hands and his favorite hound at his side. I told him I wanted to show him something, and with a grin, I allowed the magic to pool in my hands.

Rather than fill with the warm glow of life magic, my hands seeped inky black, and I could only gape in horror as it leaked out in vining tendrils that wrapped around the dog.

Looking back, there should have been some sort of violence or struggle, something to indicate the significance of what had happened.

Instead, the dog whined once, then closed its eyes and collapsed into the grass. Killed by my hands.

What happened next was a blur. I vaguely remember the hushed voices, the fearful stares . . . being packed off into a carriage and then kneeling before the king. He hadn't even asked for a defense—not that I had one. I could only stare at my hands in shock.

Death magic.

The rarest and most dangerous magic of all.

Magic that had landed me a life sentence in the Deathly Backwaters.

Within a week, we arrived at the castle. Unlike the last time I'd been here, the courtyard was barren. If the king was smart, he would have packed up and moved far away. The expense of building an entire new castle would be better than dealing with a reaver.

A surge of fear tingled down my spine as I stepped out of the carriage and gaped up at the gray stone walls, gripping my satchel tighter.

"How many guards are going in with me?"

The closest guard let out a barking laugh that he quickly smothered while Edward gave me a look that I would have labeled as apologetic on anyone else. "For this mission, it's just you."

I reeled back. "You're joking."

"The king is unwilling to risk anyone else."

"And yet the chance of success is greater with a team. Does he want to spend the rest of his life huddling in a tower?"

I would never understand his thought process. Reavers fed on a person's life force, so the more people you had with you, the less likely it would take all from a single person. It could sample small amounts from everyone without lasting effects on the victim, allowing me to work my magic.

"Fine. I'll need full access to my magic."

At the mention of my magic, suspicion flooded his expression. "It should have returned on its own by now."

So much for getting the antidote. The guard hadn't drugged me since we'd left the Deathly Backwaters, and while my magic was slowly replenishing, I was far from fully powered. Far too weak to face a reaver alone and feel good about my chances.

Who was I kidding? My chances were minimal to begin with, magic or no. Why did I agree to do this again? Oh, that's right. "You swear I'll get a full pardon?"

Edward patted his pocket where the king's letter resided. "Yes," he said, though his face reflected his feelings about letting me go after the job was completed and I knew he was remembering Granny Lois.

Well, I wasn't about to reassure him or coddle his feelings. It was clear he hadn't changed his mind about me in the last five years, and nothing, not even a command from his king, would change it now. That was fine. After this job was done, provided I survived, I was gone. With the amount of gold I'd earned, I could go anywhere and just disappear.

With the promise of a new life fresh in my mind, I climbed the steps toward the palace. My mind raced to remember everything I'd known about reavers. They were rare, and most people could go their entire lives without encountering one. Corrupted by dark magic, they had once been mages, just like me. In the early stages, they were identical to humans, but their thirst was unquenchable. Their forms mutated as the sickness progressed, and their humanity was truly lost.

The sound of footsteps behind me made me pause as I reached for the door ring.

Edward, along with five of the guards, waited behind me with bared weapons. I tilted my head. "Changed your minds then?"

"Regardless of how I feel about you personally, if you say that a team will give you a better chance of saving the king, then I'm willing to help you," he said, the muscle in his jaw ticking.

I nodded my thanks, then with a deep breath, I opened the door.

The thick stench of decay hit me first. For a mage with death magic, you might think I'd grown used to it, but it turned my stomach as much as anyone else's. I took a cautious step inside, ears trained for any sound of the reaver. I tilted my head in the direction of the western tower and my team followed. Warded or not, the reaver would be drawn to the presence of life, and I would bet good money that's where we'd find it.

Shattered urns, shredded tapestries, and bodies laid a trail of carnage that we followed, pressing our sleeves to our noses.

With each step, I called a little more of my magic to the surface, covering myself with it as though it was armor. If the reaver tried to taste me, expecting to find life, it would only encounter death.

As we approached the western tower, I dropped into a crouch and motioned for my team to stop. I whispered, "When we go inside, spread out, and don't stop moving. Your job is to distract it so I can kill it. Don't give it even a moment to lock you in its sights, and whatever you do, keep out of reach of its claws."

I could only hope it would be enough.

The reaver waited at the base of the tower, its form bent and sickly. Its clothes had long since rotted away, leaving behind tattered scraps that clung to its skeletal body. Skin that had once been full and healthy was now pale and brittle, as though the slightest touch would cause it to shatter like glass. At our approach, it twisted toward us, clicking its teeth together.

Behind me, my team spread out, but Edward remained at my side, sword at the ready.

The reaver struck with deadly speed, raking its claws across a guard's chest. It leaned in, making a wheezing sound as it drew in the guard's life force. Edward jumped forward, scoring a hit against the back of its neck, but he might as well have pricked it with a sewing needle.

The reaver turned, and I unleashed my magic.

Tendrils of magic slithered across the floor toward the reaver, weaving around its body. Before they could find purchase, the reaver sidestepped, drawing it closer to Edward.

"Look out!" I cried.

Edward darted backward, stumbling once as the reaver began to siphon from him. I should never have insisted on a team. Blocked off from a source, it would have been weakened enough for me to overpower. But out of fear, I'd stupidly brought a feast with me.

I threw myself at Edward, knocking him away.

He gaped up at me, and I scrambled away, planting myself between him and the reaver before it could attack again. It slid forward, backhanding a guard who had gotten too close, but it didn't take its eyes off me.

I readied another attack, hoping to finish it quickly.

The reaver hissed, a sharp, piercing sound that made my knees go weak and my gut turn to ice as my resolve melted away. I trembled.

I couldn't fight this.

It was too strong.

Why was I bothering to go on? If I just gave in . . . it would be over, and I would be free.

"Fight it, Lina! Don't let it get you, too." Edward's voice broke the spell.

No, I *was* strong enough.

With a desperate scream, I sent my magic spinning in a reckless wave. The reaver attempted to dodge, but it couldn't escape the torrent of death magic that buffeted it. The darkness overwhelmed the reaver and it collapsed to the floor.

Dead.

I sucked in deep gulps of air. "Is everyone okay?"

The guards seemed shaken, but otherwise unharmed. All except . . .

I approached the fallen guard who'd taken the brunt of the reaver's attack, and I knelt by his side. His breathing had grown labored, and his face was coated in a layer of sweat. He reached for my hand. "Mercy . . . please . . ."

I closed my eyes and swallowed. I could feel Edward's gaze boring a hole through my back, but I ignored it. The guard would suffer needlessly if I did nothing, and so without another thought, I allowed my magic to flow beneath his skin. The guard took one last breath and went still.

Shaking, I pushed myself to my feet and turned toward the door at the base of the tower. "We should tell your king it's safe to come out now."

A touch on the arm halted me.

"That's what you did for the old woman too, isn't it?" Edward asked, his voice surprisingly gentle. "Mercy."

I kept my gaze fixed on my boots. "Would it make a difference?"

Or would he always see me as a monster?

For the second time in my life, I knelt before the king in the throne room, but this time, instead of facing his judgment, I waited for my promised reward. With thinning red hair and a waistline that had doubled in five years, King Cyrus sat on his cushioned throne atop a raised dais as he lorded over his loyal subjects.

"Magdelina Rosewood . . ."

Hearing my former name made me jolt.

"Unfortunate circumstances have brought you to my city, but it seems I owe you a debt of gratitude for your service." The king gestured to his vizier who approached with a letter perched in his open palms. "Ordinarily, this would merit a reward. A royal pardon, to be exact."

I held my breath. This is what I was waiting for. Why I had risked death.

Freedom.

A smirk played at the king's lips. "Unfortunately, it would be unwise for me to set loose such an unholy demon to wreak havoc on my subjects. I may as well have allowed the reaver to tear through my kingdom. As such, a dangerous creature such as yourself must be locked away. Forever."

My heart thundered. What was he saying? No. I'd earned my pardon. I—

The sting of a needle bit into my arm and my magic cut off.

"Guards! Lock her away."

I barely registered the bite of the cuffs around my wrists or the guards pulling me away. As we passed through the grandiose doorway, I locked eyes with Edward, allowing him to see the depth of his betrayal.

He turned away from me, just as he'd done the last time.

Allowing myself to go limp, I let them drag me to the dungeons. I should never have left the Deathly Backwaters. I should have never allowed myself to hope for more.

Hours had passed and I had already grown used to the gentle trickling of water, the sporadic screams from somewhere in the dungeon, and the near constant parade of guards outside my cell. I was down to a single guard now. The rest had gone home, or back to the barracks for the night, I imagined. I shifted on the cold stone, hoping to ease the pressure of the cuffs where they had me chained to the wall. Would it have killed them to give me some food or water?

I knocked my head back against the wall in frustration. Was this what my life would be from now on? Caged like a dangerous animal until the king had use for me? Had Edward known that the king would go back on his word?

Scuffling from outside my cell, followed by a muffled grunt, had me staring at the cell door with wide eyes. Hinges squeaked as the door opened and someone paused in the doorway.

I squinted at the hooded figure, making out enough of his features to recognize him. "Edward?"

"I need to ask you this one thing." He stepped into my cell and held the torch up so he could see my face. "If I let you go, will you swear to leave the city without harming anyone?"

"Yes," I breathed.

As if my answer had been the dam holding him back, he rushed forward and unlocked my cuffs. He caught them before they hit the stone and lowered them gently to the floor. I rubbed my wrists. "Why are you doing this?"

"I'm sorry. I was wrong about everything."

"But—"

"No. I allowed prejudice and fear to turn me against my dearest childhood friend, and for that, I owe you a debt I will never repay. I saw your magic for what it truly is earlier today, capable of great evil, but also capable of compassion, and mercy. It's not a curse, but a gift."

He gave me a tentative smile and held out his hand. An offer.

With a deep breath, I placed my hand in his and took my first step into what I'd always longed for.

Freedom.

BETHANY HOEFLICH

Bethany Hoeflich is the author of the Dreg Trilogy. She lives in Central Pennsylvania with her husband, three children and an assortment of furry (and scaly) creatures.

Monday through Friday, Bethany is at the mercy of the sadistic whims of her scatterbrained muse, feverishly churning out the words for her next novel.

On the weekends, Bethany wrestles narwhals, participates in competitive taco-eating competitions and visits alternate dimensions through a rift in her stereotypically dark and spooky basement.

Follow her on Facebook for sporadic updates on her latest project.

facebook.com/BethanyHoeflichAuthor

C.C. SULLIVAN

LE FIGARO

THE CITY OF LIGHTS HAS FALLEN

THE SILENT WAR CRIPPLES ITS CITIZENS.

Last headline of *Le Figaro*, June 30, 2030

JUNE 2050

I'd often imagined my death—facing a firing squad or slipping off a building's rooftop—but never from the sky.

"Faith," Alexander said. "I'm sorry."

Dread seeped into my veins. "Aren't you going to give me a parachute?"

He shook his head, and I was shoved off the zeppelin.

TWO MONTHS EARLIER

A dull, monochromatic world with the pungent stench of sulfur greeted me as I closed my home's wrought-iron gate. Beyond Montmartre's winding streets, the Parisian cityscape lay sprawled out in a mélange of rooftops, windows, and alabaster white façades. In contrast, factories filled with enslaved workers spewed billows of dark fumes, and airships floated above the murky skyline.

I sprinted through Place Émile Goudeau, my strides quickening across the tiny cobblestones in the square, as I hastened to the park. Turning a corner, I crashed into someone; the force knocked me to the ground.

"Let me help," a deep, resonant voice said. He proffered his hand, and I held it to stand.

I brushed myself off, and an explosion of colors invaded my senses—brown, silver, and beyond, a splash of emerald and rose. I gasped.

"Thank you—" The words caught in my throat when my gaze fell upon the crisp, dark brown uniform and waistcoat embroidered with fine silver thread. Cascading roses and greenery hung over a garden wall behind him. "Officer! I should have been more careful."

Silence met my apology, and I kept my eyes somewhere around his chest.

"Papers, please," he said with a steely voice.

The momentary lapse of color vanished, and my achromatic world returned. My heart pounded. The postcard with the coded poem still lay snug in my breast pocket. I'd retrieved it earlier from the Poste d'Orsay and had forgotten to leave it at home. Carrying an encoded document was an act of treason, punishable by death. My trembling hand reached for my wrist wallet and quivered as I retrieved my identification booklet.

He raised an eyebrow while peering at my information. "Fée Rosegarden?"

A familiar inflection reached my ears, but I couldn't place it. "Yes, but I prefer Faith."

His lips twitched, the whisper of a smile forming at its corners. "Commander Alexander Wilde." He clicked his heels.

I extended my arm and added, "Of the Silent Army." *Our sworn enemy.* I hoped he wouldn't sense the shiver creeping up my spine as he shook my hand.

"Enchanté, mademoiselle." His tone remained cool.

Though his military cap cast a dark shadow across his expression, a hint of dimples formed. His trimmed dark hair, a goatee, and sun-kissed skin framed his piercing gaze.

My knees weakened under his scrutiny. I should have run, but my feet remained glued to the sidewalk.

He gave a curt nod. "Try not to stay out past curfew, Miss Rosegarden."

"Yes, sir." I forced a smile and dashed away.

I hurried to the pocket park with le mur des je t'aime—a wall covered with lovers' passionate messages on enameled lava tiles. I scanned the wall's façade for the hidden keys to the code—a set of cryptic characters, each part of a mechanism, like cogs in a wheel. I was Lady of the Clockwork Tracers, the fastest parkour runner in the resistance, but cryptography was another of my indispensable skills.

I leaned against my front door; my breath ragged.

Our butler, Francis, entered the foyer. He'd remained at the residence after my parents' death. "Miss Rosegarden, I'm turning in. You've made it just in time for curfew."

"Yes. I made a run for it."

Francis sighed, and Balou's paws scuttled across the hardwood floor toward me with his tail wagging.

"Oh, how I've missed you!" I got on my haunches and nuzzled my dog's coat. "You'll keep me company while I work, won't you, Balou?"

"Goodnight," Francis said.

I lifted the candelabra from the foyer's console table. I set it on the fireplace mantle in the office and sat at my desk while Balou lay at my feet, soon twitching from dreaming.

A sudden noise interrupted me.

The walls of my candle-lit library wavered, and vibrant colors came alive in the rear wall painting. A book crashed to the floor from my mother's shelf. Was my mind playing tricks, or was this another phase in our city's grim destiny?

I picked up the volume with its embossed cover and title, Grimoire, nested within an elaborate floral design. Turning to the first page, the sweet, musty scent of aged parchment filled the air as I read the inscription.

For my dearest Lys and my little star Fée, I leave you this treasure of secrets.

Yours, for always,

Émeric C. Rosegarden.

I leafed through my father's journal. He'd been a master of illusions, and a faint reminiscence of his incantations drifted at the edge of my consciousness. Though he'd not had the time to teach me his magic, I had discovered my own unique ability, a gift passed down through my mother's family—pyrokinesis.

On the oak desk, I brushed the candle's wick with my fingertip, and a small flame burst forth. In the flickering light, a childhood memory of my parents floated to the surface, then vanished. I was seven when my father disappeared. A year later, my mother died—I'm guessing from a broken heart. With Francis's help, the resistance—known as the Undergrounders within the city walls—whisked me to their subterranean city. There, I learned about my parents' other life.

A rattling sound thrummed as I set down the book. I ran my finger along the seam, picked at the corner of the thick end paper, and peeled it back. An envelope slipped out. *Lys Rosegarden* was scrawled on the front. Even though my mother had passed away years ago, I cringed at trespassing into her private life. Yet, I burned with curiosity.

A delicate fragrance of lavender and lilac wafted from the pouch when I lifted the flap. I removed a postcard with a photo of a tall monument. Written at top left was *The Eiffel Tower, Paris.* On the right was my father's message, as though he'd addressed the postcard to me.

The answers you seek are right under your nose.

I miss you.

Love always,

E.

During the war, the Silencers sprayed an inconspicuous chemical upon our city's unsuspecting citizens, leaving them existing in a gray world. The people of Paris became a spiritless society, enslaved and trapped. While fear paralyzed the masses, a resistance movement formed and went underground.

The Silencers' Forbidden Laws banished any art, music, or inventions created after the nineteenth century and destroyed all symbols of unity. I'd never seen this tower, but, peering closer at the image, I recognized the bridge in front of the Trocadero.

Bitterness plucked at the malaise wedged deep in my soul. The overwhelming pressure made it difficult to breathe. Fury gnawed at me from inside, against the Silencers' heinous dominance over our city. I'd lost everything because of them and fought against the urge to scream.

Taking a breath, I pulled out the ink-smudged postcard from my breast pocket. The sender had written a Shakespearean sonnet—a poem code. I removed the rosewood cipher wheel from my desk's secret compartment and began my cryptanalysis. It was midnight when I leaned back in my wing chair and pondered the cryptic message I'd scrawled onto the slate board: *The horned lizards hide in plain sight.*

Later that week, I hopped out of the steam-engine air cab in the ninth arrondissement. The heels of my gold-fired, cog-geared shoes clicked down the cobblestone sidewalk. My bustle skirt and ruffled blouse swished as I dashed down the street. I picked up speed to reach the bookmaking establishment where I volunteered, transcribing rankings and odds during horse races. The scoreboard was the perfect solution for transmitting messages to our agents.

I heard my name above the dreary smog and loud engines. Startled, I turned.

Commander Wilde caught up with me, sporting an off-duty uniform. He looked sharp, and I sucked in my breath. "Hello, Miss Rosegarden. I'm surprised to meet you here."

"Hello, Commander," I said, astonished he remembered my name. "I apologize, but I'm late arriving at Simonon's Wagers."

He cocked his head. "You're a bookmaker?"

Heat rose to my cheeks. "I record the bookmakers' numbers."

The corners of his mouth curled up. "Why don't I join you?"

My corset belt tightened, and I struggled to breathe. "You'll be bored."

"Nonsense. It's been a few years since I've been in a betting shop."

"Of course." I swallowed the lump in my throat and led the way.

A stale reek of cigars and dust greeted us. The bookies straightened at the commander's entrance.

"Relax everyone. I'm off duty." He grinned like a lion surrounded by a cackle of hyenas.

I took my position at the scoreboard, with the morning races about to begin.

Commander Wilde found a chair, sat balancing on its back legs, his boots crossed and perched on a nearby table. His nonchalance struck a jarring contrast to the bettors' stiff postures.

My fingers shook as I recorded the results on the blackboard, but once a plethora of digits covered the panel, my confidence and speed increased. I added the ciphers—their inclusion, less obvious now. This message was for Nick Strange, an agent I'd never met.

I wiped the chalk dust off my hands.

"Excellent work, Miss Rosegarden."

I flinched, sensing the commander's warm breath upon my nape, his presence a little too close in this crowded room. "Bookmakers' tic-tac is fascinating, isn't it?" I said to distract him.

He agreed. We left, and I heard a collective sigh behind me.

"Listen," he said, "would you consider spending the afternoon with me?"

My heart bounced in my chest. He was an authority of the highest office, and my first instinct was to run.

His eyes narrowed. "Do I scare you?"

A nervous laugh escaped me. "No," I said, a bit too quickly. I thought of all the private places close by. It was one thing to entertain the commander, another if the Undergrounders found out before I alerted them. "What do you think about the Jardin de Carnavalet?"

He paused, as if resisting the idea. "I suppose . . . It's been years since I visited."

As we entered the garden, my thoughts went to the last time I'd been here. It'd been with Nikkos, my childhood friend. *The day before he disappeared.*

"Miss Rosegarden, you appear distracted."

The commander's honeyed tone jogged me from my memory. I wasn't sure why I'd picked this place, but it had drawn me here again. "I'm enjoying the stillness. Steam-engines' clatter is hard on my ears."

"You've a sensitivity to noise?" His mouth twitched. "And you perceive things in gray tones?"

Flinching, I answered, "Yes, I have congenital amusia. Like everyone else, I developed achromatopsia—a result of the Silent War's chemicals."

His gaze slid past me, and I clenched my jaw, saying no more. He led me to a bench in the garden under a cherry blossom tree.

Its fragrance overwhelmed my olfactory sense—the one I had left to garner any visceral emotions from my surroundings.

He cleared his throat. "I've been following you around for a while . . ."

His words became drowned out by my heart pounding in my chest. How long had he been trailing me? I wiped away the tiny sweat beads lining my upper lip.

He straightened his back. "If you're agreeable to the idea, I'd like to get to know you better."

A gut feeling told me I wouldn't escape his demands. "This is a little sudden," I responded, my breathing uneven.

"Tell me you'll consider my proposal."

I gave him a quick nod and rose from the bench. "I must head back."

He smiled with hooded eyes, evidently satisfied.

One month later

We crossed paths whenever I arrived in the first arrondissement, after I'd checked the Poste d'Orsay for mail.

Alexander grew on me despite his uniformed exterior.

One afternoon, his arm brushed mine ever so lightly.

My heart thumped, blood rushing to my head. My synapses fired, triggering a sudden burst of vivid color interrupting my otherwise dreary view.

Oblivious of his effect on me, he continued, "I find you enticing in this dress." His lips grazed my ear, sending frissons up my spine.

I knew I shouldn't let myself fall for him. I couldn't allow it. Yet, no matter how hard I tried, no matter how deep I dug in my heels, he possessed an inner vulnerability which reeled me in. Despite everything the Undergrounders had taught me to hate about this enemy, I imagined *he* would save me from any harm.

Earlier, Francis had announced the Undergrounders wanted me to attend a meeting with the maquis—the resistance operating outside the city.

"Alexander, forgive me, but I must get home to attend to some matters."

"All right." He pulled me into the shadows between two buildings. "But before you go, will you allow me a kiss?"

I'd never been kissed before, not properly. We'd been meeting for a month, and he had made no advances until now. One kiss couldn't hurt, I surmised. My eyelids fluttered, and I nodded. He moved closer, his hands on the wall on either side of me.

His mouth brushed my lips, like the tickle of a feather. He leaned in, his tongue searching for mine, gently at first. His fervor increased, until a million stars exploded in my heart. I stopped him to catch my breath. My body yearned for him in a way I'd never experienced, except in my imagination. But I was crossing the line.

Somewhere amid surrendering myself to this tumultuous ocean of passion, fear wrenched me loose. With his minty breath lingering on my lips, I pushed him away and ran home.

Gloomy wisps of dusk seeped into the city as I climbed out my attic's skylight and emerged on the rooftop. I slipped out my pocket watch from my fitted leather jacket and clicked on the timer. T-minus seven minutes to the Abbesses station—a corridor to the underground city.

My rubber soles pounded on the concrete rooftops, setting my adrenaline afire. I traced my route, calculating each step from one building to another. Finding my rhythm, obstacles became advantages, from narrow brick walls to dormer windows. Through the smoky evening, I soared over the dusty urban landscape.

At Abbesses, I descended the staircase, moving with speed toward the town hall. A fleeting thought traversed my mind of a time long forgotten, when trains had traveled along these abandoned tracks, now canals. I stepped onto the water gondola and maneuvered the vessel to the private chamber. Muffled voices filtered down the hallway as I approached.

The conversation stopped when I entered the somber space. I recognized the three Maquisard who stood with Marcel.

"Welcome. Let's get started," Benoit said, a burly Maquis who led the resistance beyond the city walls. "Did your last message come from the same source?"

"Yes," I answered. "It contained the corresponding insignia."

Marcel, the Undergrounders' leader, interjected. "We follow specific directives for each poem code."

Benoit tapped his fingers on his thigh. "We suspect this message might be bait."

"You think the Silencers sent this one to draw us out?" I asked.

Marcel's shoulders dropped. "Rumor has it, people's color senses are returning."

So, others had been experiencing the same surges of color. I kept my gaze steady, not ready to divulge my own episodes. "Any intel from Strange?"

Marcel shook his head, and from the shadows, Milena coughed. She'd been my fiercest competitor for the Clockwork Tracer designation.

She folded her arms. "I'm surprised you don't have a clue what they're planning, considering your close affiliation with a certain commander."

She gestured toward me. "Like father, like daughter, no?"

The blood drained from my face, and my stomach flipped. "What are you insinuating?"

"Echoes of the past. You've decoded an important message, and now you're fraternizing with the enemy."

My chest prickled with heat. "Are you suggesting I'm collaborating?"

"You said it, not me." She smiled; her mouth stretched thin.

Marcel growled, "Enough, Milena."

My father and I? Traitors? Fire raged in my heart, and I lunged forward, ready to do her some damage. Marcel stopped me.

"I've earned the title of Lady of the Clockwork Tracer, not to give it up just like that."

"Faith has devoted her life to the underground, like her parents. Anything she does, she does so under my command," Marcel said, and covered for me as he'd always done.

I glared at Milena, fuming at her accusations, but it was too late. From the Maquis's expressions, the damage was done. She'd been waiting for this moment since we were kids.

Marcel waved off Milena and ended the gathering. "You all have your assignments. We'll meet again if needed." He turned to me. "Faith, please stay behind."

In the empty chamber, Marcel folded his arms. "You're spending a lot of time with this commander."

"He's relentless, and I can't really say no to him."

"I see. Please just retrieve messages, then get out of the inner city."

My heart plunged to my feet. His order was explicit. Despite my pulsing heart rate, I shared my suspicions about where this horned lizards' nest might lay perched.

He pulled at his goatee. "We'll look into it."

TWO WEEKS LATER

I stepped outside after my shift at Simonon's Wagers. When I spotted Alexander at the far end of the street, my spirits lifted. I hadn't seen him since the day of the meeting. The thought of his warm breath on my neck sent goosebumps up my arms.

Despite Marcel's orders, I turned in his direction, but when he shifted his position, a young woman appeared. My body stiffened, and a sudden coldness spread through my core, ice forming in my veins. Even from this distance, his focus on her was obvious. He glanced over his shoulder and caught my eye.

For a fleeting moment, I thought he would acknowledge me, but he turned and led her away. The realization hit me, and my mind spiraled. I recoiled at his rejection. I'd let my walls down when I should have remained guarded. A kiss *can* hurt, after all.

Alienated, I had no one with whom I could share my regret about Alexander. Only Balou's presence provided me any comfort. Meanwhile, another coded message arrived, this one from Nick Strange: *The horned lizards are laying their eggs.*

I waited for Marcel's orders, but none came. The silence tortured me. With nothing left to lose, I planned a mission to refute Milena's condemnation and prove them wrong about my family.

The Pont d'Iena stretched over the Seine with the Trocadero behind me. I peeked at my mother's postcard. Now, on the opposite bank, only a seven-hundred-foot-long graffitied wall stood with barbed wire running along its top plate. Had they dismantled the tower during the Silent War?

Crossing over, I slunk close to the thirty-foot-high cement structure, when a butterfly fluttered past. I observed its flight to the top of the wall and watched as it disappeared behind an invisible barrier. One of my father's notes had mentioned the power of illusion to hide objects. I gawked in disbelief.

I retrieved a small grappling hook gun—Francis's invention—and aimed upward. Secured by a taut rope, I ascended and pushed myself off the edge of the coping, vaulting over the Dannert wires, and landed with a hard thud against the inner face of the wall.

My body slumped from the dull pain of hitting concrete, and I slid to the ground. Close up, the shield was more perceptible. Reaching out to touch it, my fingers disappeared. I snapped back my hand, my digits still intact—a powerful illusion.

I took a deep breath and traversed it, finding myself in an immense compound. To my left, a colossal zeppelin sat parked on the field next to the tower. My head spun from its sheer size.

Workers crawled about like ants, hoisting metal cisterns under the belly of the beast. They were going to poison the city—again! Going home was no longer an option, and there was no time to alert Marcel. I had to stop this.

A sound alerted me to movement. To my right, a long line of men and women dressed in stately clothing exited the tower and approached the zeppelin. My hands curled into fists—the Silencers. They'd been hiding here all along. Of course, they couldn't be on the ground when they dispersed their poison.

After the never-ending queue of officers filed into the airship, a loud whoosh released, and it lifted off the ground. I dashed across the expanse and concealed myself as best I could behind the barricades. Aiming for the drop line left dangling from the ship, I leaped off a concrete barrier, soaring through the air. Latching onto it, my heart thumped against my chest. I inched my way up, praying I hadn't misjudged my ability to board the vessel.

Nearing the gondola, I sighed with relief. They'd left the rear door of the cabin ajar. I reached up and caught the frame's edge. With my other hand, I slid the door open and climbed in.

Once inside, I spied the passenger's entrance. It had a locking mechanism to keep travelers from entering the area. If latched, it would trap the Silencers on the upper level. *Perfect!*

I had reached the door when a thunderous, unfamiliar voice bellowed, "Where do you think you're going?"

My pulse quickened. I slid the latch to bolt the door before turning.

The lieutenant dragged me to the cockpit with a vise grip hold.

When we entered, Alexander's face blanched.

My gut clenched, and bile rose in my throat. *He* was the one navigating the airship, preparing to unleash the poison on innocent people? How had I fallen for such a monster?

"Get rid of this stowaway." The lieutenant's words snapped like icicles as he pointed to the hallway leading to the rear cabin door.

I stared at Alexander, but his eyes betrayed no emotion. I'd been an idiot to hope he would save me.

Alexander stepped forward and grabbed my wrist. "Why are you here?" he grumbled as he dragged me down the corridor. He opened the cabin door and seemed to contemplate what to do.

My free arm reached to grab something, anything. My fingers grazed a nearby cord just a little too far to grasp. I hoped the charge surging from my fingertips would bring the desired outcome: a last-ditch effort to annihilate this cabal.

"Faith, I'm sorry," Alexander said.

Dread seeped into my veins. "Aren't you going to give me a parachute?"

He murmured, "T-minus sixty," as feet stomped down the hallway.

Behind him, the lieutenant shouted, "What are you waiting for?" He pushed Alexander aside and shoved me off the zeppelin.

I'd shamed my family name and failed to save my city. The airship became a blur as I plummeted to earth. Somewhere the scent of burning wafted, a curl of acrid smoke winding its way, tightening around my lungs until breathing became impossible. I wouldn't feel a thing when I hit the ground. Still, my heart exploded, like a cloudburst.

I'd only ever known a gray, insipid world, never experiencing the sweetness of freedom nor the joy of dancing with a lover. A growl rumbled deep in my chest. I opened my mouth to scream, when another disembodied, bloodcurdling wail sounded above me. The lieutenant without a parachute? A macabre sense of satisfaction washed over me.

It was short-lived as I caught sight of Alexander nosediving toward me, head first. I had no time to ponder what was happening when the force of his body collided with mine. He encircled my body with his limbs, and I heard him yell, "Hang on tight!"

I clasped my arms around him as he deployed the parachute. The wind roared in my ears, then stopped. While he maneuvered us toward the tower, my heart remained lodged in my throat. My life depended on this man who'd been ordered to kill me.

We floated, descending past the tower's top platform, where I saw a flicker of light.

Alexander shouted, "Remember to roll with me as soon as we hit the ground!"

Seconds later, all went black.

A bird chirped nearby, and my eyes blinked open. In a daze, I moaned from the pain coursing through my body. Realizing where I was, I scrambled to stand. "The chemicals—"

He stopped me. "Fidget, relax. They're headed away in a blaze of fire."

"Fidget?"

"It's me, Nikkos. Nikkos Paráxenos, Lord of the Arcane Cyphers, undercover as Commander Alexander Wilde. I'm also Agent Nick Strange."

Shock rippled through my body. *Nikkos?* Now I understood why I'd gone to the Carnavalet. I shook my head at the memory when I'd leaned my head on Nikkos's shoulder and had whispered, *"I wish we could stay like this forever."* He'd promised, *"Fidget, don't worry. I'll always take care of you."*

But the person laying next to me wasn't my childhood friend. He was Alexander. I swung my fist at his chest. "Nikkos would've done everything to save me," I snapped, my chin jutting forward.

"But I saved you. And in the nick of time too!"

"But you weren't a hundred percent sure you could . . ."

He pursed his lips. "Sorry. I didn't realize the lieutenant would do that."

"You could have given me a parachute."

"I didn't have the opportunity. Besides, you weren't supposed to be on the ship! Marcel ordered you to stay put."

"I know, but when I caught sight of them loading the chemicals, I had to do something."

He sighed. "My heart dropped when the lieutenant dragged you into the cockpit."

"Yeah? Well, I thought I was going to throw up when I saw you."

The corners of his mouth curled. "So . . . I'm guessing you had feelings for Alexander?"

I glared at him sideways. "Why are you talking about him like he's someone else?"

"Because you're talking about Nikkos like he isn't me."

"If you must know, I was using Alexander to glean information."

A chuckle escaped him, and his laughter echoed across the field.

"You're an *idiot*." I blew out a puff of air, but a deep rumble began within me too. My rib muscles contracted, and I rolled around in stitches, laughing and groaning from the pain.

"I knew it!"

"Oh, shut up." Still smarting from the other day, I bit the inside of my lip. "Who's the other girl?"

"She's nobody. Marcel's orders were to keep you safe, a promise to your father." A frown formed between his brow. "Say, how *did* you do that?"

"Kiss like a goddess, you mean?"

"Set the airship ablaze."

"Oh, it worked?" I said, smiling. "Just something passed down from my mother."

"Marcel doesn't know?"

"A girl's gotta have some secrets. So, you and Marcel worked together, huh? What about Milena? Was she in on it too?"

"No. She just plain hates you."

We snickered.

"And the kiss? Was it also part of the ruse to keep me safe?"

"No," he said, his face dangerously close to mine. "That was all me . . ." He leaned down, and when his lips met mine, a shower of shimmering lights sparkled in my mind. Gazing down at me, he said, "You've been my sole reason for returning to this city. That, and your green eyes, red hair, and constellation of freckles on your nose."

"You can see in color?"

"Yes," he said, his voice measured. "That's why they sent me to a farm camp."

I pinched myself. Minutes earlier, my life had almost ended. I surveyed the tower and sat upright. *The flash of light!* "I noticed something up there. We should check it out."

We climbed to the top, where Nikkos removed the lock bar on the narrow iron door at the landing. Inside, a sparse apartment included a bed, a chair, and a desk. A Persian carpet covered its floor, and a bookshelf lined the back wall. The shield obscured any view of the city.

Nikkos and I glanced at each other.

An elderly gentleman turned and balked at Nikkos's uniform. "Who might you be?" he asked, his voice cracking.

"Nikkos Paráxenos. Resistance."

A dog scampered from behind the man and jumped to greet me, with his tail wagging.

"Balou?" I said, my mind whirling. I peered deep into the man's weathered face. My breath caught in my throat when I recognized his smoky eyes and the thin scar across his left cheekbone. "*Papa*?" All my pain vanished, and I ran to embrace him.

"Fée, you found your mother's postcards," Émeric said.

I stepped backward. "Yes. And the illusion is your making?"

"They used you and your mother as blackmail," he said, tears cresting in his eyes. "Is it over?"

"As far as we know," Nikkos said.

Émeric murmured an incantation, sending a powerful vibration through the iron structure. The shield collapsed. With the illusion gone, the sprawling rooftops of Paris appeared at all sides.

We descended and stopped at a landing.

My father's expression fell at the dismal view—soot-covered buildings, airships, and smog hovering above the skyline. "Mon Dieu!"

Crowds gathered below the tower, and a chant lifted through the air. "Pa-ris! Pa-ris! Pa-ris!"

And somewhere, a phonograph played, "'Rien de rien.'"

Nikkos slipped his hand in mine, and I smiled. Balou led the way.

The city of light shall rise again, like a phoenix from its ashes.

CC SULLIVAN

CC Sullivan is a writer from Toronto, Canada who writes in the fantasy, romance, and women's fiction genres.

She writes screenplays, short stories, and has published Book 1 of her Elements series, *Masters of the Elements*. She is working on the second book of the Elements trilogy, and on a women's fiction novel.

CC has also designed a set of journals as part of her *Intuitive Journey* series.

You can find all of her ebooks, paperbacks, and journals on Amazon. Her ebooks are also available at other distributors (nook books, Apple iBooks, and Rakuten Kobo). Digital files of her journals are also sold at ccsullivan.me

Check out her shop, *The Write Shelf*, at ccsullivan.me where you can find tools to help writers get started with writing.

In her spare time, she reads tarot cards and astrology charts, and enjoys painting, traveling, and reading.

SUSAN STRADIOTTO

Seraphina

"Did you hear his voice?" the maiden asks her owl, rubbing the black-jeweled pendant. "He can break the Lady's curse. We've met in his dreams, but there he is. Call to him, Huntress."

The owl gurgles, her amber eyes glowing at the girl. *Hoo, hoo. You are the Lady now, Seraphina. I only call the dying to cross the Bone Marsh.*

"You're wrong, Huntress. He is my fate."

Kitchi

At the marsh's edge where the sea of golden grass begins, Kitchi kneels beside his father, Noshi. Both wear only a small hide about their waists, enough to cover the loins. Beyond this small token from their last hunt, the Creator only favors hunters' functional garments. Quivers, strapped across their sun-kissed torsos, hold arrows, and on each strap, a sheath secures a curved knife to speed the soul of their next kill back to the Creator. The soil cools Kitchi's knee, and grass tickles his skin. He scratches.

Noshi nudges his son's shoulder and touches a finger to his lips. With Kitchi's attention, he points the end of his longbow in the direction of a stag strutting from the marsh. The deer freezes mid-step and whips his head around, an unfathomable show of strength to steady the twelve-pointed rack.

Kitchi stops breathing and slowly, steadily reaches for an arrow. Too late. Having already spotted the twitch in the grass, the prey darts back beneath the bog-tree cover.

Kitchi sags with defeat.

"The reason we practice stillness like Grandmother Fox." Noshi lifts his hand from Kitchi's shoulder, demonstrating the slowness necessary to avoid the rustle. "A predator must lie still and draw weapons without disturbing his prey, my son. Else the predator starves."

"I will do better, Noshi-father."

Hoo-hoo-hoot—Akk-awww!

Noshi perks, now heedless of stillness. He cups a hand around his mouth and echoes the birdcall. "Hoo-hoo-hoot—Akk-awww!"

Hoo-hoo-hoot—Akk-awww! the owl answers.

Noshi smiles. "Now you, Kitchi-son."

The boy hoots and caws, and again, the owl answers.

"Ahh!" The father releases tight shoulders. "The Creator graces us. We shall not fall prey to the Lady of the Bone Marsh and Huntress today." He tilts his head questioningly. "Shall we stalk the stag into the bog?"

Seraphina

Huntress flutters her wings. *See, Lady, the boy calls. I answer. This is not his time.*

Seraphina crosses her arms over her chest. "I will find him in his dream. He will come to me."

Kitchi

The girl with the black jewel steps from the woods, hands extended. Kitchi retreats, but still, she comes. An owl upon her shoulder caws, hoots, flutters its wings.

"Come with me, Kitchi," the girl says.

Kitchi shakes his head, holds his hands forward, and waves the girl away. "No. Huntress responded to my call. The Creator says it is not my time."

"I've come to you before, my Kitchi," says the girl, her chestnut curls cascading over one shoulder. "I chose you. I need you, Brave One. Come to me. Free me, please."

"No . . . no-no . . . NO!"

"Kitchi. Kitchi-son! Wake up."

Hands shake him.

Kitchi's eyes fly open, roaming the tent, until they find . . . "Nadi-mother." He sits, the furs falling from his chest, and rubs a hand over the thin strip of hair running the center of his head. "A dream," he breathes. "Only a dream."

"You *dream* too much while the sun shines." Nadi drops a bag of coarse salt at his bedside. "Chores. Then lessons, Kitchi-son."

Kitchi finishes salting the hide from yesterday's hunt and joins his friend Mingan, walking to the Woods Cree longhouse for lessons. Outside the house, girls are gathered, whispering and giggling. The young girl Tahki, a plain *nêhiyaw-iskwêsis* named after the cold-running river waters on her name day, steps away from the others and sways her hips, confidently striding toward Mingan and Kitchi.

Mingan pushes Kitchi toward the girl.

"Blessed day," greets Tahki.

"The Creator smiles on us." Kitchi squints up at the sun. Then he remembers he must show respect; he forces himself to lower his gaze to Tahki. But he no longer sees the plain *nêhiyaw-iskwêsis*. Instead, the girl before him has chestnut brown curls, a shawl of fur, and an owl perched on one shoulder.

Kitchi blinks hard, shoves his fists into his eyes, and backs away from the girl. Whether she is Tahki or the dream girl he believes is the Lady of the Bone Marshes, he doesn't want her to speak. He runs into the longhouse but stops and turns, drawn by his infernal curiosity. The girl now watching him longingly is Tahki, and he can't fathom why that makes his chest ache.

SERAPHINA

"See, Huntress. Kitchi aches for me too."

Hoo, hoo. Who . . . will be Lady if not you?

Seraphina purses her lips. "Perhaps . . . ah, yes!"

KITCHI

Noshi comes inside the home tent where Kitchi sharpens his

hunting knife. "Paskus says you were distracted during lessons. Nadi-mother bids me to ask you why."

Kitchi sheaths the knife and glances up at his father. "Isn't the Lady of the Bone Marsh a crone?"

Noshi draws his brows together and nods at his son's odd question. "An aged hag in tattered robes, shouldering a gray owl called Huntress. Legend says Huntress will not answer the dying, but she responded to your call."

"So the Lady should not be stalking me." Kitchi set aside the knife and whetstone, musing. "Can she turn into a maiden?"

"Not in the stories told by Woods Cree elders. Why do you ask such questions?"

"At night, I dream of a maiden with an owl. I have since the hunt. She visited last night. And . . . she appeared today in a waking dream when Tahki greeted me at the longhouse."

"Why have you not told me of these dreams before?" Noshi paces the tent, running both hands over the sides of his head along the braid marking his many moons as clan huntsman. "We must consult the elders."

Suddenly, his father turns, eyes widening. "No, this is good news. We will still consult the elders, but this is most likely a sign that Tahki wishes to take you for a mate." Noshi crouches, grinning crookedly. "I never knew you were a dreamer, Kitchi-son."

Kitchi flinches.

"The Creator's blessing is upon the Woods Cree clan. Kitchi-son, you make a father proud. Tomorrow, you will pass the hunt challenge and become a clan huntsman, be chosen as a mate, and be able to divine the future!"

Seraphina

Bent over Kitchi in the night, she waits until his eyes open. Sleepily, the amber within his eyes sparkles. Seraphina says, "Kitchi-love, bring the girl to the river within the marsh."

He rolls over, curling his blanket into his chin as if her words gave him a chill. Perhaps they did, given the unknown nature of her curse.

Kitchi

He wakes before dawn, warmth spreading in his chest. Outside, the night remains deep. Kitchi scans the home tent. Apparently, his mother and sister are hard at work, the day having already started for the clan's women. Kitchi grabs his belt and knife and steals through the Woods Cree village, quiet like Grandmother Fox, stilling when another nears. Until he finds Tahki.

Her dull eyes brighten when Kitchi approaches, but her look still chills his warm heart. Kitchi hopes the dream maiden is not the Lady of the Bone Marsh, that she doesn't intend to steal Tahki from the clan and ferry her to the woods beyond the marsh, the spirit woods. He shouldn't take Tahki to the river, but his heart urges him onward. But she comes to Kitchi in dreams. *He* is the one she wants, so all will be well for Tahki. He must learn why the maiden haunts his dreams.

Seraphina

The sun peeks over the horizon.

"Look, Huntress. They come. Call to the girl."

Huntress shakes her feathers as if reluctant to abide by Seraphina's wish. But she calls.

Seraphina doesn't breathe. Kitchi stops the girl just inside the woods and returns Huntress's call. "Hoo-hoo-hoot—Akk-awww!"

Huntress answers, *Hoo-hoo-hoot—Akk-awww!*

Smiling, clearly pleased with his talent, Kitchi turns back to the girl. He pinches his neck at the apple. "In the throat and pitch the last sound high before letting your call trail off."

No, Kitchi, NO! Seraphina covers her heart with both hands, watching. He must come to her, come to the riverbank within the marsh woods. Seraphina cannot coax him more than she already has. *Please, Kitchi! You're my fate. The only one who can free me from the curse.*

The girl attempts the call. "Hoo-hoo." And then she searches his face.

Kitchi reaches tentatively for her shoulders.

Seraphina crosses her clutched fists over her chest. *He doesn't love her, so why does he encourage her?*

But the girl's call is thin. *Too* thin for Huntress to answer.

Kitchi shifts his weight between his feet and pleads with the girl. *Does he regret coming? Will he not help me, see what we can have?* It'd happened before, but she truly believed Kitchi was the one.

"Tahki," he says more forcefully. "you must try. You have to mimic Huntress. The legend says—"

"I know the legend," she snaps. Her brows are drawn to a peak. Her shoulders lift, chest expands. She nods her head in quick jerks.

Kitchi sets his jaw and stares hard into her eyes. "Ready?" And when she nods her agreement, he encourages her. "Stronger now."

The girl takes a deep breath. "Hoo-hoo-hoot—Ak-ow."

Huntress does not answer.

Every thread within Seraphina loosens, and she exhales her worry.

The girl grasps onto Kitchi and falls into his chest, sobbing. He soothes her but pulls her along deeper into the forest, toward the river.

Toward Seraphina.

Beside the river, Huntress digs her claws into Seraphina's shoulder, stretching tall with wings spread. She takes the chain in her beak and lifts the black-jeweled pendant from Seraphina's neck.

KITCHI

Mists gather as he and Tahki reach the river's edge. "Show yourself," Kitchi commands.

The dream girl steps out, the fog swirling around her white dress. Her glorious curls glow in the morning light, and a grey owl is perched on her shoulder. A necklace with an obsidian jewel hangs from a chain in the owl's beak.

"Are you the Lady of the Bone Marsh?" Kitchi demands, holding Tahki safely behind him.

The dream girl smiles. "I am only a maiden—Seraphina. The Lady cursed me, but you, Kitchi, are my fate."

Hoo-hoo-hoot! Huntress calls, but the call is clipped. No salvation for Tahki.

Though Kitchi is safe, his heart aches for the plain-faced girl.

Seraphina lifts Huntress and tosses the owl into flight. "Fly to Tahki."

Huntress circles overhead but below the canopy of the marsh woods. In a daze, the young Woods Cree woman watches the owl, absently dancing, following Huntress's flight. Away from Kitchi she moves, and away from the clan.

Kitchi is torn, pulled toward Seraphina, but if he would be a leader to his clan, he should protect Tahki.

Seraphina

"Does the jewel call to you, Tahki?"

"It sings a lovely song." Tahki's voice sounds ghostly, her eyes cast upward. She watches the owl, her soon-to-be companion.

A slow grin spreads on Seraphina's face, and the owl swoops down. Wings beat the air around the new maiden, and the owl, Huntress, drapes the necklace around Tahki's neck. Tahki lifts her hand and caresses the jewel in its new home as Huntress settles on her shoulder.

"If that be true, the obsidian stone is yours. And Huntress, your companion. You are now Tahki Blackjewel, Maiden of the Bone Marsh."

Upon the new maiden's shoulder, Huntress calls, *Hoo-hoo-hoot!*

Kitchi

When Tahki looked at Kitchi, her gaze said many things. At once, it seemed ancient and wise. But more astonishingly, her face no longer seemed plain. She now glowed from within. Beautiful, as Seraphina had always been to Kitchi.

The mist swallows Tahki where she stands, and she disappears from his side like she never was.

Kitchi spins around, lips pursed to ask.

"When Tahki's fate walks this earth, the curse will pass to another."

She speaks. Not dream words this time. Kitchi reaches for Seraphina, not believing his ears, touches her cheek. *Real? Yes. She is.*

Eyes closed, she leans into him, kisses his palm. "Now is our time, my fate."

SUSAN STRADIOTTO

Susan Stradiotto is passionate about the written word, whether it is in her own writing or her editing practice. She is a fan of well-told stories. She spends part of her days honing her own voice and the rest editing or reading. Susan is always searching for unique voices and stories that tell a truth. As Neil Gaiman said in his master class, Write the truest story you can. She believes that is what makes a story sing.

Susan is an author of fantasy and romance and has professional editorial experience with genres such as memoir, mystery/thriller, cozy mystery, fantasy, and women's fiction. She attended Capella University for her BS in Information Technology and University of Chicago's Graham School for her professional editing certification. She lives in Eden Prairie with her husband, a hoard of Bernese Mountain Dogs, and one Miniature Dachshund.

You can see Susan's other works at https://susanstradiotto.com/susansportfolio/.

Or preorder her forthcoming urban fantasy/mystery novel, *Raine of Fire: A Faerie Detective Novel,* at https://books2read.com/Raine-of-Fire. Available 22 August 2022!

N.D.T. CASALE

SULTANA OF THE MIST

Missing half its body, the tree stands before me, filling my heart with fear.

One part of the pine exhibits luscious boughs of pointy needles while the symmetrical side has been severed away showing only the bare bark. Another pine tree is split down the middle, touched by lightning. In between them is a small hut.

The house of Zundah.

Gray vapor begins to rise up from the ground and swirls around us. According to ancient legend, Zundah is a man who could predict the future. For ones who are worthy to find him, he will give guidance to those who need it most. My handmaiden Nabila pulls her horse next to me.

"Do you think this is it?" she asks.

Ria I hear a voice in the wind. *Ria, go to the hut.* It sounds like my husband Kamal.

I dismount Sadiq, my husband's black war horse, and let him graze on the grass. My bracelets jingle as I tighten the quiver full of arrows at my back and keep my bow close. My long black hair has been woven into a tight braid that falls to the small of my back, and my jeweled headpiece glitters and reflects off my arm band despite the gloominess that surrounds us.

Nabila dismounts and comes next to me.

"Stay behind me," I command as we approach the small dwelling made of grass and mud. The door swings back as if sensing our arrival.

"Ria, Sultana of Jerdaj," a voice calls. "I have been expecting you. Come in. Do not be afraid."

Taking a deep breath, I creep toward the door. My legs tremble and my hands shake.

We enter the one-room hut, and I see a man standing before me. I clasp my hand over my mouth to stifle the scream that threatens to escape my lips, for what I see is half a man.

With one leg and one arm and a goat's tail extending behind him, his hand grips a wooden staff. He is bare-chested and muscular with a loin cloth around his waist. His face is full of scruff, his eyes narrow slits, and his nose is pointy.

"W-who are you?" I ask.

"I am the one for whom you have been searching. I am Zundah," replies the man.

He gestures toward two stools. "Have a seat."

Nabila and I sit down. Her expression of discomfort mirrors my own. I try to avert my gaze from the half-naked man.

"Ria, Sultana of Jerdaj, once a poor arrow maker from the Mist, now Sultana by marriage." Zundah scoops herbs with his hand and throws them onto the fire. "But your husband is dead."

"Yes." My voice cracks. "During the battle at sea against Evjah, he fell overboard, and his body was never found."

"And your brother-in-law has dethroned you and is now Sultan."

I feel the bitterness on my lips. "Yes, Haatim has convinced the Council that I am not fit to rule in wake of my husband's death. He claims Jerdaj was founded on the principle that a man must always sit upon the throne. Also he believes that my grief from loss makes me mentally unstable to rule."

"His claim is false," hisses Zundah, "Your husband changed the ruling when he became Sultan stating a Sultana could take over the throne and continue rule in the event of her husband's death."

My eyes widen. "Why did no one defend me?"

"Because your brother-in-law declared that you are a grieving widow and thus unfit for the throne. Those accusations alone will make a kingdom turn against you."

Leaning on a cane, he hobbles closer to me, peering at my bow and quiver. "What is it you wish to ask me?"

"How do I prove I am worthy to rule?"

"Ah, to do that you must find the Quralla?"

Quralla. The word sounds so familiar and a memory surfaces of an argument I had with Haatim before leaving the palace. His final words to me, "Your only hope to reign as Sultana would be to find the Quralla!" He laughed in my face as his guards escorted Nabila and me out of my castle.

"What is the Quralla?" I ask.

"The Quralla is the epitome of the heart's desire. Whatever you wish most in your life will be granted. You must understand the journey to the Quralla is treacherous and full of trickery. Only the most worthy are capable of opening the webs to its mystery. However, if you succeed, you will prove you are the most worthy to reign this realm."

Placing his cane against the table he grabs my face with his one hand and stares into my eyes. His grotesque appearance sickens me, but I am amazed at how well he balances on one leg.

He releases me from his grip. "You have a better chance than most." He reaches his hand into the burning flames of the fireplace, retrieves an object of curiosity, and thrusts it into my lap."

I yelp and stifle a scream. The item is not hot and does not burn me. I wrap my hands around the mass and peer closer. It is a wooden carving of . . . a frog?

"A frog?" I cry.

"This amphibian will help you on your journey to the Quralla," replies Zundah.

"It is not real. It is a carving of some material I have never seen before," I reply.

"Sometimes things are not what they appear to be. Do not judge by what you see. He will know. That is all the advice I can give you," continues Zundah.

"He? Who is he? A wooden frog is all you gave me?" I reply.

"I have given you far more than most. Now, if you and your friend will exit quietly from my domain, I have other matters to attend to. It is time for my daily meditation."

I open my mouth to say more, but the look on Zundah's face tells me the discussion is over.

"Zundah is saying we need to ask a wooden frog for the location of the Quralla?" asks Nabila as we mount our horses and head deeper into the Mist.

I grip the reins tighter between my fingers. My heart aches for Kamal. He would know what to do in this situation.

Trust the Zundah, Ria. A voice whispers. I see no one.

I look down at the oddity in my lap. *Why should I trust Zundah?* My thoughts trouble me. *The man speaks in riddles.*

I shudder to think about what will happen to Jerdaj under Haatim's rule. Haatim only cares about conquest and desires Jerdaj to become the largest empire. He does not bother himself with the welfare of the people.

A tear escapes from my eye and lands on the frog's shiny head. I wipe my lashes and a few more droplets fall onto the statue.

I feel something move in my hands, I look down and gasp. The frog no longer has a brown rustic appearance. Slowly the carving turns a mystical shade of green. Its eyes blink. I scream and throw the object into the air.

As it flies through the breeze, the figure morphs from a carving into a living creature. The amphibian touches the ground and then springs upward landing on Sadiq's head. It blinks at me with its large round eyes.

"Sultana of Jerdaj. It is a pleasure."

Nabila halts her horse and covers her mouth in shock. "The statue!" she cries.

"No, no, no, dear handmaiden, I am not a statue, I am a frog, a magical frog. Sometimes I disguise myself as a simple carving, for it gets tiring leading others on dangerous quests. Sometimes a frog needs some peace and quiet."

He lashes out his tongue and snatches a fly passing by. "Apparently Zundah felt you were worthy to call on my services. I believe I am due for a quest; the last one was some time ago."

"Did you succeed?" asks Nabila.

"Oh, no. That quest was a failure. The man I was with was arrogant and pompous, a consummate fool. He felt the advice from a "frog" wasn't good enough for him, and his lack of listening was disastrous."

"Who are you?" I ask. The chattering of the frog has heightened my anxiety. With every passing moment I feel my chance to claim the throne of Jerdaj slip away.

"I am Mahfood, the Frog of Wisdom and Guide of Mythical Quests. I know that your heart, Ria, is pure, and you love your kingdom more than anything. You wish to see goodness bestowed upon the land, not greed. I will tell you how to find the Quralla," finishes Mahfood.

"Um, thank you," I reply. My words fail me as I look at this small frog who talks to me as if I am an old friend. "Lead the way."

We continue through the section of Jerdaj known as the Mist. A place full of magic and mystery with an endless fog that surrounds the people. I take in the various memories as we ride in silence.

This is the home of my childhood. I am the daughter of arrow makers who made weapons for the palace. My brothers were soldiers and I wish to be one as well. From the time of my birth my father trained all of us in the art of fighting and weaponry. When I became an adult, I joined the castle army disguised as a man. After becoming injured, my identity discovered, I was recognized by the castle for my bravery. That was how I met Kamal and we fell in love.

"Stop!" yells Mahfood, interrupting my thoughts. We have left the Mist and now stand beside the sea. "We no longer need the horses," the frog continues as he hops off Sadiq's head. "Thank you, beautiful stallion, for bringing us to safety."

"We have to walk the rest of the way?" asks Nabila.

"We must ride the wisdom of the waves," answers Mahfood.

I turn to Sadiq. "Head to my parents' house in the Mist, my friend. We will return," I whisper as I run my fingers through his mane. The black stallion neighs and turns toward the Mist as Nabila's mare follows him. They disappear as the fog covers them.

Next to the river is a small dhow, a sailing vessel with triangular sails.

"The river is a reflection of ourselves as we navigate along the journey of life. In order to rule a kingdom, we must first learn to rule ourselves," drones Mahfood as he jumps onto the dhow. He looks at us and blinks his eyes. "Well, what are you waiting for? An invitation? Climb aboard."

Nabila looks at me. "I will take the helm. My father was a sailor."

Stepping into the boat, we watch the sails fill with air and head down the river. Before we travel very far, the shallow craft jolts forward.

"What is happening?" I ask.

"Oh, I'm sorry, you thought this was going to be an easy ride?" Mahfood hops onto my shoulder. "You thought you were going to gently sail your way to victory? Oh no, Sultana! You are going to have to prove your worth, and this is only the beginning."

I look up to see the sky grow dark. A storm is brewing. The wind howls and the little dhow tosses circles in the thrashing waves. Nabila yells instructions to me. I grab the rigging and adjust the knots. Mahfood slips into my pocket.

Stay calm, Ria, for this is merely a small difficulty. The voice whispers to me. The boat is tumbled about as the rain pours down upon us. Giant white caps crash against the craft as Mahfood yells for us to keep going. I fear the small dhow may split in two and we will all drown.

Nabila's seamanship keeps us going, and soon we find our way out of the maelstrom. Exhausted, we ride the rest of the journey in silence.

"It is not much farther," declares Mahfood. "Ah, there they are." He points to rocky cliffs that meet the sea.

As we disembark, I look up at the jagged cliffs that extend before me, towering into the clouds. Gigantic and formidable, near the top there is an opening of a cave from which extends a rocky ledge overlooking the water.

"Now Ria, this next part is important," advises Mahfood. "The Quralla is in the cave. Under no circumstance must you allow your fear to overcome your good judgment."

"What do you mean?" I ask

"It is abstract."

"Abstract?"

"Yes, it is an idea. You will not understand until you see it with your own eyes. You must climb up the cliff then enter the cave. Once you enter the cave, you will be faced with your innermost demons. You must not succumb to the illusion. Death lurks in the cave and will try to throw you off-balance. You must keep your wits about you and not be so trusting. Things are not always what they appear to be."

I take a deep breath. *Be brave Ria,* the wind whispers.

Climbing the rocks would be the easy part. As a child from the Mist, I spent my days climbing trees and rocks with my siblings. My arms have strength. My hands have grip. I had not been spoiled like those of royal blood. I was not of royal blood and had not been spoiled. I had fought for what was mine.

I walk over to the rocks and look up to the mouth of the cave: my destination. I am more than a Sultana who wears beautiful silks and fine jewels. I am a warrior, the daughter of arrow makers from the Mist. I know the struggles of the people and I know the ways to ease their suffering. I will win this war against Haatim. I am the Sultana.

I turn to Mahfood and Nabila. "Here is the plan. I will climb the rocks. Wait until I enter the cave and then climb after me. If I run into trouble, you may come to my aid. If there is danger, it will not expect you both."

Climb the rocks, Ria.

I place my foot on the stone and begin the journey to my fate. Anger fuels my mobility. My thoughts waver to my brother-in-law, who surrounds himself with luxurious comfort upon the seat that should be my throne while I risk my life to reclaim my title.

"Selfish traitor," I whisper. Once upon a time, I believed Haatim respected me as his sister-in-law and recognized me as the Sultana of Jerdaj. But he only cared about stealing my name to become Sultan for himself.

Focus Ria, focus. Justice will be served.

I am halfway up the cliff. My foot slips and I hear stones clattering below. I rebalance myself.

Keep going, keep going.

My eyes focus on the opening in the cliff above me. A circular entrance where the sunlight gets lost and darkness hides the terror within.

Giving myself one final heave, I crawl onto the rocky ledge with the cave before me.

"You did it!" yells Mahfood. "Now, do not fall prey to abstract illusions."

Still unsure of what Mahfood means. I brace myself as I walk toward the entrance. I know Death lies in wait, but I am prepared. I have been prepared my whole life. The darkness swallows me. I am trained in the Mist. I am a master of the dark.

My eyes adjust to the lack of light. I grip my bow in my hands. My body is tense awaiting a surprise. I walk into a domed room. Light from the cracks in the ceiling filters through, illuminating a dark shape sitting on a boulder in the center of the chasm. As I move closer, I see what appears to be a person.

No face gazes upon me. I burn with curiosity. Then the entity turns, and I am taken aback. I see my face, yet it is not my own. My replica has a polished appearance. Her dark hair flows to her waist and her tan skin glistens in the filtered light. I twist my bow uneasily. I look down at my mud-splattered clothes. Where is the Quralla? Where is my destiny? Aside from the creature with my face, the room is empty.

"Hello, Ria," the inhabitant calls to me.

"W-who are you?"

She laughs and slides off the rock. She walks over to me and stands before me.

"I am you. I am Quralla."

I narrow my eyes. "The Quralla is a person?"

"The Quralla is you, Sultana. You see, people always want change. They have wishes, dreams, and desires. However, it is easier to keep wishes as wishes and not act upon them. People do not understand that the first step to change is the change within. In order to obtain the life they desire, people must conquer themselves. For you are your biggest obstacle. All the feelings of unworthiness, the fear. Apprehension has become your deepest shadow, your steadfast creed. It is not Haatim who keeps you from the throne. It is you!"

"How do you know that?"

"You are undergoing this quest to take back the throne. But is this really what you want, Ria?" continues Quralla.

I sigh. What I really wished was to have my husband back. Fighting for the throne would not resurrect Kamal. It would be easier to return to my roots in the Mist and be with my family than continue to battle with Haatim over a title.

Ria! I hear Kamal in my thoughts. *You must not let Haatim win. You must fight for the crown and your home. You are worthy.*

His voice fades into the stones. I blink. Quralla rises before me, and I feel the hairs on the back of my neck stand, for it makes me uneasy to look at my replica.

Quralla smiles at me. "You are uncomfortable looking at yourself."

"It is a bit strange," I reply.

"Well, then," Quralla opens her hand, and a sword appears —"you must defeat me."

"Excuse me?"

"In order to achieve the life you wish, you must kill who you used to be," continues Quralla. "You must fight and kill me, and in doing so, kill the past version of yourself." In a quick movement she swings the sword at me and I nearly lose my head. I duck and fall to the floor. My bow slides out of my reach. Looking up, I see the handle of what could be a sword lodged in the nearby rock. I reach for it, and the shiny weapon comes loose with ease. We are now a mirror image.

Quralla brings her sword down to stab me in the stomach, but I block her advance and jump to my feet.

We launch into a battle of mirrored movements. The Quralla knows all of my favorite moves and blocks them with ease. I, in turn, do the same to her. I begin to feel myself grow tired; however, the Quralla never seems to lack energy. We pause. Our swords face outward toward each other. My arm trembles.

"Are you sure you have what it takes to rule a kingdom by yourself?" asks Quralla as she jabs forward trying to slice open my chest, one of my signature moves. Anticipating this gesture, I avoid the sharp blade.

"Are you sure the realm is ready to accept a widowed Sultana?" She taunts me.

They will love you! Do not listen to her, Ria!

The distraction allows Quralla to thrust again. I thwart her at the last second, but the tip of her sword scrapes my shoulder. The blood oozes from the wound but I do not feel the pain. My adrenaline runs high.

Focus, Ria. Victory is yours. She is full of trickery. Do not allow her to win this war of words.

I feel a renewed strength surge through my weary bones.

"Jerdaj does not need a grief-stricken woman on the throne. Let a man rule." Quralla mocks me as the clanging of our swords echoes over the stones. "You are not born to royal blood! You are not pure. You are not worthy."

I feel the rocks jab into my back as I am pressed into a corner. Quralla's sword hangs inches from my throat.

"You are a foolish woman. You are untitled, unnamed, and unworthy," hisses Quralla.

At that moment I understand what Zundah meant about the Quralla being difficult to find and treacherous to reach. If Quralla stabs me and kills me, I can be with Kamal. But then what would happen to Jerdaj and its people? Haatim would overtax the citizens and try to take over all the realms in the nearby radius to forge an empire instead of letting the people live in peace. It would be selfish of me to leave others to fend for themselves. My heart speaks. Among the people, I am loved. They need me. I cannot abandon them. I know my name. I know who I am. I am Sultana of Jerdaj.

Ria! I will always love you. You have always been and always will be my Sultana.

The confirmation of love fills me with a power I did not know existed within myself. I look at Quaralla.

"I am the Sultana of Jerdaj," I say my voice low and steady.

I thrust my sword forward. "I am the Sultana of Jerdaj!" I shout as I twist my sword against Quralla's, knocking her weapon from her grasp. Her sole defense clatters to the floor and I plunge my sword all the way through her illusion.

No blood seeps from the wound. Instead, Quralla smiles at me then laughs. "Well done." Then she disappears into the air, and I am left alone in the room.

I glance around waiting for some magical confirmation that I have won. But the cavity of the cave is still and quiet. "I do not understand," I say aloud.

A scuffle can be heard outside, Nabila enters the room with Mahfood riding on her shoulder.

"Ria, are you alright?" asks Nabila. "We waited outside but did not hear anything."

"Ah! Victory reigns," calls Mahfood.

"You were right," I reply. "The Quralla is abstract. What do we do now?"

Before Mahfood can reply, I hear a slow clap come from behind me. Turning toward the entrance, I see Haatim enter the room.

"What are you doing here?" I ask. "Who rules the kingdom?"

Worry consumes me, for the people now have no leader.

Haatim glares at me. "I have to make certain my throne is secure." He growls with menace in his voice. "Your role in the castle has come to an end. There is no need for a woman on the throne of Jerdaj." He looks around. "I do not see any wish-granting magic. I knew the Quralla was nothing but a myth."

I bite my tongue.

Nabila and Mahfood take this moment to move to the other side of the cave away from the dispute between us.

"You are a traitor!" I yell. "You have the whole Council thinking that I am unstable to rule. What kind of brother are you to betray Kamal with such a reprehensible conceit? You are selfish. You only want to be Sultan to conquer the nearby realms and forge an empire."

"What is so bad about that? If we can make Jerdaj the most powerful realm among all the kingdoms, there will be vast wealth for everyone."

"Those realms exist in peace! Their citizens are innocent! Why are you here?"

"I followed you here to be rid of you permanently. After all, you fooled a whole army into thinking you were a fellow warrior. I know you can find a way to steal the throne from me. I cannot take that risk. It is with regret, my dear sister-in-law, I must take your life," replies Haatim drawing his sword.

Clenching the weapon in my hand and remembering the wound Quralla has given me, I glance at my shoulder and see the wound has fully healed. I have no time to think as Haatim rains down jabs, and I move as quickly as I can to avoid certain death. Our duel moves out onto the rocky ledge. Its narrow confines provide little room for error.

Haatim lunges forward in a surprise maneuver. I manage to evade the sharp tip, but my foot slips. My sword falls from my hands into the sea below. I catch the cliff edge as my lower body dangles toward the gaping chasm beneath me. I attempt to pull myself up, but my arms, fatigued and weakened, begin to give out. My fate seems imminent. A shadow falls over me and I see Haatim standing above me.

"Ah, the precious Sultana finally meets her doom. I have always known you were unworthy as a warrior." He sneers. He places his sword on the ground and crouches in front of me as I struggle to keep my grip and not fall to my death.

"One push off this ledge and you shall die, Sultana. I will let you in on a little secret," continues Haatim as he leans closer. "I am the one who killed your husband."

My eyes widen and my jaw clenches.

Haatim smirks and continues proudly, "Oh yes! It was my doing. I met secretly with the Sultan of Evjah and our agreement led to war. I knew Kamal was too kind to permit his soldiers to fight without a strong leader. He had to take his place at the head of his army. He had to set the example! During our battle at sea, I pushed him overboard. Your husband never knew how to keep power. He believed too much in kindness. And it was his kindness that brought about his death."

"You are a traitor!" yells a familiar voice.

Haatim turns. I hear Mahfood and Nabila.

My heart is pounding in my ears, my palms are sweaty, and I feel my grip starting to loosen.

Mahfood hops toward Haatim. "Let me tell you something, Haatim, you are the lowest scoundrel in all of Jerdaj!"

Mahfood's moment of distraction takes Haatim's attention away from me and my brother-in-law walks toward the courageous frog. I use that moment to climb.

You are worthy, Ria. You will win this war.

The voice fills me with strength. Using my last thread of energy, I pull myself onto the ledge and feel the secure ground beneath my body.

I remember the dagger hidden in my boot.

I get to my feet and run toward Haatim. As he is about to slice Mahfood with his sword, I bury my dagger into his back and pierce his heart.

Haatim doubles forward. Out of nowhere settles a mist, surrounding him, absorbing him into its endless veils. He is finished, and so are his evil ways.

Overcome with joy, Nabila reaches to hug me. "By the Mists of Jerdaj, Ria, you have succeeded in your quest."

"Well done!" calls Mahfood "I knew you would emerge victorious."

Deep within my soul, my heart speaks to me. I run back into the cave and enter the room. The Quralla sits on the rock the same as the first time I entered. She turns toward me, and I see myself staring back at me.

"What are you doing here?" she asks.

"What are you doing here?" I repeat. "I thought I defeated you."

"Oh, honey, I am immortal! As soon as someone kills me, I come right back after they leave. It is all an illusion.

"What magic prevented Haatim from seeing you?"

"Arrogance. He was filled with his own overweening pride. He did not come here looking for me. He came here to kill you. And here you are. Now what do you want? Did you not get what you asked for?"

"No, I did not." I walk forward and take Quralla's hands. "I never told you my heart's desire. You assumed I wanted to remain the Sultana of the Jerdaj. That is true. I have proven my worth and defeated my brother-in-law. But my heart's desire is to have my husband by my side as I rule the kingdom."

Quralla sighs. "What you request reaches into deep magic, Sultana." She evaporates into the air.

I look around the empty room. I groan. "So let it be done. I shall rule the realm alone." I head toward the door.

"Ria," a voice calls behind me.

I turn to see Kamal standing in the center of the great cavern. Rushing into his arms, my heart is complete, and I kiss him.

"Well done, my Sultana," whispers Kamal in my ear. "You are a true leader."

"Sultan!" cries Mahfood as we exit the cave.

"Oh, my," cries Nabila, covering her mouth in surprise. "How is this possible?"

"He is my heart's desire," I reply, leaning my head against Kamal's chest.

"How are we going to explain this to the people?" asks Nabila.

"We say the Sultan of Jerdaj has returned," answers Mahfood. "Remember, Kamal was pushed overboard. Even though Kamal's body was never recovered, Haatim declared him dead so he could rule. It is an easy twist to say that Kamal survived, made it to shore, and has been lost in the Mist all this time. It is our courageous Sultana who has retrieved him."

"Brilliant idea," I reply.

"I was thinking," says Kamal, taking my hand as we walk back to the dhow. "When we return, I will be taking a step back from my royal duties and allowing my beautiful wife to make the decisions of the land. Your act of bravery is a shining light to all women. In my time on the Other Side, I saw the future of Jerdaj filled with many women leaders." He kisses my hand. "You are the future, Ria. You are the Queen of the Mist, The Sultana of Jerdaj. History will long remember your name."

N.D.T. CASALE

N.D.T. Casale is an Italian-American author who lives in the United States. She creates magical realms for others to escape to and enjoy.

When she is not hard at work writing, N.D.T. Casale spends her time riding horses, working out, traveling, snowboarding, and looking for her next adventure. She is fluent in multiple languages and always ends her day with a cup of tea.

N.D.T. Casale also writes under the name N.D. Testa.

Instagram: https://www.instagram.com/ndtcasale/

SKY SOMMERS

YUMIKO'S REVENGE

With a clean zing, Yumiko Blackwood sheathed her katana and adjusted the frog on her shoulder. "We're done here. Next target?" The raven-haired girl in a pleated skirt and white blouse toed the remnants of something that used to be a human being and looked around.

The manager's desk next to the dead body was the only one with decent lighting. All other working desks still had various items of *faux* clothing stuck in sewing machines. A typical Hong Kong sweatshop operating 24/7.

The workers ran as soon as she had entered the premises after hours with a katana in one hand, pressing a finger to her lips with the other. They would come back tomorrow morning to a clean environment. Yumiko glanced at the bloodless body at her feet.

Well, relatively clean.

Her magic leather footwear had already absorbed all the blood from the room. As the last remaining specks on the walls disappeared, similar sized stains of bright red seeped into her knee-high boots.

"Don't you want to have a bit of a rest? I want to have a bit of a rest," the frog mumbled and came eye-to-eye with the girl's green irises as she turned her head. The nose partition of his helmet was making it very hard for him to look cross. Cross-eyed, yes. Cross, no.

"Rest? I rest when I'm dead," Yumiko said, tilting her head and giving the frog a black wig as her bob of straight black hair swathed him.

"That's what I'm afraid of," the frog sighed, puffing her hair out of his face. "You do know why I'm here?"

"To help."

"Yes. To help you not get killed. You're an orphan . . ."

"Why does that matter? Does it make me more valuable?"

"It does," was all the frog said.

Yumiko started Googling the next Hong Kong address she had on her list of people who helped kill her parents. If the frog wasn't going to be helpful, she would do everything herself. She always had. Yumiko found her next destination and tapped the walking option in the map app. When the diagram lit up and the arrow all but crawled out of the phone to show her the way, she finally flipped the light switch and started up the stairs.

In one swift move, Yumiko swiped the frog from her shoulder. Sitting in her palm, the frog looked at her through slitted eyes. The neon signs blinking behind her head were making him change color like a chameleon.

"Frog. Help me or get lost."

The frog's mouth drew into a fine, wide line.

The girl threw him carelessly toward her shoulder and he had to scramble back onto his perch, mumbling something about no respect for gods.

For ten minutes, neither of them said anything as the kind lady in the map app dictated their movements through the Wan Chai District.

Yumiko stopped before a decrepit forty-story building. *Public housing. Curious.* "Last address," she said and stared some more.

"Are you sure the last person on your list lives here?" the frog asked. "Didn't you save the best for last?"

"The person who gave me the list did not lie. He wouldn't dare. I severed his thumb," Yumiko said.

"A thumb? Why a thumb?"

The girl looked at the frog like he was daft. "So they would know it was me. The gokudō don't go for thumbs."

"Ah, despite your wonderful torture techniques you don't want them mistaking you for Yakuza. It was before I volunteered to help you, so enlighten me, oh Vengeful One . . ."

Yumiko raised an eyebrow.

"Have you thought that maybe the person who gave you the list, he . . .?" the frog asked and got a curt nod, "he knew what you were about to do and wanted to throw someone into the mix who he wanted to get rid of? Ever thought of that?"

Yumiko eyed him warily. "You say he put someone who didn't kill my parents on the list because he wanted them dead?"

The frog shrugged. "Come on. Someone who lives in this place"—he gestured at the grey crumbling high-rise, the balconies of which were adorned by colorful threadbare laundry drying in the smog —"couldn't have profited from their death."

Yumiko paused. "Maybe they did and maybe they didn't. Perhaps they didn't profit, but they helped. In which case, they die." Yumiko started toward the elevator, which to their surprise, turned out to be in working order.

When Yumiko exited the elevator on floor thirty, everything was eerily quiet.

"I don't like this," the frog said and adjusted his helmet.

"Neither do I, but someone's gotta do it," Yumiko spat.

As she neared door 950, the red arrow climbed out of her mobile phone and pointed at the door, all but jumping and whistling to get her attention.

"I should never have given you my phone with all its magical apps," the frog said. "Or the magic boots."

"Normal phones work and I could have lived without the boots. All I need is my katana." Yumiko unsheathed her sword, put the frog onto the ledge of the balcony and said, "Sit still, I'll be a moment."

The frog rolled his eyes at her and blew a raspberry. "Sever heads first, ask questions later. We have talked about this. You have to make sure the poor dear who lives did actually help to kill your parents before you dispatch them."

The girl stole a cold glance at the amphibian and brought her finger to her lips.

Before she could knock, the door opened and Yumiko clutched her katana with both hands, prepared to let it sing.

A boy of five peered out, his eyes widening. He scrambled back, leaving the door open and Yumiko saw a man and a woman emerge from the tiny adjoining room. Yumiko could see the whites of their eyes. The woman crouched down and held onto her child, shielding his eyes, whispering something comforting to him. The man and the woman didn't look like anyone she knew. Could the frog have been right?

"Anyone else in there?" Yumiko asked and all three shook their heads.

"Ask them if they know him," the frog croaked.

"*How* do you know Yoshinori Shinobu?" Yumiko asked. She had to be sure.

"We . . . I . . ." the man faltered. "My brother owed him money. A lot of money. My brother is dead. So is his family. We are the last remaining relatives."

Yumiko nodded. Only then did she sheath her katana, earning a silent gasp from the dwellers. They couldn't have been her father's informants. Or Boss Yoshinori Shinobu's either. The frog was right. She had been purposefully misled.

"Leave this place," she ordered the family. "I was sent by mistake. There might be more 'mistakes' coming." The head of the family nodded and took a step back. "If you are ever in trouble, ask for Yumiko-san and come tell me your grievances. In person." Yumiko nodded at the boy and closed the door between them, hearing them collectively exhale.

Yumiko picked up the frog and shoved him onto her shoulder.

"For the record, I'm not going to say anything. Nothing at all," the frog whispered into her ear.

Yumiko didn't say anything either, just shook her head, her hair slapping the frog about as if he was stuck in a carwash.

On the way down, in the elevator, the girl tapped something into her phone without looking at her list. The last name and address on that list had been memorized a long time ago.

"Aren't you glad I was there to prevent you from making the worst mistake of your life?" the frog said as Yumiko tapped her Octopus card at the tourniquet of the subway station.

"This is you not saying anything?" Yumiko mused as she located her train. "You knew, didn't you? Would you have let me kill them?"

"I didn't know. But I suspected. Your opponent is the leader of one of the Yakuza families who, in his expansionist plans, is attempting to get Hong Kong under his thumb. He has an army. You are alone and a teen. You need to start thinking like him if you want to beat him."

"I don't want to beat him. I want to kill him. There's a difference," she hissed.

"Potato, pot-ah-to. At least don't just rely on your own brains and resources. Use mine. Would you have been that careful if I hadn't told you someone might be out to use you? No. You would have swung your weapon first and asked questions later. And at least one member of that family would be dead and an innocent's life would be on your conscience."

Yumiko toed the flyaway newspaper on the floor of the subway train, bit her lip, and nodded.

"Now, will you listen to me?"

The frog got another nod and patted his protégé's neck. "Good girl. Now, let's go kill the last baddy, shall we?"

Yumiko hopped off the subway train at the Diamond Hill MTR station and headed toward the exit. Five minutes later she was standing in front of an iron gate that stretched a hundred meters to her right and the same to her left. The sign on the gate read: Nan Lian Garden, 7:00 a.m. to 9:00 p.m daily.

It was 8:30 p.m. The gate was already closed.

Yumiko muttered, "Last orders," and grabbed for the hilt of her katana.

"Wow-wow-wow, hold on a minute, girly. You're going to take on someone in"—the frog glanced at the descriptive plaque—"thirty-five thousand square meters of beauty? Alone?"

Yumiko puffed a stray hair out of her face, assessing the fence for where she could jump it. "I have you for company, and yes. You have a problem with that?"

The frog put up his digits. "None whatsoever. I've fought in more picturesque places than this one. What I meant was—we need backup."

"Why?" Yumiko grabbed one of the iron bars and *hunhed*. "No zing. We could jump."

"You can jump. I could crawl right through. And what do you mean no zing? You thought it was electrocuted and you put a hand to it; are you daft?" the frog accused.

Yumiko shrugged. "I bet he's in there with a thousand bodyguards."

"All the more reason to call for backup."

Yumiko inclined her head. "Who did you have in mind?"

A slow, wicked smile spread over the frog's face. "You'll see." Then he yelled at the top of his lungs, "Oh, Gabriel, Loretta, whoever is up there—help, *ANY* help needed in Nan Lian Garden, Hong Kong, Earth dimension. Now! Send Vic!"

A heartbeat later, a pair of warriors materialized next to the gate, green goo dripping off their drawn swords. One warrior was tall and dark, the other ginger and short.

"What in the name of smelly goblins did you do that for, Victor?" said the boy with red hair and a high-pitched voice. "We were finally having fun! Why did you pull us out of Hel?"

"I didn't," said Victor, lowering his sword as he assessed the surroundings.

"I did," said the frog.

The newcomer eyed Yumiko. She eyed him right back. "Who the hell are you?" Victor asked.

Yumiko felt the frog lean on her neck and hop sideways. "Hello, Victor."

"Boss?" Victor said as the youth stepped to his side.

"That's your boss? Since when?"

"Former boss," the frog said and Victor nodded.

"If she's the damsel in distress, then pardon my disdain, but I don't see the kind of distress that warrants the services of three guardian angels," the younger warrior said.

"Two. You're not a guardian." Victor glanced at his compatriot and then to the former frog.

The youth's nostrils flared in offense. "Are we saving this girl from you?" he asked the former frog. "You're sitting way too cozy on her shoulder for someone who is about to attack."

"He's the one who called me in," Victor said.

"Us."

"Me."

"Kids," the frog admonished.

"Why are we here, Boss? Don't tell me, you're back to your old ways of villainy." Victor smirked.

Yumiko tapped the frog's shoulder with her finger and smiled. "I always knew you were a dark horse, frog."

"Enough chit-chat. Do you want your revenge or don't you?" Boss asked Yumiko, who nodded once.

"Revenge? You interrupted my vacation for revenge?" Victor looked nonplussed.

"The last of my parents' killers is in there." Yumiko nodded toward the iron gate and the beautiful park that lay behind it. "The baddest of them all. With a gazillion ninja bodyguards."

"And you were going to go in alone?" the younger warrior inquired.

Yumiko shrugged. "I've got my frog."

Silence settled.

"Wow. You sure know how to get people emotionally invested," the youth said and bumped Yumiko's shoulder, turning to go.

Yumiko blinked. "So, you'll help?"

Victor's mouth stretched into a grin of pearly whites. "We'll help."

Behind them, the iron gate creaked open.

"Now, are you ladies going to stand around here all day or shall we get moving?" the youth said, pocketing something that looked like a claw.

"What have you been teaching our new recruits?" Boss asked Victor who gritted his teeth.

"Not a new recruit. And, unfortunately, some things they pick up all by themselves."

The youth stuck out his tongue at Victor and asked Yumiko, "Do you know where your 'baddest of them all' is or do we have to comb the entire park for him?"

"Why do you immediately assume it's a him?" Victor asked, slinking in after the youth.

"It's a him," Yumiko said, following them. "My source says he's on top of the Chi Lin Vegetarian Dim Sum restaurant."

"So, past the Pavilion of Absolute Perfection and the nunnery and into the pits of that park?" the frog asked.

"Nunnery?" the youth asked. "We're not going to . . ."

"No."

"Are you absolutely sure?"

"Yes," the frog said.

"How come?"

"No nuns. Only Buddhist monks. And the eatery is far from the temple."

"Sounds like you've been here before," Victor said, ducking down at the base of a red bridge while the rest of them walked on.

"You don't need to hide. Lots of tourists come here. It's a family park," Yumiko said. "Why don't we walk to the restaurant like normal people and save our strength for the fight?"

"Normal people?" the youth gestured at his grimy self. "I know you've been hanging around with a magic frog and that has shifted your view of normal, but have you met Victor?"

"Hey," Victor protested.

"Cosplay," Yumiko said.

"Bless you," the youth said.

"She means people going around in fancy dresses, like their favorite characters, and nobody giving a damn, dear," the Boss said.

"Like Halloween but all-year-round?" Victor asked and the youth snorted. "So, we walk through the park and anyone who sees us will think what?"

"Role-play," Yumiko said.

Fifteen minutes and a lot of photo snaps peppered with tourist admiration later, the quartet was standing in front of a two-story house built into a granite rock. The lower level was hidden behind a waterfall wall and housed a vegetarian restaurant.

"There are customers in there," the youth pointed out.

"Potential hostages," Victor nodded.

"And he's up there," Yumiko pointed upward, where she knew her target was waiting behind armored walls and a ton of loyal bodyguards.

"You were right about the gazillion goons," Victor supplied and drew the sword sheathed between his shoulder blades as men in black suits with black ties filed out, filling the rooftop terrace. The young warrior swished out a scimitar while Yumiko's katana was already catching the last of the dying sun.

The frog hopped off Yumiko's shoulder, transforming into a regal-looking, olive-skinned man mid-flight.

Behind the water curtain, a firework of white flashes dotted the window.

"Tourists," Victor hissed. "I bet they think this is a performance."

"Frog?" Yumiko whispered to the man in a midnight blue Hindu sherwani etched in gold, sporting a wide silver belt.

"You know I was never just a frog, little girl," the spry geriatric said.

"Grandpa?" said the youth with red hair, and everyone turned to stare at him.

"Erm . . ." the former frog raked his hand through his curly, salt-and-pepper hair. "Grandpa? Who are you?"

"I'm Ellinora . . .Ellie." When that elicited no response, the petite warrior added, "Melisandra's youngest?" The youth wiped the grime off which only made a tad of a difference, revealing two chocolate brown eyes and a button of a nose.

"You're a girl?" Yumiko asked.

"Yeah, so are you," Ellie said. "What are you, twelve?"

"Fifteen."

"Fifteen?" Ellie turned to Victor. "Parents dead? Isn't she a tad young to recruit?"

Victor and the former frog shrugged while Yumiko narrowed her eyes at them. "Orphans are special, huh?"

The man Victor had referred to as Boss started untying his metal belt without taking his eyes off the balustrade of the terrace.

"Erm, Grandpa, a belt, really?" Ellie asked.

"This is Urumi, child. The deadliest sword there ever was," the former frog said and flicked the hilt. The zinging *whoosh* ended with a slap. The metal curled around a wooden pillar in the fence separating them from the tiny pond which surrounded the eatery. As he recalled the weapon, the middle half of the pillar fell.

The guards on the terrace took a collective step back. Satisfied with the effect he had made, the Boss said, "Here's the battle plan. Victor and I storm the terrace. You girls secure the tourists."

The two girls looked at the older man, one with judgment, the other with curiosity.

"He's *my* target!" Yumiko protested, while Ellie smirked and said, "What makes you think I fight like a girl?"

Victor rolled his eyes and went to bolt the restaurant door from the outside, yelling "Stay inside, you'll disturb the set!"

"What's the holdup?" came a booming bark from above and the pack of bodyguards filed in two halves, letting someone through.

"Well, well, well, who do we have here," said a man whose belly jiggled with every step he took. He cooled himself with an ivory fan.

"Yoshinori," Yumiko hissed, looking up. She would recognise that portly bastard anywhere.

It's not just the feet and dead eyes of your fallen family you see from under a bed. She had seen the ballooning figure, the double chins, the shining bald spot. Also the cruel eyes, Jabba-the-Hut mouth and fat fingers with rings on them. All while she lay in the blood seeping from the bodies of her parents.

"Kumichō Shinobu to you, girl," the man's mouth drew into the hard line she remembered so well. The Boss and Ellie flanked her at both sides while Victor waved and smiled at the people ogling them through the waterfall obscuring the restaurant window.

"You're not my boss. You're a dirty gokudō," Yumiko spat.

The man *tsk-tsked*, "Ninkyō dantai, girl, get it right."

"Your organization is as chivalrous as I'm forgiving. My parents were not part of your organization. What did they ever do to you?"

"They got in the way. Your police chief father, he shouldn't have poked his nose where it didn't belong," the fat man *tsk-tsked*. "Your mother . . . well, she was just in the wrong place at the wrong time."

"They were home."

"You weren't. Otherwise, I wouldn't have to deal with you right now." The man cringed as if he was smelling something unpleasant.

"You purposefully fed my informant a wrong address." There was no hurt in Yumiko's voice, only calm.

"Yes, and he fed you all of my other accomplices. Thank you for dispatching them so I didn't have to. I could only hope the family in Wan Chai would dampen your plans. But you are so hell-bent on revenge that even killing innocents in that dump didn't deter you." He shook his bald head and smiled. "Maybe I could have a use for your bloodthirst. Except if you killed them, then you are blind to bad decisions. I can't have blind mice walking my streets." Yoshinori held up his hand. "Enough chit-chat. Bring me her head." The man turned and went back inside, his bodyguards closing ranks like the Red Sea after Moses.

The first twelve cupboard-sized men in black drew their swords and jumped off the balcony.

In a flash, the Boss let out his white wings, whipped out his Urumi and stepped in front of Yumiko who assumed her battle stance. The former frog said, "Change of plans."

Then all hell broke loose.

Yumiko's katana zinged left and right, creating a myriad of flying limbs and high-pitched cries while the Boss made wide berths of space with each snap of his sword. With every whip Urumi made, the Boss sent fallen warriors onwards, making them and their body parts disappear mid-flight as he released his hold.

Victor and Ellie worked in unison, twirling around in a clockwise motion as they progressed up the stairs, leaving a trail of bodies in their wake.

Ten minutes later, Yumiko's magic boots were lapping up the blood as she ascended the stairs. The Boss gathered his Urumi and retracted his wings on the go. The balcony was littered with men in black suits. Victor wiped his weapon on the sleeve of one of the fallen and looked rather cheerful. "Weren't there more of them?' he asked. The Boss nodded."Where did you send them then? Valhalla or Hel?"

"Both," said the former frog. "Some will serve as permanent nightmares for their sins. Others deserve Valhalla."

Victor smirked, stuck the weapon back into the sheath lodged between his shoulder blades and the hilt disappeared from view. Ellie still held her scimitar aloft, just in case.

"Good battle," Yumiko said, nodding to everyone in appreciation. "But Yoshinori is still inside. He is mine."

Ellie smiled, "Yes, and he's alone."

Inside, they saw Yoshinori pushing a button on the wall and the metal blinds *whooshed* toward the blood-spattered terrace.

"Oh, no you don't," Victor said and stuck a penknife into the window frame, aiming a kick at the glass. The window withstood the assault, while the metal blinds stopped at the penknife mark.

"Yumiko, boots," the Boss said, motioning toward the window.

Yumiko approached and, looking at Yoshinori's grinning face, aimed a swiping kick at the illusion of safety between them.

The glass shattered into a million pieces, making the whites of the man's eyes pop as he scrambled away.

Yumiko stepped over the shards only to see a flash in front of Yoshinori's face accompanied by a bang, much too loud for this closed space. The world slowed and she saw a bullet flying toward her. Victor moved swiftly into the trajectory of the bullet, extending pitch-black feathers that closed around them in a *whoosh* as he jerked toward Yumiko.

"You really should be more careful," Victor squeezed out. "Now go get your revenge." He leaned onto the wall for support.

Yumiko's eyes focused on Yoshinori who was cowering behind the kitchen island.

"You."

Using the chair as a step, Yumiko hopped onto the kitchen island and twirled for momentum, her katana slicing through air.

Whoosh.

Yoshinori's head rolled into the kitchen's corner and bumped against a cabinet door, leaving a bright red mark. The white marble floor was quickly changing its color scheme.

Yumiko hopped into the spreading puddle of red goo, splashing more specks onto the cupboards. The puddle paused and retracted itself toward her boots. Her boots flashed bright red and settled back to their usual black color.

She looked around, spotted a black duffel bag on a chair and headed over. Yumiko opened the bag, paused for a second and went to open the side window. She looked down and noticed tourists were climbing out of a window.

"Was beheading one of the Yakuza clans always your plan?" Victor rasped from the opposite side of the room as he gouged the bullet from his feathers. Ellie stroked his shoulder and craned her head to see better into the kitchen.

"No. But it was my father's," Yumiko said, picking up the duffel bag and upending it outside. Bills of various currencies floated down, eliciting an *aaahhh* from the crowd. Next, Yumiko went into the kitchen, picked up the head and stuck it into the bag. "I'll have this stuffed."

The four of them walked out onto the terrace, which seemed pristinely white, if it weren't for the bodies littering it. Victor molded his wings into his back.

Yumiko surveyed the surroundings. "It seems the tourists want to go home. We can only hope they think this is a movie set."

Victor smirked, said, "Allow me," and hopped down from the balcony. He was greeted with a wide berth and interested stares.

"Shooting a movie, folks. See the drones? No? You just missed them. Thanks for staying outta the way, don't disturb the set. I believe you've already been paid?" He gestured toward the money littering the ground.

"Are you sure they won't call the police?" Ellie asked.

"I dispatched most of the fallen. They can't see the terrace from there and Yumiko's boots have taken care of the gore. Besides, they were paid," the Boss said and locked eyes with Victor. The guardian angel nodded and pointed the tourists toward the garden gates. Haranguing the crowd while blocking their phones and cameras wasn't difficult for his six-foot frame in a sea of people who barely came up to his chest.

Yumiko gripped the duffel bag. "My father is avenged."

"You're not afraid of the consequences?" Ellie asked.

Yumiko looked her in the eye. "I am the consequences."

"And you are formidable. Isn't she, Ellie?" the Boss said.

Yumiko eyed the former frog and decided to ask, "You and the other man have wings. What are you?"

"I'm a guardian angel," the man said. "Yours for the moment."

Yumiko nodded as the blood seeping from the duffel bag dripped all over her boots which were much too happy to lap it up.

Ellie wolf whistled at Yumiko's boots. "I thought it was weird that you would choose crystal shoes to go into battle, but now I see they are not quite what I thought they were."

"Where do you see crystal shoes?" Yumiko asked and Ellie pointed at her boots.

The Boss frowned at Ellie. "The shoes are on loan. They change the way they look and perform different functions based on the need of the person wearing them."

Ellie threw her Grandpa a knowing look. "Oh. So, if you need a prince to chase you, they slip off; if you need to clean up, they absorb blood. What else do they do?"

Yumiko eyed her feet. "Useful footwear. I'm inclined to keep them." She started down the steps. Her boots extracted all the remaining specs of blood from their surroundings with every step she took.

The Boss looked at his protégé's back and told Ellie, "Her revenge is complete. She has no need for the shoes. They will be returned whence they came." At Ellie's raised eyebrow, he said, "Magic Kingdom."

Ellie *hunhed* and ran down the steps after Yumiko. "I know you're fifteen and all, but you can call me up for a fight anytime. That was fun!" Ellie smiled, her pearly whites lighting up her grimy face and grabbed Yumiko's hand to shake it with vigor.

Victor materialized at her side. Ellie grasped his waist, waved at Yumiko, and told the former frog, "Don't be a stranger. Back to Hel, Victor, we have dirty goblins to quarter!" A black cocoon of light enveloped them both and gone they were.

When Yumiko and the Boss walked out of the garden, Yumiko headed for the black limousine parked under the No-parking sign. Four men in black suits, identical to the pack of bodyguards they had just dispatched, tapped their earpieces and looked worried.

She thrust the duffel bag at the man closest to her, making sure he saw the drops of red seeping through onto the pavement. The men in black froze. Keeping her hand on the hilt of her katana, Yumiko said, "Open it."

The guard did as he was told. Seeing the contents, he paled and almost dropped the bag.

"Yoshinori Shinobu is dead. I'm in charge. And we are going to do things a lot differently from now on."

The bodyguards all straightened and stood at attention, the
on this tiny girl of fifteen with one grimy warrior by her side. T
one still holding the bag tapped the driver's window. The man got out and opened the passenger door.

To the angel at her side Yumiko said, "Get in."

The former frog did as he was told, except it was a frog who hopped into the car. The driver who saw this, kindly dropped his jaw. "A battlefrog demon . . ."

Yumiko kicked his shin. "Open," Yumiko motioned at the trunk.

The driver complied hastily.

The girl threw the duffel bag in there and got into the back seat.

As the limousine pulled away from the curb, thus began the reign of Yumiko-gumi, the most feared female Yakuza boss of all ages. Her empire stretched from Japan to Macao, and from the time Hong Kong became her permanent residence, its streets had never been safer. Yumiko-gumi's rule was as terrible as it was fair. Crime was almost eradicated. With Yumiko-gumi and her forces of fairness keeping the precarious balance, the police suddenly had no reason to be corrupt.

The lady was revered and adored. Her success was only partly attributed to the personal battlefrog demon she had at her beck and call. Anyone who said differently hadn't seen her wield her katana every morning on the top terrace of the Chi Lin Vegetarian Dim Sum restaurant in Nan Lian Garden.

SKY SOMMERS

Sky Sommers was born to Estonian-Russian parents and for most of her life has lived and worked in Tallinn, Estonia, with brief escapes to all but the top and bottom continents in search of her muse. Her debut e-book in 2012 was about ancient goddesses running amok, trying to get their wilted powers back. She then proceeded to indie publishing her own books and found her way from Greek and Arthurian myths and legend to fairytales retold for young adult and adult audiences. So far, Thumbelina has been updated for suspicious adults, more sinister versions of Cinderella, Red Riding Hood and the Wizard of Oz are out and a new Goddesses series is in the making. All her books are peppered with dry humour, linked by some character or another and she loves making you choose at the end depending on whether you are an optimist or a pessimist. She lives in a house with a small garden with her husband and mostly one, but on occasion plus four kids. No dog.

If you want to know more about Yumiko's magic shoes, you can read Cinders: Necessary Evil
https://amzn.to/33Kj9Rn

If you love short fairytales by indie authors, there is another charity anthology coming out in July 2022 that features Sky's To Snare A Prince, a short & sweet fairytale from the Magic Kingdom
https://amzn.to/3FSsgMT

You can best find & interact with me on Instagram:
https://www.instagram.com/sommers_sky/

ARIELLE WILLOW

The Readers of the Great Backwaters have always been the most revered healers of the land, with one exception.

One hundred years ago on the longest night of the year, the Great Backwaters was plunged into darkness. A powerful Reader, a rare magic user who could see, interpret, and mend the soul threads of life and connection, turned against his oath of healing. He ripped through the colorful and patterned tapestries of everyone around him, radiating shadows through the surrounding villages. He tore through connections that began with every birth—children's energy intertwined with their parents', playful twists of early friendship, cautious braids shaped from young romance, and thick knots formed as love or friendship deepened. Not even the strongest bonds marked by glowing light survived. All that remained were the frayed cords, wounds on the soul from pain and heartbreak to grief and loneliness. Readers have always vowed to weave their own threads of light and strength into tapestries, supporting their neighbors and friends as they reform broken tapestries. But the Dark Reader renounced his oath.

A great sorcerer, Grandmaster Onyx Clearwater, gathered the strongest magic wielders to bind the Reader, using the power of the winter solstice. They cut all the Dark Reader's soul threads and banished him to a prison outside of time. He was stuck at the age of twenty, never granted the release of death from old age. And because tapestries are woven when one soul's energy entwines with another's, even his name was bound so he could never seize a connection formed by someone speaking it.

"Not another one," grumbled Riannon Cyanriver as she plucked the smooth, milky-white stone out of her trouser pocket and tossed it over her shoulder onto the path behind her. At her last count, Riannon had evicted eleven stones, all different shapes and colors, but all as smooth as glass. Riannon sighed and called out to the strangely quiet forest around her, "My pack is heavy enough, thank you. I don't need more weight in my pockets. I just spent a week healing dozens of people from the surrounding villages, and I need to get home." Riannon received only silence in response. Apparently, the Fae were thoroughly enjoying this game. Riannon sighed again and continued along the dirt trail through the forest.

Riannon was used to the tricks of the little forest Fae: pinecones appearing in coin pouches, tiny handprint-shaped smudges of pollen on tunics, bright flower buds stashed in food supplies. The fair folk enjoyed harmless mischief with the infrequent travelers through the Silver Forest, but they were not usually so persistent. On her last journey, the Fae politely ceased their mischief after she gifted them the last of her honey from her pack.

After finding the first few stones in her pocket, she offered fresh blackberries and a dollop of sweet cream she'd received as payment from the villagers. Sweet cream was a well-known favorite of the Fae, and yet, they continued to fill Riannon's pocket with a new stone as soon as she removed the previous one. Riannon counted five more paces, reached into her pocket with the barest hope she would find it empty, and then grinned when all she felt was the soft cloth of her trouser pocket.

"Thank you!" She called to her forest friends. *They're finally bored with this game of pocket rocks,* Riannon thought. *I didn't want to insult them by not playing. Now, I can focus on getting home to the Festival of Harmony.*

The Reader quickened her pace and thought about what this day meant to her. The Festival of Harmony took place during the winter solstice, when magic and energy flowed the strongest. By tradition, each village's magic wielders used this energy to fortify the binding of the Dark Reader. Over the last hundred years, the Festival had morphed into a joyful celebration of life and community. The magic users perfunctorily completed their task when the sun passed below the horizon, and then the fun began. Children ran races, lovers snuck away for moments of passion, and friends of all ages competed to make as many people smile and laugh as they could. Riannon's mentor, Elder Zia Lightblossom, kept hinting that Riannon might meet a suitor there this year. Riannon usually responded by teasing Elder Zia about finding her own Harmony romance.

Despite this lighthearted bantering, Elder Zia always insisted Riannon was home long before sunset so she would be ready for the ceremony. Riannon happily complied with this directive, because she was excited for the Festival to begin. As a Reader, Riannon would be surrounded by almost blinding brightness as the threads and cords wove together to form the immense tapestry of her community. This light strengthened Riannon and soothed her soul. For once, she could receive healing instead of giving it.

Riannon grinned as she got closer to home. She checked her surroundings and noted the familiar landmarks along the path. She estimated she was about an hour from her village. Looking up briefly to track the sun in the sky, her smile dimmed as she realized sunset was also about an hour away. Riannon grimaced, imagining the earful she would get from Elder Zia if she was late. *I'm twenty years old and I'm still afraid of angering my mentor.*

Riannon turned her gaze back toward her destination, determined not to let anything else distract her. A line of smooth stones lay horizontally across her path. "Not again!" Riannon complained. "I don't have time for another game!"

She stared at the strange little boundary line, trying to understand what the fair folk wanted this time. The stones reminded her eerily of a ward, like the tradition of lining windows and doors with salt to keep away evil spirits. Reflexively, she reached into her pocket like she had so many times before on this path, and her fingers brushed against a cold, smooth stone.

"What is this? What does this mean?" she called, looking around at the Silver Forest for a glimpse of the fair folk. Nothing but silence. Again. She debated what she should do, trying to ignore the goosebumps rising on her arms. *I can turn around and take the path that skirts the forest, but I would miss the binding ceremony. The Fae are probably just being silly. This is the quickest way home, and I always take this path.* Riannon scanned the forest ahead of her, and nothing looked unusual. She needed to get home and had to make a choice now. After a deep, calming breath, Riannon stepped over the line of stones and continued on her way.

The forest gradually darkened around her as sunset approached.

Riannon was about ten minutes from home when the branches overhead blocked so much light that she could no longer see the trail ahead. Reluctantly, she stopped and searched in her pack for a small lantern. She had just lit it and started forward when she saw the slight glimmer of a soul thread.

Well, that's strange, Riannon thought, frowning at the thread. *I don't see the rest of the tapestry. Is it a loose edge from someone too far away? Maybe Elder Zia sent someone to look for me. She must be getting worried. I'm never this late for the Festival.*

Riannon took only one step when a thought struck her like a slap. *Could this be a Shadow Thread?* She squinted and tried to make out the colors and shape of the cord. She thought she saw a darker, oily shine, but she wasn't sure. The lantern only lit a few yards ahead, and this thread was in the deeper shadows.

I can't see any colors from here. But it can't be. No one has seen one since the Dark Reader was bound. She needed to see it more clearly. The Reader was almost positive she would recognize the tapestry of a villager if she stayed on course. Still, Riannon hesitated to move forward. Elder Zia had warned her to flee immediately if she ever saw a Shadow Thread. She had gone on a long-winded lecture about the danger of Shadow Threads and how they could corrupt anyone who went near them.

Riannon was torn. She was so close to home and didn't want to disappoint her mentor. Riannon spoke out loud as she considered what to do, trying to guess what her mentor would do. "I can run. I *should* run. Elder Zia made it very clear there is nothing I can do. I should turn around, go right back through the Silver Forest, and find a different way home."

With a sigh, she looked at the path she'd already traveled. Then she turned right back around and continued in the direction of home. *It's dark, and late, and I'm being paranoid. It can't be a Shadow Thread. If I go back through the forest, whoever Elder Zia sent for me could get lost in the dark. I'll run into them soon, and then we can both get back to the village for the Festival.*

The soul thread continued to reflect a bit of the lantern light, but it always seemed just at the edge of her vision. Riannon felt like a child playing hide and seek, unable to find the villager in the dark. She kept increasing her pace and chased the wisps of the oily thread around curves in the trail, growing more frustrated.

"Oof!" Riannon yelped as she fell to the ground on her hands and knees, her lantern rolling ahead of her. She glared back at the offending root that had tripped her. Her palms hurt, and she mumbled curses at the root, the path, and the whole Silver Forest. She looked around to find her lantern and froze; her breath caught in her throat.

A campfire glowed in a small clearing where the path should have been, with a dingy wood cabin at the far edge of it. Terror spread over Riannon, chilling her with the barest touch of a winter wind. It became more tangible and grew rapidly from a light breeze that ruffled her hair to a strong gale, forcing the healer to her feet and toward the fire. Riannon struggled desperately but the wind pushed harder.

When she was just a few feet from the campfire, the air suddenly went calm. She lost her balance and fell to her hands and knees again, pain sparking through her sore palms. Riannon lifted her head, ready to curse quite loudly this time, but an image in the flames caught her attention. No sound left her lips as her body froze.

A tall, masculine figure raced along a path through dense trees. Riannon recognized the last stretch of the way toward her own village. *The Silver Forest!*

The image shifted, and now the figure burst through the doorway of a small home. Riannon could see the figure's face: blue eyes opened wide, cheeks flushed with exertion, mouth opened in a yell.

He looks terrified.

She saw the man fall to his knees on the floor, his arms wrapped tightly around a young toddler. Tears flowed down the man's cheeks, and he rocked the child back and forth. Riannon could see his lips form the same silent words over and over, "My son. My son. My son." Completely absorbed in the story before her, Riannon didn't notice the tears starting to glide down her own cheeks.

The scene changed, and now the man knelt surrounded by people. He sobbed as he lowered a small figure wrapped in white cloth into a freshly dug grave. Riannon could see the ragged and heartbroken gashes in the man's tapestry, mirroring the rough edges of the hole in the ground. The man abruptly threw his arms out wide and let out a horrific scream, startling the villagers trying to comfort him. Riannon's heartbeat thundered when she saw what he was doing. Rushing toward his fingertips were dozens, and then hundreds of soul threads, unwinding and tearing apart from the tapestries around him.

Villagers started screaming too, their bodies shuddering as their tapestries were ripped and shredded. She focused on the man's face, and she was surprised to see confusion and fear in his expression.

One last shift, and the man was running away from the crowd back toward the forest. His tapestry looked like a tangled knot of broken cords, and at the very center, Riannon saw a bristling mass of oily darkness spreading outward.

Riannon stared in horror at the blackening tapestry, her mind filling with pieces of understanding. *He's the . . . But he's a father . . . He's supposed to be evil . . . He was so scared . . .*

Something pressed against Riannon's shoulder, and she screamed, her body released from the fire's thrall. She leapt to her feet and twisted around. In front of her was the figure. The Dark Reader.

"Hello, little healer," he said, the fire reflecting in his coal-black eyes. He was so close. She could feel the odd chill of his breath on her skin.

"You. You're a . . . You're the . . ." Riannon tried to say, but she couldn't complete the sentence, not yet ready to accept what she had seen. A deep laugh spilled from the man's lips, and Riannon cautiously edged sideways, trying to put space between them.

The Dark Reader's mouth twisted into a smirk, and he allowed her to take a few steps, his unsettling eyes tracking her every movement. He raised his hand toward her, palm up, and curled his fingers into a tight fist. Riannon doubled over, pain like icy fingers gripping her heart. "Tsk. Tsk. You do not get to walk away from me," the man said, his tone disconcertingly calm, almost pleasant.

"W-wh . . ." Riannon struggled to speak, wheezing with the effort.

The man sighed and loosened his fist. Immediately, the pain

decreased, though a claw of ice still lingered like a sharp nail splitting the skin above Riannon's heart. In a cracked voice, Riannon asked, "What have you done to me?"

The man's eyes twinkled with amusement. "You're a Reader. You tell me."

Riannon pushed through her haze of fear and pain and focused on her tapestry. "No . . ." The word was little more than a rasped breath.

"Oh yes," the man said with glee. Riannon barely heard him, transfixed by the edges of her tapestry. Thick threads tore free from their patterns, twisting through the air and into his clenched fingers.

Even after what she saw in the fire, she didn't want to believe what was happening. Soul threads were the bonds of energy and life between people. Readers healed by mending and adding connection to a tapestry. They weren't supposed to be able to take connections away. But the grieving father in the vision pulled threads from the villagers surrounding him. And that same man stood in front of Riannon now, gripping her threads in his fist.

"Little healer!" the Dark Reader snapped, his calm demeanor fracturing. Riannon looked up toward his inky eyes. "I'm tired of waiting. I've been alone for so long, and I'm ravenous."

"Ravenous?" Riannon echoed, her thoughts hazy and muddled. She was still trying to understand how this man had seized control of her threads, and now he was talking about being hungry?

"You're so strong, so bright," the man murmured, caressing the soul threads between his fingers. "Almost as powerful as I was, before—" The Dark Reader's voice cut off abruptly, and his eyes unfocused. Fleetingly, Riannon thought she saw a hint of the blue she had seen in his eyes in the vision. Then it was gone.

"Your magic radiates around you," the man resumed. "The winter solstice has filled you to the brim, and I want that energy. I *need* it."

She wasn't sure the Dark Reader was even seeing *her* anymore, just the light of her tapestry. He reminded her of a starving predator, driven by the visceral urge to fill the emptiness inside him. He took one step toward her, eliminating the little gap he had allowed her to make. Cold emanated from his body, and she felt it crash against her like a wall of snow.

Riannon instinctively jerked back, but he gripped her threads tighter, not permitting an inch of movement. Pain flared through her again, and it cleared the remaining fog from her mind. Anger quickly replaced it. She couldn't stop herself from yelling, "You're mad! Absolutely deranged!"

The Dark Reader's focus sharpened, sentience returning to his expression. He bent his head down and stared intently at Riannon. Her heart raced with rage and terror, and she dropped her gaze before she said something even more foolish. His breath frosted against her forehead, icy tendrils stroking along her temples and down her cheeks. The man lifted Riannon's chin so that she was forced to look at him directly. He tilted his head, considering her.

"You surprise me, little healer. You have a spark of fire in you. I could use that," he mused. "I'll give you a choice. With your energy and my skill, we could channel immense magic from the solstice and sever the binding keeping me trapped here. You can join me, be by my side, as we seize control of the Great Backwaters."

"Why on earth would I do that?" Riannon asked. "I *heal* people. That's my calling. I've spent my entire life training to repair the damage and pain in tapestries. Those are my people! My family, my friends, people who trust and need me. Why do you think I would give that up to join you?" Her last word dripped with disgust.

The Dark Reader's mouth curved into another cruel smirk. "Because you're already on the path to darkness. For such a powerful Reader, you're really quite oblivious. Look at your tapestry."

Riannon finally saw it then: inky, glistening threads wriggling from The Dark Reader's fingertips on her chin, twisting around the frayed edges of her tapestry, multiplying as they crept closer to the heart of it. Shadow Threads. Riannon felt so foolish, remembering Elder Zia's warnings. So many more emotions rippled through her: dread, anger, regret, and worst of all, hopelessness.

"Ah, now you understand." The Dark Reader's grin stretched wider. "You have two choices. You can accept your defeat, and I'll make sure your energy isn't wasted. I'll even be gentle as I consume your light. Or you can join me." He held her gaze for a moment, and then he lowered it to focus on her lips. In a softer, lower voice, he added, "Your fire fascinates me." His thumb brushed over her lips, pausing in the center and gently pressing down, parting them.

The healer shuddered at the Dark Reader's touch. She felt disoriented, uncertain about what was happening. His thumb felt like ice, and yet, it was strangely comfortable. Her fingers and toes were getting colder too, tentacles of frost spreading slowly like the darkness edging along her tapestry.

The man dipped his head lower, and Riannon felt his chilly lips brush against her ear. He murmured his offer. "I can show you how thrilling it is to grasp all the magic you could desire. You are becoming like me. Soon, you'll crave the dark and the power. We can take what we want, let it satisfy us. Let me show you."

Riannon tried to hold on to her thoughts, but they were racing so fast. She couldn't make sense of the moment. *He wants to kill me. No. Yes. He wants me. Yes. No. He wants . . .* Something was wrong, but something was right too. His fingers on her chin. His thumb on her lips. His lips on her ear. Too many sensations.

Then his icy touch retreated, severing each point of contact with her. "What do you choose, little healer? Will you join me? Or will you sacrifice yourself in a misguided attempt to protect your people? Either way, I win. Once I have your light, I can sever my bounds. You should feel grateful for my offer."

Riannon felt jumbled and foggy. Did it even matter what she chose? Her tapestry was warping and darkening, and soon she wouldn't be herself. She struggled to concentrate on his question. Her thoughts were even more fragmented, broken into little shards. *Join . . . Desire . . . Fire . . . Sacrifice . . .* Riannon seized on that last thought, forcing the fog away with effort. With her last moments of clarity, the healer made her choice.

The Shadow Threads were now covering more than half of her tapestry, and Riannon smiled at the sight. She felt a bit of tension leave her body as the Dark Reader loosened his grip on her threads. She cautiously lifted her hand toward his cheek, testing what he would allow, until her icy thumb rested on his lips. Her eyes traced the same path. She saw his lips turned up in a wicked smirk, as though he never doubted she would join him. She dared to look higher, and she met his gaze fully. The Dark Reader waited for just one heartbeat, and then pulled her hand away to press his lips directly to hers.

Riannon felt her threads fall completely from his hand, and she sensed him drop his guard too. In that instant, she shoved her magic at him. Brilliant white light shattered through the clearing, fracturing the dark like lightning in a midnight sky. Riannon channeled everything she valued and loved—her family, Elder Zia, the villagers she healed, even the Fae who tried to warn her—into the Dark Reader. Bright, colorful threads unwound from Riannon's tapestry, winding themselves through his. His Shadow Threads burned in the light, revealing a faded pattern beneath their ashes.

Riannon was fading, draining her magic to heal this man. A rainbow of hues saturated the tapestry, working from the edges toward the center. Riannon shaped a final bright cord from the last of her life's energy. This cord wound to the heart of the man's tapestry, to the hole left when a father lost his son and accidentally wounded others in his grief. A hole with ragged edges of guilt and blame toward himself. Riannon's thread spread and spiraled like a glistening web, connecting all the edges into a new pattern, glowing with the light of forgiveness. Gentle, blue eyes were the last thing Riannon saw before she severed her connection and let go.

Riannon opened her eyes and was surrounded by a blanket of light; soul threads of every color and every size wove around her like a cocoon. Peace enveloped her, and she envisioned this as the road to her afterlife. She remembered Elder Zia's warning about Shadow Threads corrupting her. She smiled, wishing she could tell Elder Zia that there was light on the other side of the darkness. She closed her eyes and drifted.

Sometime later, Riannon opened her eyes again. Instead of her vision of the afterlife, she was in her bedroom at Elder Zia's home, bundled tightly in her favorite threadbare blanket.

"Are you ready to rejoin the living?" asked Elder Zia, pressing her hand to Riannon's forehead. "You've thawed out finally." Elder Zia declared this brusquely, but Riannon saw the lines of worry on her mentor's face.

Riannon opened her mouth to form a question, but she didn't know where to begin.

Thankfully, Elder Zia understood. "I kept watching for you to return for the Festival of Harmony. Right before the sun dipped below the horizon, a strange man emerged from the forest with you in his arms. You were as cold as ice and still as death. I thought you were gone, until I saw a faint thread connecting you to him. We had been ready to shore up the binding, but instead, we channeled our magic toward you. Every single villager joined the gifted around you.

"I wish you could have seen the tapestry they formed. The Festival of Harmony is always bright, but I have never seen a tapestry as blindingly brilliant as the fabric that wove around you. I asked the man to carry you here to continue your healing. You slept for three days, getting a little warmer each time I checked. And now here you are, and you'll be fine. Though I can see I've worn you out already. Go back to sleep and we can talk more later." Elder Zia settled back into a rocking chair by the bed.

Riannon had so many more questions. How did she even get into the Dark Reader's prison? How did she get out? Who brought her here? Nothing seemed to make sense. She didn't have the energy to ask yet. Riannon was drifting back to sleep when Elder Zia said, "I almost forgot to tell you. It turns out the man who brought you here is a healer, and I asked him to stay in town while you recover. He can tell you more about how he found you." She grinned and gave her apprentice a knowing wink before adding, "He has the gentlest blue eyes I've ever seen."

ARIELLE WILLOW

Arielle Willow, an artist and forever daydreamer, is now branching out on yet another creative adventure. Arielle borrows from her background in radio news, amateur art, and mental health to craft stories with characters you could imagine in your own life, if you lived in a world of magic that is. Arielle dreams up her stories while living her (not so secret) life as a tattooed, motorcycle-riding, gardening faerie in the Midwest. To keep up with Arielle's newest ventures, follow her on Amazon
amazon.com/author/ariellewillow

and Goodreads
goodreads.com/ariellewillow

ASHLEY STEFFENSON

A LESSON IN REFINEMENT

At the screeching whistle of a teapot Adara dropped her feather duster and hurried into the kitchen. Leafy strands of hair fell around her green tinted face. She swiped them impatiently behind her ears and twisted her hair back into a tight bun. Adara placed the teapot on the counter in front of a row of neatly labeled jars. From a small cupboard, she withdrew a China teacup and saucer. Adara poured herself some tea and sat at her dining table where Fernis' teacup and saucer still remained. Staring blankly at the cup adjacent to her, Adara recalled the bitter times. The great division between the two of them. What was the last thing she said to him? Why don't you make like a tree and leave? Adara sighed. He had left. And she hadn't seen him since.

Adara finished her tea, rinsed her dishes, and placed them in the precise place she had retrieved them from. A knock sounded on the door as she wiped the table spotless. She brushed invisible crumbs from her green dress, and went to answer it.

"Adara Plumwasp, dryad of the Plumwasp Woodlands?" A voice snuffled from the other side of the perfectly arched oak-wood door.

The sun glinted off the fine leather boots of Sir Prindlewood, the courier from the palace. Adara's eyes widened a little and she curtsied respectfully. "Yes, I am Adara. To what do I owe the pleasure?"

"The Duchess of Eryas Palace requests your musicianship for the anniversary of her birth." Sir Prindlewood's beady eyes traveled around the cottage, resting for a moment on a small violin at the foot of a crisply made bed. "You are to report to the palace at eight o'clock sharp." Without waiting for a reply, Sir Prindlewood displayed a piece of paper with the details written in calligraphy.

Adara closed the door and set the piece of parchment on her vanity next to an old photograph. In it were two young dryads, a boy and a girl. The boy had his arm around the girl, and they were both smiling, actually, they were laughing. Adara couldn't remember what had been so funny. A sad smile curled her lips. "Wish you were still here, brother."

The festivities were a bright light in Adara's memories as she glanced around. Fireworks lit up the night sky like rainbows of starlight. The sounds of flutes and strings drifted through the air as musicians performed their evening gaieties and different outfits lit up the evening in a riot of color. Adara's smile waned as a dull ache grew in her chest like wood rot. Even though it had been over a fortnight since Fernis' disappearance, the festivities reminded her of the times they used to play for the Duchess' special occasions together.

"Adara - " a fair woman in her thirties greeted her. She had thick brown hair pulled into a loose bun at the nape of her neck. Stray hairs framed her olive-toned face. "It is good of you to come and play for me tonight."

"Of course, Duchess Carolinda. It is an honor."

The Duchess smiled, a warm smile that mended a part of Adara's aching heart. "Come. I have a place all ready for us."

Carolinda led Adara to an amphitheater in the center of the palace garden. "I know you and Fernis played together on the stage in the courtyard, but since this will be your first time playing without him, I thought it might suit us better."

Adara swallowed down the lump in her throat. "Of course, Duchess."

As the amphitheater filled, Adara could overhear people making comments about how exciting it was to be in the presence of one of the best musicians in the realm of Eryas. Others commented on her fine choice of dress for such an occasion, and her perfectly groomed appearance. The guests were seated as the Duchess made her usual opening announcement thanking them for coming. Once she took her seat, Adara began. Every note she played was perfectly in tune. Every scale she ascended was flawless and every chromatic scale was without error.

Adara concluded her performance to an enthusiastic round of applause.

"Beautiful, as always." Carolinda wrapped her in a warm embrace as the crowd dispersed and handed her a small glass bottle with a cork. "For playing for me this evening." Adara gave the bottle another look. "Thank you, but what is it?"

"You wouldn't believe me if I told you." Carolinda's honey-brown eyes sparkled mischievously. "Don't open it until you're back home."

Adara returned to her cottage late that evening. She almost forgot about the small glass bottle and considered leaving it till the morning, yet her curiosity got the better of her. She popped the cork. Whoosh!

The trees creaked outside, and dust whipped into the air. The cottage shook violently. Glass jars shattered onto the kitchen floor. Bottles clattered around them. The dining room table was knocked askew. Adara's tight bun came undone as she yelped in fright when a ghostly figure appeared. Heart pounding, she clambered across the bed and withdrew a dagger from underneath the wardrobe. The room went still as Adara stared at the creature before her. It's upper half was that of a man and its lower half snaked into the bottle. A cascade of black hair parted around a glowing green face.

Breathing heavily from shock and the exertion of clambering over the bed, Adara attempted a commanding voice. "You clean up this mess right now!"

The genie snapped his fingers and the room righted itself. "Ah. You are a dryad," he observed. "I've never served a dryad before. A forest spirit, yes?"

"Plumwasp spirit," she corrected him.

The genie chortled. "Tell me Miss Plumwasp spirit, what was the first thing to break in your cottage upon my summoning?"

Adara's brow furrowed. "Why does that matter?"

"It will tell me what needs mending in your life. You see, unlike other genies, I grant only one wish. You do not get to choose your wish. The broken objects do that for you. If I deem you worthy of my aid, I may choose to help you at my own discretion."

Adara pursed her lips, trying to think of the first broken object. "The bottles."

"They were glass?"

Adara nodded. "Filled with different herbs and spices."

"I see..." The genie glided back and forth in the air. It looked like he was pacing. Lost deep in thought.

"So, what does it mean?" Adara asked.

"Hush," he snapped.

Adara flinched and raised her dagger defensively.

"Broken glass can have many meanings. I am filtering what it means for you." His eyes fell on Fernis' old teacup and saucer. "Aha. You are grieving."

Adara's heart twisted in her chest. "Perhaps... a little," she admitted.

"You are. The broken glass represents your broken relationship with someone. Inside, you are ruled by regret. Who have you wronged?"

"That is no concern of yours," Adara muttered.

The genie turned to face her square on. "It is if you wish to receive my help. Tell me. Do you desire to see whoever it is you wronged again?"

"Of course I do."

"Are you ready to change?"

"What do you mean?"

"In order for me to grant your wish, you must be willing to surrender the rotting parts of yourself. Think of it as being refined. Letting go of your old self, and bad habits."

"I... suppose." Adara chewed her bottom lip and her frown deepened. "But what bad habits are you referring to?"

"I can see from your cottage that you are a tidy spirit. There is nothing wrong with that. There is only something wrong with it if it becomes your only focus. Have you always been this way?" Adara groaned, massaging her temples. Her head hurt. The genie's questions felt like thorns in her side. Twisted roots in her heart. She was not in the mood for philosophical questions. But, she knew Carolinda wouldn't have given her the bottle in the first place if there was no purpose behind it. More than anyone, Carolinda knew Adara wanted her brother to come home.

"I don't think so," she finally answered. "I started cleaning more after Fernis left. It was a way for me to occupy my mind because I..."

Adara paused. She wanted to say she felt bad, but she wasn't ready to admit that to this strange new being.

"Felt guilty?"

Adara's eyes snapped towards the genie. How did he know what she was thinking? She mulled over a response. "I didn't mean some of the things I said to him."

"Him being?"

"My brother."

The genie nodded thoughtfully. "You were living in denial."

"Look, if all you want to do is reveal my misgivings, I'm not in the mood for it right now," she huffed."I'm tired. So, if we could continue this conversation in the morning I'd appreciate it."

"There will be no need for that, Miss Plumwasp," the genie replied.

"My name is Adara. And why is that?"

"The first step to healing is to recognize the root of your rot. You just did."

"How?"

"By recognizing that you cleaned because you felt bad for treating your brother harshly. You see, not only does broken glass represent broken relationships. For you, it represents the fact that you are easily damaged. In other words, you are more sensitive than you let on. You started cleaning because you were in pain. The only way for you to mask the pain was to occupy your mind with something else."

Adara sighed, lowering her dagger in defeat. She felt depleted of energy. And as much as she hated to admit it, there was truth to the genie's words. "So can I expect your help or not?"

"Refinement of the heart is no easy feat, but you have proven yourself. I will help you."

One Month Later

"It is unlike you to request anything of me." Adara and Carolinda sat together on a weathered stone bench in the palace garden. "How can I help you find Fernis?"

Around their feet the bright sun glinted off the buttercups turning them gold. The garden always seemed a brighter place after a good rain. Or perhaps the refining Adara had done with the genie simply made her heart feel lighter.

"I need a map to the Living Highlands…" Adara felt awkward asking for a map. She had never traveled anywhere. Would she even know how to read it?

Carolinda's eyebrows rose.

"And a horse… If you can spare one."

Adara found herself holding her breath as she waited for the Duchess to respond. It felt so very uncomfortable asking for a favor from another. Especially Carolinda. Adara couldn't remember the last time she had asked anyone for help. Why was that? Perhaps it was a fear of rejection. "As much as I wish to be of service to you, all our palace steeds are off fighting in the war." The corner of Carolinda's lip turned up apologetically. "But, perhaps this will suffice," she turned to one of her guards and he disappeared in the direction of the stables. "Nobody has ever requested a map of the Living Highlands before…" The guard reappeared, leading a brown, miniature pony. Carolinda smiled. "His name is Peanut."

"He's awful small," Adara noted, taking the lead from the guard.

"Ah, but not many can match his endurance. Now, I must tell you Adara," she looked deep into the dryad's eyes. "There is a reason nobody has ever requested a map of the Highlands before. Do you know why?"

Adara shook her head.

"They are said to be cursed. That whoever journeys up their steep slopes will fall victim to his own misgivings."

Adara shuddered. "You mean, someone's misgivings could be their downfall?" Carolinda nodded solemnly. "We have lost many good men to those Highlands. It is said that once someone becomes lost in their misty recesses their bodies become blackened trees with gnarled roots mirroring their misgivings. Their faces carved into the trunks never to see the light of day."

"That's horrible!"

"Truly. It is a foul fate." Carolinda's face was grave.

"So, why journey to the Highlands in the first place?" Adara wanted to know. "If all they grant is death?"

"It is said that if one's heart has been truly refined, he will break the curse, thus releasing the souls of the entrapped." Carolinda took Adara's small hands and squeezed. "I urge you to reconsider your options. Were you explicitly told that Fernis was in the Living Highlands?"

Adara nodded slowly. "The genie told me…"

The Duchess' face grew pale. "Then I am afraid you have no choice. If you want to free your brother you will need all the help you can get. And if you are working on refining yourself as much as you say you are, you may emerge victorious. Come, I will retrieve a map for you."

The next morning Adara sat at her dining room table with her tea, the map of The Living Highlands spread where Fernis' teacup once sat, untouched. She outlined what she thought would be the most direct route to the base of the Highlands. A nicker sounded and Adara glanced up. Peanut's small head peeked through her open window. She smiled and held a carrot to his muzzle which he chomped on happily, making a mess on the floor. Adara filled a haversack with food and water, wrapped a green cloak around her shoulders, and exited the cottage.

Outside, she saddled and bridled Peanut. "Are you ready, my friend?"

Peanut nicker-snorted in response as he searched for any remaining treats in Adara's hand. His untrimmed whiskers tickled her palm, and she chuckled. "Let's go."

As they traveled through the woods, Adara found her mind was swimming with all sorts of what ifs. What if Fernis wasn't in the Highlands, and the genie had tricked her? If he had been turned into a black tree, what if she couldn't free him? What if she turned into a tree herself? Just like the other poor souls whom Carolinda had mentioned? They had all thought their hearts were pure enough to enter The Living Highlands, but none of them returned. What if she was just another poor unfortunate soul journeying straight to her death? She shivered on top of Peanut and the pony's ears flicked back as if telling her to stop over-thinking.

At length they neared the tree line of the Plumwasp Woodlands and Adara could see the Highlands

in the distance. Dark specks dotted the hillside enveloped in mist. They stood like scattered black knights. Tall, yet lacking in procession.

Adara rode Peanut through the lowlands to the base of the nearest knoll. The pony began to prance in anticipation as she dismounted.

"Don't worry, you're staying right here," she promised, removing the pony's saddle and bridle. But he just stood there, ears pricked and nostrils flaring, watching her.

Adara smiled. "I'm not going back with you. I need to find Fernis." Her gaze drifted to the specks dotting the hillside and dread crept into the pit of her stomach. "I don't even know if I'll make it back..." She began to feel nauseous. No, she wasn't going to turn back now. Fear was another piece of rot. A piece of her that needed refining. There were so many things she did because of fear. And so many things she didn't. Like apologize to Fernis in the first place because she was afraid he wouldn't forgive her. She had to trust, to believe that her refining with the genie had paid off. And there was only one way to find out. Taking one deep breath, Adara stepped through the barrier of mist at the base of the knoll.

The path beneath her feet faded the higher she climbed into the mist. Queer noises sounded all around her. Grunts, screeches, and scuffling in the undergrowth. Adara could not see what made the noises as an early dusk greeted her. The strange scent of unknown critters and must hung in the air, thick and foreboding. The wind picked up, and with it came the voices. Shivers vined up her spine and Adara quickened her pace until she could no longer hear the whispering laments.

She passed several looming shapes in the gradually thickening fog. The trees watched her. They seemed to close in, drowning out the light. Their branches all pointed in different directions as if a strong wind had warped them. Once or twice Adara was sure she saw heavy-lidded eyes staring back at her through the fog. A bent elbow here. A silent scream there. Heart palpating in her chest, she grew weary. Gnarled roots dipped in and out of the ground all around her. They looked like feet in flight. There were faces of men and women, even children. Adara shivered, pulling her cloak tighter around herself. The exertion of climbing the hill was no match for the dread that began to creep into the pit of her stomach again. Adara's heart grew heavier with each step she took, and she wondered if the curse was taking its toll. Finally, she neared the top of the knoll where a lone, blackened tree greeted her. It was smaller than most of the others. Slowly, Adara approached.

Adara's mouth went dry. Etched painterly into the trunk was -

"Fernis!" She placed her hands on either side of his face. Tears swam in her eyes. It looked as if he were in a deep sleep. "I'm so sorry," she sobbed. "I never should have told you to leave." Leaves and bark began to encompass her. She felt her body constrict with the weight of it all. Adara could feel her arms and legs grow stiff. The scent of cedar swam in her nostrils as darkness pressed in on her vision. A sad smile curled her lips as her brother's face disappeared from view. It's okay, she thought. We're Plumwasp spirits. And our spirits never truly die.

ASHLEY STEFFENSON

Adara will return in "Troria Shedo", coming 2023.

If you enjoyed this short story, check out "Estellia", the prequel to "Troria Shedo", now available on Amazon.

Ashley Steffenson is a born and raised California girl turned Southern. She earned her BA in Intercultural Studies and loves incorporating unique fantasy cultures into her realms. Ashley resides in the deep south with her husband Cody, and their three wily cats - Ember, Milo, and Piper. Currently, she is working as a Librarian Page at their local library. In her spare time she enjoys video-gaming, spending time with family and, of course, reading and writing. She also enjoys making candles for her small business, Estellian Treasures, which was originally inspired by her debut novel.

ESTELLIA is her first novel. A sequel titled TRORIA SHEDO will be released in 2023.

Instagram: @authorashleyanne @estellian.treasures

Facebook: Ashley Anne Steffenson

ELENA SHELEST

The orchard was quiet when Marko hid between the blackberry bushes with his bow and arrows at hand. Surrounded by a sturdy fence, rows of fruit trees spread in front of him, casting long shadows under the moonlight. Several of them stood empty of fruit, their branches broken and charred. Marko spent the last three nights trying to catch the mysterious thieves. Best hunter in the area at seventeen, he never failed to capture whatever he set his eyes on. The problem was, he couldn't keep his eyes open long enough, and there was something unusual about his inability to resist dozing off at exactly the same time. But tonight he had a new plan: sturdier snares and a bitter concoction from the local healer to keep him awake.

As before, around midnight the wind blew harder, whispering a strange birdsong through the leaves. It had lulled Marko to sleep on previous nights, but now he suffered only a few yawns. Half an hour later moving torches descended from the sky. He restrained himself from running to the well to grab water and only gripped his bow tighter. The moving bonfires got closer, taking on the shapes of large birds. Each was the size of a swan with a long, graceful neck, a wide span of wings, and a tail of long fiery feathers. The strange beings glowed brightly with an orange and yellow light that played across their plumage like a gem reflecting the rays of sun. He couldn't look at them for more than a few moments.

The five birds landed on one of the trees and pecked at the apples. Marko held his breath, waiting. Finally, one of his traps snapped, and the beautiful intruders let out a panicked cry. Marko sprinted into action, running the few steps that separated him from the tree. The creatures rose into the air—all but one; its foot caught in his snare. The rope ignited as the bird struggled. Marko threw a net around its body and yanked hard. The being tumbled to the ground, letting out angry cries and scorching the grass. Its companions circled nearby, ready to attack.

My bonds won't hold up, Marko thought. *The whole garden will burn!*

Marko aimed his bow at the writhing ball of fire, willing his hands not to shake. "Dare touch me or this place and I'll kill you with a single strike!"

He had heard of these creatures, and if the myths were true, they were intelligent enough to understand his words. His prisoner stopped writhing and let out a strangled sound, sending the rest of the flock away. It stood up, disintegrating the thick ropes into ashes. A flash of light surrounded its body, and for a moment Marko closed his eyes. The glow pulsated before fading into low embers, revealing a woman of otherworldly beauty. A wreath of shining flowers adorned her long red hair and her embroidered dress was filled with precious stones.

"And what are you planning to do with me, boy?" she asked in a melodic voice. "Don't you know who I am?"

Marko swallowed against his dry throat. "You're a firebird."

"I am Elina Silverheart," the woman said, her tone regal and full of indignation. "Tsarina of the Enchanted Borderlands. Bow to me and ask for forgiveness."

Marko frowned. Royalty or not, he had a task to complete. "You might be a tsarina somewhere else, but here you're a thief."

Her eyes flashed. "You would dare hurt the immortal firebird?! The one who brings healing, longevity and happiness?"

"So far you've been nothing but a thorn in my side. So, what is it going to be, tsarina? What's the price for your life?"

He kept the string of his bow tight, his hand steady, keeping up the bluff.

"I will fulfill any wish," she finally said. "Whatever your heart desires."

"And promise not to return here?"

She nodded.

Marko narrowed his eyes. "How can I be sure you won't trick me?"

"I will bind myself with an unbreakable oath."

Once again, the woman morphed before his eyes into a fiery bird that rose into the air and twirled. Marko adjusted his aim. A single fiery feather fell on the ground, pulsating with heat until the glow faded, turning it to gold.

"Say your oath," he ordered.

Fiery sparks circled in a whirlwind around the firebird as she sang the words. "I promise to fulfill one of your wishes, whatever it might be. But it can only touch one person, change one life. And when you wish for something, you have to desire it with all your heart. Then and only then will it come true."

Marko furrowed his brow. "What do you mean by all of this?"

"It has to be your heart's greatest desire," she continued to sing. "When you know beyond a doubt what you yearn for most of all, hold this feather, turn around three times, hit your right foot on the ground, then say, 'In the name of Elina Silverheart, Tsarina of the Enchanted Borderlands, I wish.' Whatever you utter will come true. One wish. One life. Don't forget."

Then she flew away. And Marko let her, feeling as if she had fooled him. At least the orchard was finally safe and his duty fulfilled. He picked up the feather that stretched from the tips of his fingers to his elbow and tucked it inside his jacket. It sparkled like pure gold but was soft to the touch. If anything, he could sell the wonder for a good price.

It was still dark when Marko hurried home. He enjoyed the fresh air and the stillness of the night, letting his thoughts run freely. Should he wish for wealth? What would he do with it? He made enough coin from the sales of wild game to never be in need. Should he wish for the most beautiful maiden? Marko sputtered. No, he enjoyed his freedom. He couldn't wish for his people to be free of Tatar's attacks as the tsarina promised to only change one life and not an entire nation. Then what?

By the time Marko got home, he was in a lousy mood. He could not sleep after the potent herbal brew, and the golden feather underneath his hunting jacket burned a hole in his thoughts as if cursed. At sunrise, he changed out of his clothes, washed, and put on a new linen shirt. Instead of the cloth sash most men wore, he kept his sturdy leather belt. It was broad enough to hide the feather underneath along his waist. Today their village celebrated the end of the harvest, and he ran out after a quick breakfast, not wanting to waste another moment inside.

It was a perfectly sunny September morning. Despite the early hour, a crowd had already gathered on the fields for the annual festivities. The harvest had been collected days ago, but workers left a few ceremonial sheaves for decoration. Young women with wreaths made of wheat and barley threw teasing glances at Marko as he passed by. Several men stopped and thanked him for the deer he donated for the celebration. Dishes overloaded the tables. Women dashed about, swatting the children who tried to sneak a few treats early. Elders smoked the pipes and tuned their instruments for the upcoming dance.

"Hey, stranger." Marko's friend Ivan caught up with him. "Rough night?"

"Lousy hunt?" another chimed in, joining them.

"We might have something to cheer you up," a third young man shoved him on the shoulder and winked. "The *tabor* is here. *Tsigane* could cure anyone's sour mood."

Marko's curiosity got the best of him, and he followed his friends. The Romani nomads visited their area from time to time, performing during the festivities in exchange for coin and feasting. This time it was a large tribe with several carts and a dozen horses. They pitched tents and sat around, practicing their acts for the evening. Men threw a few sharp glances at their group. Several girls in brightly colored dresses watched them too, whispering between themselves and giggling. Marko frowned and turned away, chased by a cheery "hey, handsome!" and more laughter.

"We should split," one of Marko's friends suggested. "We'll never get any attention next to you."

The opposite sex did seem to favor Marko, not that he paid them any mind. He was taller than his peers and broader in shoulders, with sun-blazed skin, black hair and sharp gray eyes. But having two able hands to provide for others seemed more important to him than good looks.

"Suit yourself," Marko grumbled. "I'm going back to where the food is."

He hurried away, turned the corner, and almost tripped over something sprawled on the ground.

"Saints! What in the. . ."

It was a girl, and she was trying to crawl. She finally gave up, rolled on her back, and frowned at him, her long dark curls sprawling haphazardly around her pretty face. She looked about his age, but something was off. Marko stared in confusion at the strange angle of her shoulders. Her wide sleeves twisted up her arms that were too skinny to be of much use, hands curled in. The rest of her was hidden behind a loose shirt and a pleated skirt. One foot peeked out and was warped as well.

"What are you gawking at, oaf!" she demanded, her dark eyes flashing daggers.

"I'm . . . I didn't mean to. Let me help." He came to his senses and bent down but was unsure how to pick her up.

The girl swatted him. "Leave me be, fool! Did I ask for your help?"

"You look like you need some, and I'm not leaving you here to trip someone else." He gathered her in his arms despite her fierce protests. Her body was too light. Did they starve the poor thing? "Where shall I place you?"

The girl only pursed her lips. Fine, he'd figure it out himself. Marko spotted the carpet with a few pillows lying near one of the carts and propped her up between the cushions.

"Be gone before I curse you," she hissed.

Marko arched his brow. "Can you really do that?"

"I can tell your fortune." Her dark eyes narrowed. "Or misfortune."

Marko laughed. "Well, I'm fortunate enough to not be scared of a snobby girl who thinks she knows better."

He got up and turned to leave.

"Wait!"

"What? More insults to share?" He faced her again with arms crossed over his chest.

She sighed. "Words are the only weapons I've got. Sometimes they get away from me. I'm sorry."

"No offense taken."

"Would you sit with me then?"

Marko scratched his head but obeyed. "Sooo, what's your name?"

"Guess."

He snorted. "How?"

"My name means 'renowned warrior'." The girl let out a bitter chuckle. "I guess I can lash out with my tongue."

"You're pretty good at it too." He grinned. "But I don't know a single word in Romani."

The girl rolled her eyes. "I just gave you a hint. You're not very bright, are you?"

"Speak for yourself," he retorted.

The girl pouted but didn't stay silent for long. "What's your name?"

"Marko."

"What do you like to do, Marko?"

"I'm a hunter."

"So preying on helpless animals."

"Are all girls the same?" he scoffed.

"No," she retorted. "I seem to be a bit different."

Marko opened and closed his mouth, unsure if he could ask what was wrong with her. The girl laughed at his obvious embarrassment. She was lovely, her skin darkened by the sun, a bright blush on her cheeks and a sparkle in her eyes the color of chestnuts. Marko caught himself staring.

"Ah, that's where you're hiding, Lash! Hopefully not giving away free fortune-telling." A robust woman came around the cart and melted into smiles when she spotted Marko. "Come later, young man. She'll be at the festival and will tell you everything you want to know. Bring coin, silver or gold, we take it all."

Marko stood up.

"Lash then." He grinned at the girl behind the woman's back. "I'll see you later, Lash."

He returned to the main area and found his wayward friends. The day passed by in a flurry of games, dances, food, and more food until Marko could barely breathe. When the sun began to set, he spotted a colorful tent and the woman in front of it who came to collect Lash earlier.

"Ah, here you are," she murmured. "Come inside, don't be shy. Find out what awaits you. Uncover your heart's greatest desire."

Marko stiffened at her words. The firebird's warning about the wish was like a fresh wound. Maybe this girl could help him sort things out, and he did want to see her again.

He dropped a few coins in the woman's outstretched hand. She gave him a syrupy smile and opened the flap of the tent. The area inside was small but cozy, filled with oriental rugs and brass lanterns. Lash sat propped up on the pillows in a long black dress, her head covered by a red shawl. Her eyes were closed, ornate shadows falling on her beautiful features. Marko stood still, forgetting to breathe. She looked up, surprised at first, then delighted, nodding for him to take a seat.

"So you found me."

"So I did." He sat on the rug in front of her.

Lash smiled. "You want to know your future then?"

"No. Who does?"

"You'd be surprised."

Marko shook his head. "I want to live one day at a time and enjoy it. No use of worrying about what's to come."

Her smile widened, revealing a dimple on one cheek. "I like you."

"Oh, now you do?" He meant to be sarcastic, but his neck burned as she nodded. "Eh . . . does . . . is this stuff about fortune telling for real?"

Marko would have scoffed at anything supernatural before his encounter with the firebirds, but maybe he needed unusual help for his unusual problem.

"People are easily impressed," she said with a smirk. "I'm much better at reading faces than palms. You know, I sit all day and watch and watch."

He didn't know, and he couldn't possibly understand what it would be like to not have freedom to move about. Just the thought made him uneasy.

"But when I get it right, people get really impressed and believe anything else I tell them after. Like this." She dropped her smile and stared, her gaze boring into his, her voice dramatic. "You're after something. A challenge you came across recently, a riddle you're not able to solve, and it's bothering you."

Marko grinned. "You're good."

"You're looking for answers, but sometimes there are simply no answers."

Her voice dwindled into a whisper, and Marko wasn't sure anymore if she was talking about him. The girl looked exhausted.

"Do you want to get out of here?" he asked before he could stop himself. "To see what's outside?"

Her eyes brightened. "Yes, but—"

"Then I'll come back. In a minute. So that your guard won't suspect me."

Lash giggled. "That's my aunt. And she'll be looking for me if I disappear."

"Well, tell her someone came to take you back to camp because you got tired."

"My back does hurt from sitting up for too long."

Marko frowned. "Why do you let her use you like this?"

"She's not using me! It's my work. I like meeting people. But I want to go with you."

"An oaf you barely know?"

Lash giggled. "I've already said sorry. And you're forgetting I can read people. I see you have a good heart, even if you like to kill helpless little animals."

"I kill big ones too." Marko winked and ran out.

He found a wheelbarrow, lined it with several soft wool blankets, then rolled it to the back of the tent, untied one corner, and carried Lash out, laying her carefully among the quilts. Lash's cousin, who came with food, agreed to conceal her absence. Marko grabbed the handles and pushed the wheelbarrow around to Lash's delight. It was already dark outside, but multiple bonfires lit the field. Young people danced, kids played games, and men challenged each other in wrestling or knife throwing. Marko fed her every delicacy there was at the celebration until Lash complained that her stomach would burst.

"You're too skinny and weak. You need to eat," he said when Lash turned her nose from a piece of apple cake.

She glared at him. "Take me home. Now!"

"Is your aunt mistreating you? Tell me," he insisted.

"My aunt is the only family I know!" the girl yelled as she tried to either sit up or fall out of the wheelbarrow. "She has been taking care of me ever since my mother died and my father left. No one is mistreating me, you fool! Take me back."

Marko knelt on the ground next to the cart and gripped the side to keep it from tipping over. "Then explain if I'm so dense!"

Lash looked away from him and watched a group of youths holding hands in pairs and running through the tunnel, her gaze filled with silent longing. "I don't know what's wrong with me. It started when I was about ten. I stumbled a lot and dropped things. Others thought I was just clumsy. But my aunt knew. My mother had the same thing. It's like . . . I'm melting away. What I miss the most is riding a horse, pretending I am one with the wind."

Her faint wistful smile made his insides twist. Marko picked the girl up and marched through the field, ignoring her demands to know where he was taking her. The lights and sounds of the festival were behind them, but he didn't stop until they reached the stables of the nearby homestead. An old herdsman sat by the shed, and Marko proceeded to sweet-talk him into letting them borrow a horse. He finally agreed but must have noticed that Lash couldn't hold on when they mounted. He brought a blanket and a few long straps of leather which Marko wrapped around himself and Lash with her back against his chest.

"Do you even know how to ride?" she grumbled.

"Wait and see."

Marko nudged the mare to a trot then a full gallop as they passed the outer gate into the vast grassland beyond. Lash whooped, hollered, and laughed against the wind. Finally, they slowed down, and he circled an arm around her to adjust her body, trying not to think of her warmth next to him.

"Have you always lived here?" Lash asked as they rode through the moonlit steppe.

"Yes."

"It's so strange."

"What?"

"To be in one place. Don't you get tired of it?"

He took in the endless span of land around them. "No."

"Can't imagine. I'm always looking forward to where the road takes us next. I love watching all the changes. And it makes me feel like I am moving, going somewhere, even though I can't take a single step."

"But you don't have a home to go back to."

"My people are my home."

He didn't understand this strange girl or her world or why he was drawn to her, but it seemed like Lash knew what she wanted from life, no matter the limitations. Did he?

"Thank you for taking me riding," she said.

"Are you ready to fly like the wind again?" he asked.

She nodded and Marko sent the horse racing through the night.

They spent the next three days together, accompanied by Lash's cousin. Marko took Lash riding again and even carried her into the forest to show his snares. She told him about all the interesting places she'd seen: big cities with houses made of stone and church steeples as high as the trees. He said that he still preferred the trees and that his village was better than any city. She pouted and called him ignorant, then marveled at his knowledge of tracks and plants. One day, on a pretense of trying some wild honey, he took Lash to the healer who gave him the sleep-deterring brew.

"I've seen your friend's condition before," the healer told Marko when they stayed alone. "Although it's different in everyone, there is no cure. Some people who have it don't live long. I think the girl knows it too. She told me her mother died young."

Marko couldn't sleep that night. Every moment they spent together made him care more about Lash until she filled all his thoughts. Maybe because they talked the day away, and he shared things he never told anyone else. Lash was a good listener, and when she looked at him with her big dark eyes, it was almost as if she could reach into his very soul. He could see it clearly now—Lash was that one person whose life he had to change.

In the morning he rushed to the Romani camp, but several men blocked his way.

"The girl is getting attached to you even if you mean no harm," their chief said when Marko begged for a chance to say goodbye. "We're leaving in the morning, and she's already crying her eyes out. Leave her alone."

The men promised to be less friendly if he came again. Still, Marko decided to sneak into their camp at night. A few hours after sunset, he put on his hunting clothes, hid the feather, and set out to the valley. He knew which tent Lash was sleeping in and moved unseen past the guards. After slipping inside, he found his friend. Marko rubbed Lash's cheek until she opened her eyes, staring at him through the dark. He scooped her into his arms still wrapped in the blanket and walked out.

"Are you out of your mind?" she whispered.

He grinned. "Yes."

"If you get caught—"

"I won't."

Carefully, he retraced his steps, carrying her beyond the vicinity of the camp.

"I can't believe you stole me in the middle of the night. But I'm glad you did. I am so selfish," Lash lamented. "I couldn't bear to leave without seeing you one more time."

Marko held her tighter but didn't say a word until they got to a small overgrowth where he spread covers on the ground, making a seat for Lash. Reluctantly, he let her out of his arms and started a bonfire to keep them warm.

"There is something I have to tell you," he began.

"I have to tell you something too. I'm leaving in the morning."

It was bound to happen, but Marko's heart still sank. He couldn't possibly ask her to abandon her family and stay behind with someone she barely knew, to change her way of life for him. The road called to her. Lash's eyes traveled over his face as if trying to memorize his every feature, silently pleading for him to let her go.

"You know, at night we can both look at the same stars and remember each other," she whispered. "I never had a friend like you, aside from my cousin. No one *saw*, really saw me like you did. I will never forget our time together as long as I live."

At that moment, Marko understood what the healer meant. Lash knew that her days were numbered, and she was determined to enjoy them to the fullest, to see every little detail around her and commit it to memory. Marko's chest tightened. He knelt before her and took her limp hands. "If you could wish for one thing, Lash, what would it be?"

She tipped her head to the side, her cheeks colored slightly with the warmth of the fire. "You will laugh . . ."

"I won't."

"It's rather silly, but here it goes. I've never been kissed, and before I die—"

He pressed his lips to hers, soft and warm, and held them there for a moment, relishing their closeness. Heat engulfed Marko's face as he pulled away. "I've . . . I might not have done it right."

She smiled. "It was perfect. Thank you for this too."

"Don't thank me, Lash! I should thank *you*. Don't you see how you've changed me?"

Tears spilled out of her eyes and she tried to wipe them on her shoulders. "You're breaking my heart, Marko."

He embraced her, letting her soak his shirt while hiding his own tears in her hair.

"You'll forget me soon, Lash," he said. "Your life will be full of exciting things, new places, new people. Maybe you will come back here one day to tell me the stories."

She shook her head. "I shouldn't have let you get close, Marko, but you made it impossible to resist. I hope *you* forget me because I won't be coming back. My mother . . ."

"I know. But it doesn't matter. You're going to be well."

Marko sat her up, then took out the golden feather. It shimmered, reflecting the light of the fire. He told her about his night watch at the orchard, the firebirds, and the promise to fulfill his heart's greatest desire. She listened intently until he told her of his wish.

"I can't let you use it on me. Who am I to you? A stranger passing by." She had a stubborn look on her face. "This is not right, even if it works."

Marko placed the feather onto her lap. "I can't think of any other reason to use it."

"But there is no time limit. You might need it later for something important."

"And how do you suppose I'm going to live with myself knowing that you . . . that . . ." He took in a ragged breath.

Lash pressed her lips into a determined line. "I shouldn't have come here. Take me back."

"I'm going to do it whether you want me to or not," he said, trying to rein in his frustration. "Why wouldn't you let me help make things better for you?"

"Because I can't repay such a debt!"

"Who's talking about repayment?! Did I request anything in return?"

"Still, I won't let you! Doesn't the person you wish to help have to agree first?"

"Then if I can't do this one thing, I don't want it for myself either." He picked up the feather, stepped toward the fire, and raised it over the flames.

"Stop!" Lash yelled. "You're the most stubborn, impossible, reckless—"

He rushed to her side and kissed her again, putting an end to the argument. "Please. Let me try this."

Finally, she sighed and nodded.

He stood in front of her, then turned around three times, hit his right foot on the ground, and held the feather up. "In the name of Elina Silverheart, Tsarina of the Enchanted Borderlands, I wish to see Lash's body restored."

For a moment nothing happened. Then the feather began to transform, turning into a fiery torch. It burned Marko's fingers, and he let go, but it remained floating in the air, growing until it morphed into a firebird. Elina Silverheart flapped her wings, looking over Marko and Lash.

"I heard your wish," the tsarina sang.

"Fulfill it then. Like you promised." Marko said firmly.

"What you're asking is hard but not impossible. The girl would have to come with me and live among us. She will listen to our songs and drink the living water from our stream until her strength returns."

Lash shook her head. "I can't leave. My relatives will worry, and my tribe . . . they will suspect that Marko took me."

"I will stay in the forest until they leave. Let everyone think that we ran away together," he said.

"Marko, that's even worse! How can I do this to you?"

He knelt in front of her again and kissed her knuckles. "Don't worry, I stay in the forest all the time anyway. I'll go to another village and sell my game there." He smiled into her teary eyes. "Maybe it's time for me to see the world too."

"How will I find you then? I want to find you," she pleaded.

Marko turned to the tsarina.

"I'll leave a mark on you, boy, then will show the girl how to track it." The firebird swooshed next to him, grazing his left shoulder with her wing.

Marko hissed and grabbed his arm. Lash shrieked. His sleeve was singed and skin burned.

"Now decide. Do you accept my offer?" Elina Silverheart sang.

Lash kept shaking her head no, but Marko cupped her face and made her look at him. "You will go with her. Then return to me. I will wait."

Lash agreed then, her eyes filling with what looked a lot like hope.

He smiled and kissed the tip of her nose, then stepped aside. "Take her now, Tsarina, and make her well. It is my heart's greatest desire."

The wind picked up around them, swirling embers of fire until everything was filled with light. Lash called his name, but it was as if from a distance, and when everything settled down, she was no longer there. The firebird vanished with the last of the embers. Marko tried to ignore the hollow feeling in his chest. He wanted to be happy for his friend. More than a friend, he hoped. The enchantress never said how long it would take for Lash to get better. What if it was long enough to forget him? After all, they only spent a few days together. But even if he never saw her again, he would do the same thing.

Marko wrapped his burned skin and gathered his belongings, then walked home where he packed his hunting gear and said goodbye to his family. The sun began to rise, covering the fields in early morning fog as Marko left his village. He looked up at the vanishing horizon, remembering the girl who liked to watch the road as she traveled, and walked bravely into the unknown.

If you want to find out what happens to Marko and Lash next, sign up for my once-a-month newsletter—the story is coming out soon: https://www.subscribepage.com/slavic_fantasy

Several more stories with elements of Slavic fantasy have been written. They are all about the Ukrainian settlement near Hortitsa Island. You'll be the first to know when they are published.

ELENA SHELEST

Elena Shelest immigrated to the U.S. from Ukraine at the age of 15. She currently resides in Oregon with her husband, two busy kids, and three pets.

Elena is a full-time nurse, an artist, and an avid reader of fantasy and inspirational books. She is hoping to encourage her readers to be able to look beyond what's possible and believe again that everyday miracles do happen.

To read other books by this author, see her Amazon page: https://www.amazon.com/Elena-Shelest/e/B07XFBFSHB

To read more magical short stories about the birthplace of Ukraine, sign up for my monthly newsletter: https://www.subscribepage.com/slavic_fantasy

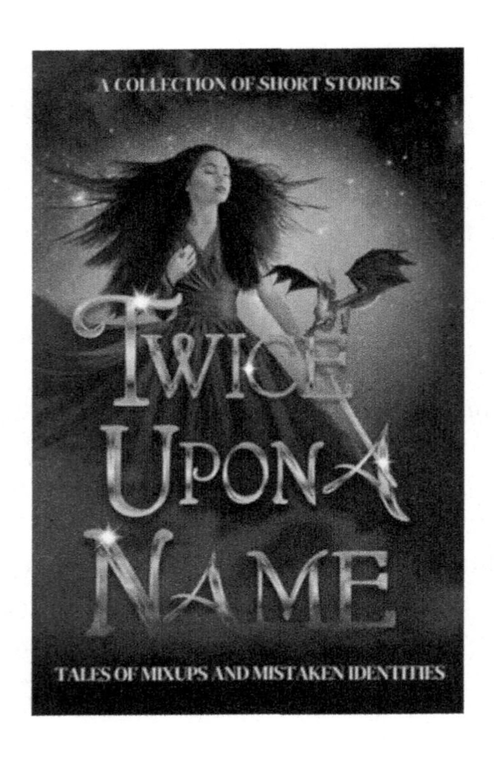

Double the name and double the magic, mystery, and mayhem

Once upon a time, a fairy tale name generator issued a challenge to a group of authors. Volume Two of these quirky stories brings double trouble.

In this clean YA anthology, spy on thieves discovering their princely identities, accompany villains seeking redemption along with accident-prone geese, and rejoice in the reunion of siblings separated at birth. Side with twins split between good and evil, giggle over mistaken identities, and discover the secrets of royal doppelgängers. When fates are intertwined by a namesake, mayhem and mischief are sure to follow.

Venture into this collection of adventurous stories by award-winning and up-and-coming authors and see if what happens once... happens twice!

Pssst...some characters from Once Upon A Name might make a comeback, but the two sets and all stories in them can be read as standalones.

All proceeds donated to charity in support of reading and literacy.
Preorder your copy today!
https://books2read.com/TwiceUponAName

Made in the USA
Middletown, DE
21 April 2022